LESS THAN HERO

LESS
THAN
HERO

|||| A NOVEL ||||

S. G. BROWNE

GALLERY BOOKS

New York   London   Toronto   Sydney   New Delhi

Gallery Books
A Division of Simon & Schuster, Inc.
1230 Avenue of the Americas
New York, NY 10020

First Gallery Books trade paperback edition March 2015

GALLERY BOOKS and colophon are registered trademarks of Simon & Schuster, Inc.

For information about special discounts for bulk purchases, please contact Simon & Schuster Special Sales at 1-866-506-1949 or business@simonandschuster.com.

The Simon & Schuster Speakers Bureau can bring authors to your live event. For more information or to book an event contact the Simon & Schuster Speakers Bureau at 1-866-248-3049 or visit our website at www.simonspeakers.com.

Interior design and interior illustrations by Robert E. Ettlin

Manufactured in the United States of America

1   3   5   7   9   10   8   6   4   2

Library of Congress Cataloging-in-Publication Data is available.

ISBN 978-1-4767-1174-4
ISBN 978-1-4767-1178-2 (ebook)

For Guy and Jenn
Thanks for your generosity. You're both super.

LESS THAN HERO

From the *New York Post*, page 3:

MIDTOWN HALLUCINATIONS HAVE
POLICE SEEING DOUBLE

Doug Drury and Kim Woody were enjoying a wonderful day exploring Manhattan when the California couple decided to grab some lunch at the Carnegie Deli. That's when their afternoon took a turn for the bizarre.

"This guy sitting at a table near the window jumped out of his chair and started yelling for everyone to hide," Doug Drury said. "He claimed there were flying sharks circling above us; then he dove under our table and grabbed on to my legs like they were a life preserver and he didn't know how to swim."

The man in question, identified as Brad Thompson from Manhattan, continued to rant and rave about sharks and other invisible creatures before he was eventually subdued by police and taken into custody.

"I don't know what happened to him," Robert Solis said. A longtime employee at Carnegie Deli, Solis said he's seen it all. "But I've never seen anything like this. He totally flipped out. It was like he was on a bad acid trip or something."

While the afternoon theatrics had everyone at the Carnegie Deli buzzing, it wasn't the only unusual incident in the neighborhood. Ten minutes later, the patrons and employees at the Starbucks on West Fifty-Second were treated to a surreal strip-tease show.

According to witnesses, a dark-haired woman who was standing in line waiting to place her order suddenly shouted out, "Oh my God!" and started taking off her clothes. David Kasama of Sacramento, California, had a front row seat.

"She kept shouting, 'Help! Help! I'm on fire!' as she pulled off her clothes," Kasama said. "Then she ran over and grabbed a pitcher of water and dumped it over her head. It was pretty hot, if you know what I mean."

After dousing herself with water, the woman told everyone in Starbucks they were all melting like wax candles before she ran out the door.

Debra Dunbar was found twenty-five minutes later in the Pulitzer Fountain at Fifth Avenue and West Fifty-Eighth. She was taken to New York Presbyterian Hospital for evaluation.

chapter 1

I 'm sitting on a chair in an examination room with a disposable thermometer in my mouth and a blood pressure cuff around my upper left arm. On the walls around me are posters of vascular systems and reproductive organs. Fluorescent lights wash away any shadows. A clock ticks away the afternoon. Outside the closed door, someone asks for a breath mint.

My lips have gone numb.

This has never happened to me before. Usually I don't get anything more than cotton-mouthed, drowsy, or light-headed. Occasionally I develop rashes or feel like I have food poisoning. More often than not, I'll get a headache. Nothing major. We're not talking migraine and vomiting. That would be serious. What I get is pretty typical, nothing 400 milligrams of ibuprofen won't fix.

But numbness in my lips? That's definitely a first.

The medical technician sitting across from me removes the thermometer and the cuff, then records my temperature and my blood pressure on a chart attached to a clipboard.

The technician is male. Mid-thirties. Prematurely gray. He has a zit coming in on his chin. His breath smells like nachos.

"How are you feeling today?" he asks.

"Good," I say, though my lips feel like they're made of rubber.

"Any problems with your vision?" he asks, looking down at his clipboard.

I shake my head and say no.

"Cognitive functions?"

No.

"Speech?"

No.

"Numbness or tingling in any of your extremities?"

Technically my lips aren't my extremities, but I tell him just in case and he writes it down in his notes.

"Have you experienced any nausea or flu-like symptoms?" he asks.

No.

"Memory loss?"

No.

"Hallucinations? Seizures? Rashes?"

Sometimes just hearing the word *rash* makes me want to itch, but I answer in the negative three more times.

"Any bloating or rapid weight gain?" he asks.

No.

"Are you feeling dizzy or light-headed?"

Most of the time, the questions are the same.

Nausea. Headaches. Dizziness.

Frequently they'll throw in night sweats or loss of appetite, with an occasional sinus inflammation and the odd sexual-performance question. But I've never been asked about an irregular heartbeat. Or renal failure.

"No," I tell him. "No dizziness."

The tech takes a few more minutes to run through the rest of his questions. By the time he sends me off for my blood and urine tests, my lips have returned to normal.

In another room, a phlebotomist wraps an elastic tourniquet around my arm and sterilizes the soft flesh just inside my left elbow.

The phlebotomist is female. Early forties. Blond with frosted tips. She's had Botox injections around her eyes. Her breath smells like peppermint.

I'm not a big fan of needles. Even after more than five years, I still have to look away. So I take a deep breath and stare at the wall as she draws half a dozen blood samples into evacuated tubes. Normally before drawing samples, she's supposed to ask a list of questions and record my answers on a form:

Am I on anticoagulation therapy?

Do I have a history of fits?

Do I have any bleeding disorders?

Have I fasted?

Instead, she asks me the questions while taking the samples, except for the one about fasting. This test doesn't require me to fast. I'm not a big fan of fasting. I'm not Baha'i or Buddhist, and I've never spent forty days and nights on a mountain with God, so abstaining from food and drink has never been my strong suit.

After the phlebotomist draws my blood, she hands me a sterile plastic specimen container and points me to the bathroom.

"Try to catch the urine in midstream," she says. "It makes for a cleaner sample."

I nod as if this is something I've never heard before. As if this is my first time.

Urine samples are standard procedure. While I'm not always asked to give blood, I almost always have to leave a sample of my urine. I've heard some guys have a hard time peeing on command into a cup. I've never had a problem, so I provide a midstream catch, deposit the specimen container in the cabinet, grab my backpack, and head to the waiting room—not a waiting room in Brooklyn with soft-cushioned seats and diffused lighting and copies of *Rolling Stone* and *National Geographic*, but a waiting room in Queens with hard plastic stacking chairs and fluorescent overhead lights and copies of *Us* and *People*.

Randy stands at the front desk, hitting on the receptionist.

The receptionist is female. Late twenties. Jet-black hair. She's wearing too much foundation. Her breath smells like cloves.

"Cardio is my nirvana." Randy clasps his hands behind his head and flexes his biceps. "I run every day. I love working up a good sweat."

Randy is a six-foot-tall, two-hundred-pound walking erection. In the three years I've known him, I've never seen him pass on the chance to chat up a woman.

"I hear sweat's a big turn-on for women," I say.

"Lloyd, my man!" Randy gives me a bro shake followed by a pound hug, even though we've seen each other almost every day for the past week.

Randy may not be subtle, but he wears his affability, like his muscles, for everyone to see.

"Where's Vic and Isaac?" I ask, looking around the otherwise empty waiting room.

"Totally Eagles," Randy says.

Randy likes to make esoteric references to song and album titles by classic rock bands, leaving out the titles and figuring everyone knows what he's talking about.

"Already gone," he says, with a wink to the receptionist.

"Thank you for coming in, Mr. Prescott." She ignores Randy and hands me some discharge literature and an envelope with my name on it. "We'll see you for your follow-up on Tuesday."

"What about me?" Randy asks. "I'm free Friday night."

"I'm sorry, Mr. Ballard. I don't date patients or clients. Plus I have a boyfriend."

"What if I wasn't a patient or a client?" Randy asks.

"I'd still have a boyfriend."

"Que sera, sera." Randy shrugs and turns to me, his face lighting up with a smile as big as Long Island. "Hey, wanna grab some grub?"

chapter 2

R andy and I head back to Manhattan on the J train after chowing down on a couple of slices from Alfie's. It's a forty-five-minute ride back to the Lower East Side and we've used up most of that time talking about baseball and sex and playing a few games of Guess That Prescription Drug.

"Can it cause suicidal thoughts or actions?" I ask.

"Yes," Randy says.

"Hallucinations?"

"Yes."

"Seizures?"

"Yes."

"Shortness of breath or trouble breathing?"

"Yes."

That could be any number of antidepressants or antibiotics, but I'm guessing Randy didn't pick an SSRI.

"Yellowing of the skin?" I ask.

Randy shakes his head. "Nope."

That rules out most of the antidepressants, though it's not like you've won the lottery just because your medication doesn't turn you into Homer Simpson.

When playing Guess That Prescription Drug, we tend to stay away from side effects like diarrhea, dizziness, headaches, loss of appetite, nausea, and vomiting, because almost every pharmaceutical drug can possibly cause at least two or more of those. Instead, we focus on the more severe side effects.

"Severe blistering, peeling, or red skin rash?" I ask.

"Yes."

"Burning, numbing, or weakness in the extremities?"

"Yes."

"Inability to move or bear weight on a joint or tendon?"

"Yes!" Randy says. "You are so Van Halen right now."

I run through a possible list of Van Halen songs in my head. "Hot for teacher?"

"On fire," he says, as if it should be obvious.

"Right. How did I not know that?"

"I don't know. It's only the final track on one of the greatest debut rock albums of all time."

Randy's knowledge of classic rock is rivaled only by his enthusiasm for getting laid.

"Is it cipro?" I ask.

"Nailed it!" Randy gives me a fist bump as the train pulls into the Marcy Avenue station. "Speaking of nailing it, did I tell you about the cute little blonde technician who works at the Montefiore Medical Center in the Bronx?"

Randy proceeds to tell me about the cute little blonde technician in more detail than I care to know. While he's telling his sordid tale, three young white punks get on and stand in the middle of the car wearing sunglasses and wife beaters, with their pants halfway down their asses like they've never heard of a belt.

"So how are things with you and Sophie?" Randy asks.

"Good," I say, as the doors close and the train continues toward Manhattan.

"You two been together what? Four years now?"

"Five," I say.

Randy nods and whistles. "I don't think I've been with the same woman for more than five hours."

Randy's not a big fan of long-term commitment.

"You ever think about getting married?" Randy asks.

"Sure," I say.

When I think about marriage, it's always more in theory. Like time travel. Or the conspiracy to assassinate JFK.

It's not that I don't like the idea of marrying Sophie. I like it just fine. And when I graduated from high school, I figured I'd be married by the time I hit thirty. But now that I'm here, getting married seems like something grown-ups do.

"Yo man," one of the punks says, loud enough for everyone to hear him. He has a buzz cut and a soul patch growing on his chin like black mold. "This car smells like piss."

"Yeah," the second punk says, this one with a clean-shaven face and blond cornrows. "Like someone rolled around in it."

"Or took a bath in it," the third punk says, his head shaved down to a cue ball.

They laugh at their show of bravado and continue to stand in the middle of the car, daring anybody to make eye contact. Cue Ball makes a show of sniffing at the air and takes a few steps in our direction, while Cornrows and Soul Patch follow his lead, sniffing at some of the other passengers like dogs.

Marcy Avenue is the last stop on the Brooklyn side of the

East River, and it's about an eight-minute ride to the Essex Street station, so our only options are to avoid eye contact or move to another car for the next five minutes. But New Yorkers like to act as though nothing bothers them, so everyone stays put and keeps their eyes trained on their books or on their iPhones or on the advertisements above the windows on the opposite side of the car, one of which is for depression.

Are you feeling anxious? Have you lost interest in activities you used to enjoy? Are your dishes piling up in the sink? You just might have clinical depression. We can help!

"I think it's that motherfucker over there," Cornrows says, nodding toward an apparent homeless man sitting by himself at the other end of the car. The three punks make their way toward where the man is sitting and start harassing him.

"Yo man, you stink," Soul Patch says.

"Yeah," Cornrows says. "Why the fuck did you bring your smelly ass onto this fuckin' car?"

"Now we have to breathe your fuckin' stench until we get to the next fuckin' stop," Cue Ball says.

"Leave me alone," the man says, his voice high-pitched and pleading. "Just leave me alone!"

They continue to berate the homeless man, who cowers in the corner, taking their abuse. No one in the entire subway car says anything. No one does anything. It may as well be happening on another planet.

I feel bad for the guy. The problem is, I don't know if the three assholes are carrying knives or guns, and I don't really want to find out. I'm not much for fighting, especially when the odds are in favor of me getting my head kicked in.

While my cupboards might be full of empathy, I haven't exactly stocked up on heroism.

The thugs keep at the homeless guy for a couple of minutes. When it starts to look like they're about to escalate their verbal abuse to something more physical, Randy stands up.

"Hey," Randy says. "You heard the guy. Why don't you leave him alone?"

The three punks stop their badgering and turn to look at Randy.

Cue Ball takes a step forward. "What the fuck did you say?"

He stares at Randy from behind his sunglasses, flanked on either side by his buddies. Everyone in the car seems to be holding their breath, as if anticipating someone getting hurt. I'm sort of anticipating the same thing.

"I asked you to leave him alone," Randy says.

While Cue Ball is a couple of inches taller, I'd say Randy outweighs him by a good twenty pounds. But I don't know how much size matters in a street brawl, even if it's on a subway train.

"We're not looking for any trouble," I say, trying to think of something to keep Randy from ending up in the hospital. But even to my own ears, I sound like a pussy.

"Yeah, well, trouble is what you got." Cue Ball starts to walk toward us, with Cornrows and Soul Patch following his lead.

The people sitting in our general proximity finally decide this would be a good time to get up and find another place to sit. I'd like to join them, but I can't bail on Randy.

Shit, I think. Then I stand up to let Randy know I have his back.

Randy flexes his hands and fidgets, shifting from one foot to the other, like a boxer dancing around on his feet. While Randy occasionally moonlights as a bouncer, he's always struck me as more of a lover than a fighter, but he's not backing down. Me? I've never been in a fight before in my life, never even thrown a punch, and I don't really want to break my perfect record. Or my face.

It's only another minute or two before we reach the next station, and I'm hoping we get there fast enough for me to avoid words like *fracture* and *contusion* and *hospital*.

"You should mind your own fuckin' business," Cue Ball says as he and his buddies close in.

Yes. I agree. We should mind our own fucking business. But it's a little too late for *should*s.

I take a deep breath and curl my fingers into fists as my heart pounds inside my chest like it knows I'm about to get pummeled and is trying to warn me. My own personal robot shouting, *Danger! Danger, Will Robinson!*

Next to me, Randy continues to fidget while Cue Ball gives us a cold, icy smile. Then the smile vanishes and I tense up, expecting the first blow to follow. Instead, Cue Ball gets this look on his face like he's having a heart attack or crapping his pants. The next moment his face and arms break out in hives and he starts scratching at himself and shouting *"What the fuck!"* over and over.

Cornrows and Soul Patch don't want any part of whatever's happening to their buddy and back away. Randy and I do the same, just in case whatever Cue Ball has is catching, and watch as he continues to suffer from what appears to be some kind of allergic reaction. To what, I have no idea. Maybe he used the wrong detergent. Or ate Moroccan food. Or wore a cheap polyester blend. But at least it looks like no one's getting pummeled.

When the train pulls into the Essex Street station, Cue Ball's skin has turned bright red and blotchy, and he's covered in hives. No one offers him any comfort or sympathy, not even Cornrows or Soul Patch, who have retreated to the other end of the subway car as if their buddy is a nuclear bomb.

The doors slide open and all the passengers scramble out of the car as fast as they can, including Randy and me. Even Cornrows and Soul Patch make themselves scarce in a hurry, leaving Cue Ball behind to deal with his own shit.

"Hey!" he shouts. "Hey, man! Someone fuckin' help me!"

As we head for the exit, Randy says, "What the hell do you think happened to him?"

"I don't know," I say, checking my hands and arms. "Whatever it is, I hope it's not contagious."

"No doubt," Randy says. "Hey, speaking of contagious, did I tell you about the receptionist at the med-lab facility in Brooklyn?"

||| chapter 3 |||

I'm a professional guinea pig.

I take generic painkillers, heart medications, antidepressants, and other experimental drugs being developed and tested for consumer use.

Drugs for ADHD, insomnia, and urinary tract infections.

Drugs for schizophrenia, impotence, and Parkinson's disease.

Drugs with names like clonazepam and naproxen and Adderall.

Not exactly something you go to college for, or intern at a prestigious law firm to gain experience as, or dream of being when you're a kid.

"What do you want to be when you grow up, Lloyd?"

"I want to test drugs that might make me vomit or experience uncontrollable flatulence."

This is why they have high school guidance counselors. Someone to give you direction and a sense of purpose. Someone to help you come up with a plan for a future that doesn't involve selling yourself for medical research or starring in bad porn. Not that I've ever had sex for money, but sometimes you do what you have to do in order to make ends meet.

And sometimes you end up doing it for so long that you can't figure out how to stop.

Most prescription drugs go through three trial phases before they hit the market. In Phase I, experimental drugs and treatments are tested on more or less healthy subjects in order to determine efficacy and study possible side effects. Phase II clinical trials deal with dosing requirements and effectiveness, while Phase III trials involve test subjects who suffer from the condition the new drug intends to treat.

I'm in the first category.

Over the last five years, I've participated in over 150 clinical trials. During that time, I've consumed chemically enhanced sports drinks, been given pills laced with radioactive tracers, had extensive X-rays, worn a twenty-four-hour catheter, and taken a medication that turned my sweat and urine a bright, fluorescent orange.

I was like a human highlighter pen.

While test subjects in Phase III trials often enroll in a study in order to gain access to a new drug that might help them, healthy guinea pigs in Phase I trials can't expect any medical benefits from the drugs we're testing. And every time we volunteer, we take a risk that something might go wrong.

I suppose no matter what you do for a living, there's always a chance something might go wrong. You could get hit by a bus. Or suffer a brain aneurysm. Or have a gas main blow up beneath your cubicle.

You never know what wonderful surprises life has in store.

But chances are, when most people go to work, they don't have to worry that their jobs might lead to multiple organ failure. Or cause permanent damage to their immune systems. Or result in the amputation of their fingers and toes.

These aren't hypothetical worst-case scenarios. This is what happened to half a dozen guinea pigs who participated in a study for a prospective treatment for rheumatoid arthritis and leukemia.

So yeah, shit happens. But sometimes life provides options you never thought you'd have to take, so you take them in spite of the risks. Plus it's not like I'm volunteering just to accumulate a bunch of karmic brownie points.

In a typical month I make over $3,000, sometimes twice that, but I've never made less than $2,000. Generic testing studies usually take place over a couple of weekends and pay anywhere from $600 to $2,000. One time I took home $5,000 for a study on a new prostate drug, but I had to spend two weeks in a research dorm getting prodded by lubricated index fingers. Another time I was paid $4,500 for a twenty-eight-day sleep deprivation study. While I only received $500 for a one-week Paleolithic diet study, it didn't require a washout, which is the thirty-day waiting period required between some studies to make sure you don't have any drugs in your system that might impact test results.

This is presuming guinea pigs tell the truth about the drugs we've tested. Since there's no shared database among all of the various research companies to keep track of who's volunteering how many times a year, most of us bounce from one research facility to another to maximize our earnings.

While honesty may be the best policy, it doesn't always help to pay the rent.

The best-paying studies are lockdowns: inpatient trials that require volunteers to check into a research facility for several days or weeks. That way, researchers can control diet, check blood and urine on a regular basis, and monitor medical status around the clock.

I'm not a big fan of lockdowns. One, I can't stand institutional food. And two, you usually end up rooming with other guinea pigs, not all of whom are people you want to be around for two weeks in a row, 24/7.

But the money is hard to turn down.

A few weeks ago, Randy and I and five other guinea pigs we know each earned a $3,300 paycheck for taking part in a twenty-two-day lockdown in which we were tested to see how multiple drugs interacted with one another. The drugs, which have already been approved by the FDA, are used to treat schizophrenia, depression, and bipolar disorder.

A lot of these drugs I've tested—the ones that have already passed the final stage of clinical trials and are now legally available by prescription and advertised on television—come with a host of common side effects in addition to their advertised health benefits.

Diarrhea. Nausea. Vomiting.

These are the less serious side effects. The ones that don't require you to call your doctor or make you wonder if it's too late to take out life insurance.

But then there are the more serious side effects, the ones you hear rattled off on a commercial like a contest disclaimer.

May cause seizures. May cause loss of consciousness. May cause severe or persistent cramps. Only one entry per household. Must be eighteen or over to be eligible. Residents of California and Arizona must pay sales tax.

Then there are the drugs that actually cause the very problem they're supposed to be treating.

Drugs to treat diarrhea that can cause diarrhea. Drugs for sleep disorders that can cause insomnia. Drugs to combat depression that can cause suicidal thoughts.

One drug—an anti-inflammatory taken for arthritis, tendinitis, bursitis, gout, and menstrual cramps—suggests that you stop taking the medication and seek immediate medical attention if you experience any of the following:

Slurred speech.

Blistering or peeling of the skin.

Coughing up blood or vomit that looks like coffee grounds.

There's more, including jaundice, bloody stool, numbness, and chills. But if I'm having trouble speaking and my skin is blistering and I'm throwing up something that has the consistency of Starbucks Breakfast Blend, I'm thinking maybe this drug needs to be taken off the shelves.

It makes you wonder how something like *this* gets approved by the FDA while the federal government continues to debate the benefits of medical marijuana.

Still, the safety of these drugs is dependent upon a pool of willing volunteers who have a lot of time to spare. This isn't something computer engineers or college professors or lawyers or CEOs or members of Congress do. This is something the poor, uneducated, and desperate do, so that others who can afford it get new and improved drugs.

We're like pharmaceutical soldiers, fighting on the front lines of medical science to defend your right to life, liberty, and the pursuit of antidepressants.

chapter 4

"Anyone else sign up for the lidocaine spray trial?" I ask.

I'm at Caffe Reggio with Randy, Frank, Charlie, and Vic. We get together once every month or so to share information on clinical trials and the companies who run them. Guinea-pigging can be a lonely existence, so it's nice to have a support group of your peers to help navigate the waters of clinical trials. We're kind of like our own little brood. A family of professional slackers living on the fringe of acceptable employment.

"Is that the study on premature ejaculation?" Charlie asks. "The one where they numb your penis?"

"Don't say *penis*," Vic says. "It makes you sound like my mother."

Charlie is a twenty-four-year-old high-school dropout with freckles and red hair that has never met a hairbrush, while Vic is a former middle-school math teacher with a shaved head and black Ray-Ban prescription glasses that make him look like the offspring of Mr. Clean and Buddy Holly.

"What should I say instead of *penis*?" Charlie asks.

"I don't know," Vic says. "How about *cock* or *dick*?"

"Okay," Charlie says. "Then you're a dick."

Charlie and Vic are like a married couple who are always getting on each other's nerves. It would make sense if they were gay, but they're not. At least not openly. Still, sometimes I wish they'd go to couples counseling.

"Maybe you should sign up for the trial," Vic says. "Give them some pointers on premature ejaculation."

"I don't have a problem with premature ejaculation," Charlie says, without much conviction.

Charlie dropped out of high school after his junior year to take care of his father and stepmother, both of whom had developed lung cancer. His father lasted another year, leaving his estate to Charlie's stepmother, who died before she could update her will, so everything passed on to Charlie's stepsister, leaving him with nothing. After flipping burgers and delivering pizzas for a few months, Charlie volunteered for a one-week study on antiseizure medication for $1,500 and has been guinea-pigging ever since.

"Who's behind the lidocaine spray trial?" Randy asks.

"Covance," I say.

Trials for new drugs used to be held at universities, which tended to conduct their research in a deliberate fashion. When the universities couldn't keep pace with the growing financial pressures to bring drugs to market faster, pharmaceutical companies moved most of their clinical trials to the private sector, creating contract research organizations that specialize in drug studies. And they're always looking for healthy test subjects—more than ten million in any given year.

"I got disqualified from one of their trials," Charlie says. "They told me my cholesterol count was too high."

"What was your diet like the week before the test?" Frank asks. "Did you eat a lot of foods high in salt or saturated fats?"

"I don't know," Charlie says. "I don't remember."

"What the hell does that mean?" Frank takes a bite of his cannoli. "You either know or you don't. Jesus, Charlie. Don't you keep track of what you're eating?"

Frank, our stocky guinea pig patriarch with a receding hairline and a fluctuating waistline, is always telling us to pay attention to everything we put into our bodies, since it can have an impact on our livelihood. He takes being a guinea pig very seriously.

"I try to keep track," Charlie says, looking like a scolded puppy. "But sometimes I get distracted."

"Excuses are the currency of the weak-willed," Frank says. "Take responsibility for your actions, Charlie. No one owns them but you."

Frank had a business with his former wife selling her artwork out of their home in Queens. When she filed for divorce, she kept the business and the house and Frank got a severance package. Out of a job, a home, and a marriage, Frank took a ride on the depression train from Burger King to Dunkin' Donuts to the Aqueduct Racetrack, where he lost his entire divorce settlement. Facing homelessness, he signed up for a four-week gastrointestinal disorder study that gave him room and board for a month and paid him $3,200. The rest, as they say, is history.

"Have you gained weight?" asks Vic.

"What the hell does my weight have to do with Charlie's inability to keep track of what he's eating?" Frank says.

While Frank's always been a little on the *before* side when it comes to his weight, he does look like he's packed on a few extra pounds.

"Maybe you shouldn't be so hard on Charlie," Randy says.

"Maybe you shouldn't bother to take pride in what you do." Frank stuffs another bite of cannoli into his mouth.

Frank seems to be a little more irritable than usual, although he's not the only one who runs low on a sense of humor every now and then. When you spend your existence taking experimental prescription drugs that give you headaches and constipation and insomnia, irritability is just a comment away.

"So is Frank being more of a dick or a cock?" I ask.

"It's a matter of semantics," Vic says. "A personal choice, really. It just depends on what you're comfortable with."

"Yeah, well," Frank says, "I'm comfortable with the both of you kissing my ass."

"Speaking of kissing asses," Randy says. "I hooked up with that hot phlebotomist from the research facility over by Murray Hill."

"You mean Megan?" I ask. "The redhead?"

"That's the one." Randy leans back in his chair with his hands behind his head, the proud purveyor of promiscuity. "I ran into her at Billymark's West and we started talking and drinking and doing shots of Jägermeister. The next thing I know, we're back at her place and she totally lets me Led Zeppelin her."

"What does that mean?" Charlie asks.

"You know," Randy says. "In through the out door."

Frank throws his fork down on the table. "Great. Now I can't eat the rest of my cannoli."

"You can also call it the Pink Floyd," Randy says.

"Because you're comfortably numb?" I ask.

Randy rolls his eyes. "No. Because you're going to the dark side of the moon."

"Of course," I say.

Charlie looks around the table. "What's in through the out door?"

"That reminds me," Vic says, adjusting his glasses. "The Bauer Research Facility in Newark has a serious issue with fecal matter."

And the conversation turns back to business.

Vic taught math in middle school for seven years until he got fed up with a bunch of bureaucratic policies that handcuffed his ability to actually teach, so he offered to beat some sense into his new principal. It didn't matter that Vic never physically touched anyone. The fact that he threatened his boss was enough to get him fired. While criminal assault charges were eventually dismissed, none of the school districts in New York or New Jersey wanted anything to do with him. Eventually Vic discovered the glamorous life of guinea-pigging.

I met him a few years ago during a one-week lockdown to study the effects of several different antibiotics. Once the study was over, we went out for drinks to celebrate our payday. Vic brought along Randy, whom he'd known for about a year. Not long after that, Charlie and Frank joined the club.

Sometimes Blaine and Isaac show up, expanding our number to seven, though they usually only make it to poker nights. More often than not, when we're talking business, it's just the five of us.

"When's the next poker game?" Charlie asks.

"We'll get to that in a minute," Frank says, the patient father, his earlier rancor about Charlie's lack of attention to detail forgotten. Or more likely shelved. Frank's never far from his anger. He likes to keep it handy.

All of us have been guinea pigs for at least five years, and over the past three we've met on a semi-regular basis to talk about recent and upcoming trials, comparing notes and grading clinics, factoring in variables such as the friendliness of the staff, how much they pay, and whether or not the receptionist and venipuncturist are hot. At least that's one of Randy's criteria.

Randy blew out his knee playing pickup basketball six years ago. Since his injury wasn't on the clock, neither of his part-time jobs—as a bouncer and working the counter at a liquor store— paid health insurance or unemployment. While he received some temporary disability payments, they weren't enough to cover his rent. When his medical bills piled up and forced him to file for bankruptcy, one of his former coworkers told him there was easy money to be made volunteering for a testosterone study. After that, he was hooked.

Once the business portion of the meeting is over, talk turns to poker night, which Charlie volunteers to host as Frank orders another cannoli.

"You planning on leaving any for the rest of us?" Vic asks.

Charlie laughs through a mouthful of cappuccino, which he sprays across the table.

"Goddamn it, Charlie!" Frank says, wiping Charlie's cappuccino off his face.

"Don't blame Charlie," I say.

"Yeah," Vic says. "He's not the one eating all the cannoli."

"Fine," Frank shoves the plate away from him. "You want my cannoli? You can have my goddamned cannoli."

"I don't want your cannoli," Vic says.

Charlie raises his hand. "Can I have your cannoli?"

"Sure," Frank says. "Have it all."

"Thanks!" Charlie says.

While being a professional guinea pig wasn't on my short list of dream jobs—which included professional golfer, travel writer, general manager of the Mets or Yankees, and *Playboy* photographer—it does offer a low-stress work environment and a flexible schedule with a minimum amount of responsibility. Plus I get to enjoy hanging out with a group of misfits like me and sharing moments like this.

"Totally Simon and Garfunkel right now," Randy says.

Vic looks at Randy over the top of his glasses. "You realize nobody has any idea what you're talking about."

One of the drawbacks, however—other than the risk of multiple organ failure and getting your fingers and toes amputated—is that you can't always depend on a steady monthly income to pay the rent. And it's hard to hold down a part-time job when you have to take three weeks off so someone can collect your blood, urine, and semen while pumping you full of antipsychotics.

So sometimes you have to find other ways to make ends meet.

chapter 5

Get a job you lazy bastard!" a middle-aged man says as he drops a dollar into my hat.

I thank him and wish him a nice day.

"Shove this up your ass!" A twenty-something guy displays a George Washington around his middle finger before flicking the dollar at me.

I give him a nod and a smile.

"You're lousy in bed." A thirty-something woman throws a handful of singles in my face. She gets a couple of steps away before she turns around and marches back over to me. "You're the worst fuck I've ever had!"

I press my hands together in front of me and bow my head.

I'm sitting on a bench in Central Park near the Naumburg Bandshell, watching the tourists and locals walk past. Summer is in full bloom, delivering warm days and blue skies, which is good for business. Any panhandler worth his alms can make enough from Memorial Day to Labor Day to support himself for the rest of the year.

None of the other guinea pigs panhandle in order to earn some extra cash. Randy does some part-time gigs as a bouncer to help during the lean volunteer months, while Charlie, Vic, and Frank pick up temporary shifts here and there making deliveries, working flea markets, putting up drywall, or taking any other short-term work they can find. But I don't like driving in Manhattan, I hate flea markets, and my carpentry skills peaked with Lincoln Logs. Besides, why would I want to work for someone else when I can be my own boss?

On a typical four-hour shift, I earn $10 to $12 an hour, which is better than minimum wage, and I don't have to pay any taxes or deal with any corporate hierarchy or worry about making an off-color joke and getting sued for sexual harassment. And during the summer and peak tourist seasons, I can take in $15 an hour without even breaking a sweat—$20 an hour if I put a little effort into it. You can't earn that much slinging mochas or working on a burger assembly line at McDonald's. True, I don't get any health benefits or food discounts and I have to deal with getting heckled by teenagers, but I get fresh air and sunshine and the chance to meet new people.

"I hope you rot in hell, you son of a bitch," a man says and gives me the change out of his pocket.

I give him the peace sign and tell him to come back again.

Other than writing words on a piece of cardboard and picking high-traffic locations, panhandlers don't need any specific skill to earn a living. You don't have to know how to juggle or perform magic tricks or play a musical instrument. Those are buskers, performing for tips and gratuities in parks and plazas and transit centers. Sometimes even in restaurants, bars, or cafes.

Billy Joel was a busker who cut his musical teeth working in piano bars. Some other famous buskers include Joan Baez, Bob Dylan, George Burns, Steve Martin, and Penn & Teller.

Most decent panhandlers tend to steer clear of buskers and respect their space, choosing instead to find locations where they can benefit from the crowds without encroaching on the performance. But there are panhandlers who hover around buskers, intercepting customers and taking the potential donations for themselves.

In the busking community, these are referred to as *spongers*.

Other panhandlers run little extortion schemes, harassing marks until the busker pays the panhandler to go away. Some panhandlers also steal donations, instruments, and props.

These are the ones who give the rest of us a bad name.

I could earn more money if I learned a skill like juggling or playing the harmonica or making balloon animals, but performing for my tax-free donations would mean having to practice, and I've never been a paragon of self-discipline. Plus large crowds give me performance anxiety. And most of the guys I know who make balloon animals are pedophiles in training. So instead I just come up with creative signs that help me to generate some supplemental income.

MY PARENTS SNORTED MY COLLEGE FUND

CREDIT AND DEBIT CARDS NOT ACCEPTED

MY OTHER JOB IS GETTING HIT BY A ROLLS-ROYCE

That one doesn't always work, but it makes me laugh. And a happy panhandler is a prosperous panhandler.

"You deserve your miserable existence." A woman crumples a dollar into a ball and flings it at me.

I thank her for stopping by.

The sign I'm displaying today says:

WILL TAKE VERBAL ABUSE FOR MONEY

When I first started using this sign a couple of years ago, I received the standard insults and derogatory comments meant for me and my wasted life. For what I represented. For what I'd become.

A social tumor.

A rash on the ass of civilization.

An oozing pus bag of failure.

More often than not, the insults weren't accompanied by a donation but by malicious laughter. Sometimes people spit on me, which isn't technically verbal abuse, but when you're a panhandler, you can't expect everyone to be on the same page.

But after a while, once people saw me around Central Park with my sign on a regular basis, they started to feel comfortable with me, to understand the freedom I was offering, and they started to open up. Now when most people approach me, rather than showering me with personal attacks and derogatory invectives about my existence, they vent their frustrations about anything that's troubling them. The problems that they're unable to deal with.

Jobs. Relationships. Family.

"I hate you, Mom." A young woman wearing a Columbia University sweatshirt tosses a dollar into my hat. "You've ruined my life."

I get that a lot.

It doesn't matter if the object of their frustration and anger is male or female, mother or father, husband or wife. I'm an androgynous receptacle of disparagement. An ambiguous catchall of angst.

Sophie is concerned that I'm allowing myself to take on the projected anger and frustration of the people who pay me to hear their confessions of hostility and resentment. She thinks I'm putting myself at spiritual risk.

"The human psyche is like a sponge," she says. "You can't help absorbing some of their negative energy."

While I appreciate Sophie's interest in my spiritual health, I don't share her concerns. It's not like I'm holding on to any of the rancor directed at me. I don't take it personally. I don't bring my work home. Plus, in a way, I feel like I'm providing a valuable service. Earning the money they toss and fling and throw at me.

I'm kind of like a mendicant therapist. A panhandling priest. Absolving my flock of their sins in exchange for whatever they care to leave as a contribution; offering a sliding scale of emotional succor.

"Go fuck yourself, Kaufman." A guy in a suit donates a dollar to my cause. "I don't need this job or your bullshit TPS reports."

In some countries, begging is tolerated and even encouraged. In Buddhist countries like Thailand, Cambodia, and Vietnam, monks and nuns traditionally live by begging for alms, as did Buddha himself. A number of religions hold that a person who gives alms to a worthy beggar gains religious merit—a sort of spiritual credit they can cash in when their time on this plane of existence has come to an end.

Even in traditional Christianity, the rich were encouraged to serve the poor. Talking about criminals, prostitutes, beggars, and other people generally despised by society, Jesus is supposed to have said, "I am the least of these." So apparently giving to a beggar is the equivalent of giving to Jesus.

Not comparing myself to the Son of God, but at least it's good to know he thought so highly of panhandlers.

So I sit and I listen and I smile and I thank my flock for their words and their donations and their abuse, and after four hours, I've earned eighty-seven dollars and change—which is a good seven dollars more an hour than I typically earn using any of my other signs. At that rate, doing this full-time, I would earn more than forty-five grand a year.

Tax-free.

But if I used the same sign every day, it wouldn't carry the same weight. I'd become just another unimaginative panhandler, preying on the goodwill of my customers—which is why I like to mix things up. Plus it makes me appreciate days like this.

Besides, with all of the competition out there, HOMELESS & HUNGRY: PLEASE HELP just doesn't cut it. You have to be more original. You have to come up with something that stands out in the crowd. Otherwise, you might as well be a mime.

As I start to collect my money and my sign, a teenager on a skateboard rides up, calls me a dream-crushing asshole, then throws a handful of quarters at my feet.

At least I know I'm making a difference.

I pick up the quarters, which have scattered across the concrete, and call out a thank-you as the kid rides away. At the same moment, my lips go numb like they did at the research facility in

Queens last week. This is followed by an overwhelming sense of exhaustion, as if I got run over by the Sandman.

The kid glances back and gives me the finger as I close my eyes and let out a yawn that seems to last forever. When I open my eyes again, the numbness in my lips is gone and I feel refreshed. As if I just took a power nap. I'm wondering what the hell that was all about when I notice the kid on the ground in an unconscious heap, his skateboard rolling away.

I look around to see if anyone noticed, but no one's paying attention, so I walk over to see if the kid's okay. He's on his back, out cold, his head turned to one side. His lips are moving but I can't hear what he's saying, so I kneel down next to him.

"Hey. Hey kid, are you okay?"

He moves and I think he's coming around, but instead of opening his eyes and sitting up, he rolls onto his side, puts his hands under his head, and curls up in a fetal position.

I think about calling 911, but other than a couple of scrapes on his knees and elbows, he doesn't look like he's suffered any serious injuries. Besides, what am I going to tell the emergency operator? That there's a teenager with a skateboard sleeping in Central Park? Like that's news.

Instead I sit down on a nearby bench and watch over the kid, wondering if I should do anything or just mind my own business. I'm still sitting there a few minutes later when he suddenly yawns and stretches and opens his eyes, then sits up and looks around like he's trying to figure out how the hell he got here. When he sees me, he gives me the finger, gets on his skateboard, and rides off without a word.

Most people wouldn't understand what I do or why I do it. They wouldn't choose it as a lifestyle. They wouldn't encourage their children to pursue it as a career.

This is an example of what not *to do with your life*, they would tell their sons and daughters while standing in front of the Professional Guinea Pig display, which is located in the Museum of Natural History right between Drug Addict and Reality Television Star in the Hall of Social Failures.

This isn't the way I imagined my life turning out.

To be honest, I don't know what I imagined. The problem is that I never had much imagination or ambition to begin with and just sort of drifted along as I got older, waiting for something to happen. I haven't so much participated in my life as I've watched it like a spectator, hoping my team finds a way to win.

Not everyone has their shit figured out. Sure, some people do. They're the ones who actually stick to a plan and make all the right choices and end up with the life they imagined.

The rest of us don't really have a plan but just make it up as we go, like Indiana Jones. For some, things work out and they end up rescuing the girl and having a ride named after them at Disney-land. For others, they discover that trying to win the lottery isn't a viable plan for living happily ever after, and end up as a disappointment to their parents.

Sorry, Mom. Sorry, Dad.

I did attend college and earned a bachelor of science in marketing, but only because I couldn't think of anything else I wanted to do. I just buzzed around from one major to another like an aimless honeybee that had lost its magnetic compass and graduated with a BS in marketing because that was the major I was pollinating when graduation rolled around.

When my parents call every few months to ask me how I'm doing, I tell them I'm into volunteer work, which isn't exactly a lie. But even if I was affiliated with the Red Cross or the Leukemia & Lymphoma Society or the Peace Corps, they would still think I was wasting my life. They've never accepted that when it comes to my goals, I'm about as ambitious as a suntan.

I'm sitting on a bench at the south end of the Mall in Central Park, doing a little sun worshipping while eating a black-and-white cookie from Greenberg's. About thirty feet away from me, a Fairy is perched in front of the Japanese maple that's the centerpiece of the Olmsted Flower Bed. The Fairy wears a seafoam-green sleeveless dress with matching green wings and a yellow chiffon skirt that conceals her feet and the pedestal upon which she's standing. Her face is painted a soft white. Not so much that she looks like a mime, but just enough so that she appears otherworldly. She holds a single red rose in her left hand. In front of her sits a painted yellow wooden box with a narrow opening for donations.

The Fairy stands perfectly still.

She's a living statue, the hidden pedestal she's standing on adding a good twelve inches to her height, making her appear more than six feet tall and giving her added stature . . . which is important if you want to be noticed.

For the last hour, dozens of people have walked past her, some stopping to smile or take pictures, most giving a cursory glance, while about two out of ten walk up to the Fairy and deposit a single dollar into the yellow box at her feet.

The moment the dollar falls into the box, her face animates and she comes to life, one hand reaching into a satchel on her hip. She removes something from the satchel and holds her hand out in front of her, fingers pressed together and pointed down. When the person who donated the dollar holds out their hand in response, the Fairy sprinkles a pinch of pixie dust into their open palm, then turns her hand over and blows the remaining pixie dust into the air, coating the person with fairy magic.

It's an elegant display, smooth and graceful, as if her limbs are gliding through water.

Most of the customers don't know what to do. Some of them just laugh or smile and continue on their way, while others blow the pixie dust back at her, which kind of defeats the purpose. After all, she's a fairy. She doesn't need any more pixie dust. But the act of reciprocation seems like the appropriate response. Every now and then, however, someone walks away looking sour and annoyed while brushing the pixie dust off of them.

Some people just don't appreciate fairies.

In addition to the Fairy, there are a number of living statues in Central Park, including the Historian out behind the Met, the Eggman over by Strawberry Fields, and the Silver Skater across from the Wollman Rink.

While those are all good locations with significant foot traffic and the opportunity to attract large crowds, they're actually better suited for street theater, acrobats, or puppeteers. Sheer volume can work against a living statue, causing potential customers to pay more attention to everyone else around them rather than to the silent street performer standing off to the side. By design, the living statue doesn't stand out in a crowd or attract attention. Sometimes the location itself can be a liability.

In busking parlance, the location is called *the pitch*, and the right pitch is essential to success. Standing in front of the Olmsted Flower Bed that complements her costume and character, where everyone walking south along the Mall beneath the canopy of American elms can't help but see her, the Fairy has picked out the perfect pitch.

In the time I've been sitting on the bench, she's had a total of fourteen paying customers. At $14 an hour, presuming she were to do this for eight hours and make one dollar per customer, she'd take home $112 per day. With a regular schedule, that comes to $560 per week, about $2,300 per month, or $30,000 per year.

But this isn't a nine-to-five job. And the foot traffic changes from hour to hour, week to week, season to season. Plus fairies don't tend to work during the winter. So even if she takes advantage of the summers and holidays and weekends, which are prime busking times, the best she can hope to make is about $20,000 per year. Still, it's tax-free, with low overhead and fresh air in a beautiful park with trees and sunshine. That's better than earning twice that amount sitting at a desk and having to deal with a middle manager who's projecting his insecurity issues onto your performance review.

Once I've finished my black-and-white cookie, I get up and walk over to the Fairy. Her blue eyes stare forward, fixed and vacant, her mouth open in the faintest hint of a smile, her head cocked slightly to one side as if she's listening to some distant music, her arms perfectly still.

The Fairy is a vegan. Mid-twenties. Short brown hair. She has a dimple near the left corner of her mouth. Her breath smells like fennel.

"Are you going to be here much longer?" I ask.

Buskers often vie for prime locations, sometimes sharing pitches on a rotational basis. Otherwise it's first come, first served. Every now and then, a busker will send someone to fend off a pitch until they arrive, though squatting is frowned upon in the busking community. Snake charmers are the worst offenders, with contortionists coming in a close second. Plus they're fucking prima donnas.

For the most part, the buskers in Central Park tend to get along with one another, but fights can and do happen. I've seen competing street musicians nearly come to blows. And it's not uncommon to see a fire-eater and a ventriloquist slugging it out in front of the Hans Christian Andersen statue.

But I'm not interested in sharing her pitch. One, I'm not a performer. And two, this isn't a great place to panhandle. Instead I just wait to see if she's going to acknowledge my presence. But she doesn't show any indication that I'm standing directly in front of her. Not a flinch or a twitch or a blink. Her lips don't move and she doesn't look at me. She's a statue made of flesh and white paint and seafoam-green silk.

I reach into my wallet and pull out a dollar and drop it into her yellow donation box and let her go through her routine because I know that's what she has to do; then I hold out my hand to receive my pixie dust as she offers a smile and leans down toward me.

"I'll be done at seven," she whispers as she sprinkles the pixie dust into my palm and blows the rest into my face. "Can you pick up some organic spinach on your way home?"

S ophie and I live in a one-bedroom, fifth-floor walk-up on the Lower East Side across from Seward Park. We're just a few blocks from the Tenement Museum and right around the corner from the Doughnut Plant, the best doughnuts in Manhattan.

That's a personal endorsement, not a statement of fact.

I don't get to frequent the Doughnut Plant as often as I'd like because Sophie encourages me to live a food lifestyle that minimizes the consumption of cooked oils, wheat gluten, and processed sugars. I counter that the Doughnut Plant uses all-natural ingredients, but I tend to lose those arguments more often than not, which pretty much screws me on my doughnut fetish.

"Can you pass the spinach, please?" Sophie asks.

We're eating a dinner of soy-marinated baked tofu with brown rice and fresh organic spinach. On the linoleum floor next to us, Sophie's seven-year-old cat, Vegan, laps up a bowl full of rice milk. Vegan only eats cat food made with organic animal products. He also doesn't consume any dairy products, even if they're made with non-GMO ingredients or come from cows that aren't factory-farmed or injected with HGH. According to Sophie, this is a decision Vegan came to on his own.

I tend to think Sophie has more than a little influence on Vegan's diet, but even though we've lived together for the past five years, I still don't feel it's my place to question Sophie about her cat.

I take another bite of tofu as Vegan looks up at me and lets out a meow, which to me sounds like Cat for *I could really go for some prime rib*.

Or maybe I'm just projecting.

When Sophie's not a living statue in Central Park, she's the night manager at the Westerly Natural Market, which offers a huge selection of nutritional supplements, organic produce, all-natural groceries, and environmentally friendly body-care products. She started out as a part-time clerk during college but quickly worked her way into a job as full-time manager.

"So how are the boys?" Sophie asks as we continue to eat our organic, gluten-free, animal-friendly dinner.

Sophie always refers to the guinea pigs as *the boys*, never individually by name. It's like they're all one person sharing the same body. Or some mythological creature like a Chimera or a Gorgon, with Vic and Charlie and Randy as different snakes weaving around my head.

"Frank's a little crankier than normal," I say. "I think he's going through menopause. And Randy's been educating us on classic-rock-themed anal sex."

"I tried that once in college," she says matter-of-factly. Like we're talking about acupuncture. Or blowfish. "It wasn't my thing. Would you like some more spinach?"

I take another helping and wonder how anal sex has never come up before. Probably because I've never been interested in going in through the out door and Sophie never mentioned any interest in taking a trip to the dark side of the moon.

But then I guess some relationships are like that. You come together due to the serendipitous circumstances of your life without thinking about what's going to happen next, and before you know it, five years have gone by and you're sharing an apartment and joint custody of a cat and discovering that your girlfriend had anal sex in college.

When Sophie and I met, I was twenty-five and doing freelance marketing for a start-up company that had taken on too much debt and was hemorrhaging money. The owner blamed everyone and everything but his own bad decision-making and fired his entire marketing staff, which consisted of me.

Since I'd been hired as an independent contractor, I couldn't collect unemployment. So while I looked for another full-time marketing job, I got a minimum-wage gig as an office clerk. When my life savings started to get sucked down the fiscal drain of rent and monthly bills and Chinese takeout, I got another minimum-wage job working five nights a week making pizzas and I started eating Top Ramen for lunch and dinner. But you can't make a living on minimum wage. At least not in Manhattan. Five years ago, even if you worked two full-time minimum-wage jobs at eighty hours a week, you'd barely earn a whopping $30,000 a year. Before taxes.

The great lie about a college education in the infancy of the twenty-first century is that it guarantees a job that will allow you to live the lifestyle portrayed in all the beer commercials and car advertisements you see on TV. The reality is that you have a lifetime of student loans to pay back while you send out résumés and serve pizzas and wonder when your proverbial ship is going to pull into port to help you navigate your ocean of debt.

So there I was, my savings dwindling down to pocket change, struggling to pay my bills even after canceling cable TV and my health insurance, trying to figure out how the hell I was going to make rent without having to get yet another part-time job or move to Washington Heights.

It was near the end of October and I was walking through Central Park, watching the pigeons milling around on the ground in front of me, the first real autumn chill blowing off the Hudson and the leaves from the American elms turning yellow and falling to the ground like broken promises, when I looked up and saw Sophie standing perfectly still in front of the Olmsted Flower Bed, holding a rose in her left hand and wearing the faintest of smiles. As if she had a secret. As if she knew something I didn't.

I watched as people brought her to life with their donations and received their pixie dust, unable to look away, my gaze drawn to Sophie like a magnet to metal. Like a compass to north.

After a few minutes I decided I didn't have anything to lose but a hundred pennies. So I walked up to her, told her I'd gotten laid off, was working sixty hours a week and running out of money, about to lose my apartment, that I didn't believe in God but I believed she'd appeared to me for some divine reason, and that I could use a little pixie dust to change my luck. Then I gave her a dollar and watched her go through her routine and I wished for a job with the Yankees or *National Geographic* when she blew her pixie dust over me.

Before I could thank her, she leaned forward and whispered: "Do you like cats?"

One month later, I moved in with her.

"Would you like some more tofu?" Sophie asks.

While Sophie has removed her wings and chiffon skirt, she's still wearing her makeup and has pixie dust on her hands and in her hair.

"Thanks," I say, helping myself to another helping of baked, marinated, coagulated soy milk.

Sophie started her living-statue act during the fall of her junior year at NYU as a project for her Behavioral Psychology class, only to discover that she enjoyed being the Fairy so much that she kept doing it even after getting an A in the class. At the time I met her, she'd been the Fairy for two years.

Before I met Sophie, I didn't know anything about fairies. When I Googled them, most of what I got was useless crap about tiny winged creatures and fairy godmothers and a bunch of Tinker Bell porn.

"That's not uncommon," Sophie once told me. "Most men are drawn to the fairy energy but they don't know why, so they sexualize it just like they do everything else they can't understand."

According to Sophie, there are a lot of different types of fairies, including Dryads, Pixies, Flower Fairies, Cloud Fairies, and Earth Fairies. Sophie is an Earth Fairy, as she loves nature and animals and has plants all over the apartment: dracaena, ficus, English ivy, spider plants, Chinese evergreens, golden pothos, and bamboo palms, all of which are supposed to improve the quality of the indoor air.

I suppose they do, but most of the time I can still smell Vegan's litter box.

After I moved in with her, it didn't take me long to discover that Sophie's living-statue act isn't an act at all. Even though she doesn't wear her makeup or her fairy outfit all the time or stand still for hours in the corner of the apartment while I research potential clinical trials on my laptop, Sophie is truly a full-time fairy, spreading her good cheer by volunteering at the SPCA three days a week and giving half of what she earns in Central Park to the Bowery Mission. She also sprinkles her magic pixie dust everywhere, even in the apartment, and I'm constantly following her around with a dustpan and a brush, sweeping it all up and recycling it.

That's very important to Sophie. To recycle her pixie dust. To never throw any of it away.

"It's cosmic," she says. "It floats around and settles on those who need it the most."

While I humor Sophie about her pixie dust, I don't believe there's anything magical about it. It's just glitter that gets on everything and in everything and I'm pretty sure has been the cause of more than one serious rash.

After all, you can't change someone's life by sprinkling silver metallic glitter over them.

"Can you take Vegan to the vet tomorrow?" Sophie asks. "Mandy's out sick and they asked if I could work a double shift."

"Sure." I take a bite of tofu and glance down at Vegan, who stares up at me with either contempt or hunger, I can't tell which. "What's the matter with him?"

"His upper-respiratory thing has come back," she says. "I think he might be allergic to the new food we've been buying."

On cue, Vegan sneezes.

I notice he has pixie dust on top of his head and stuck to his nose and I wonder if the upper-respiratory infections Vegan sometimes gets are related to his diet or to the good fortune Sophie sprinkles around the apartment.

Fortunately, Sophie's job compensates her well enough that she can afford Vegan's vet bills, which she usually pays with some of the extra money she makes as the Fairy. I chip in for groceries and rent and utilities, splitting most of our costs, though Sophie gets some of our organic food at discount. And between the money I earn volunteering for clinical trials plus the tax-free income I take home from panhandling, I earn more than $50,000 annually.

Not bad for someone who makes his living taking experimental drugs and begging for money in Central Park.

A few minutes of silence pass before Sophie says, "So how was your diabetes trial?"

The trial Randy, Vic, Isaac, and I recently wrapped up was a one-week, outpatient, placebo-controlled, double-blind study for an investigative diabetes drug.

"Fine," I say, as if I don't have any idea where this is going.

Every few weeks we have a conversation about volunteering for clinical trials, with Sophie trying to convince me to stop. After nearly a year of this, I can tell what's coming next. It's like a guided tour I've taken so many times that I know the route by heart.

"Have you thought any more about looking for something with health benefits?" she asks.

Up here on the left, we have passive-aggressive pragmatism.

"Yes," I say.

"And?"

"And I'm still thinking about it."

I'm not, really. But admitting that I'm not looking for another job is one thing. Admitting that I don't have the confidence or the ambition to make a living doing something other than volunteering for clinical trials is a whole other kind of honesty.

"I wish you could find something in marketing," she says.

And up here on the right, we have unreasonable optimism.

"I wouldn't get your hopes up," I say. "It's been five years since I worked in marketing, and my résumé isn't exactly up to snuff."

"Well, I know you'd be great at it."

Sophie's always trying to make me feel better about myself, telling me I'm good enough and smart enough to do anything I want—be it marketing, teaching, acting, or running my own business.

The people who love us see all of our potential and promise and the bright, shiny edges, while we often focus on our failings and missed opportunities and the dull, tarnished surfaces.

This tends to be the self-image default setting when you don't believe in yourself.

And although our loved ones and ardent supporters do their best to encourage us and make us believe in what we have to offer and how talented we are, sometimes the stories we tell ourselves have more power. And the more often we tell ourselves these stories, the more likely we are to believe them.

"What about working with me at Westerly?" she asks. "I can see about getting you an interview there."

And if you look out the window to the other side of the road, you can see a disaster waiting to happen.

"I don't know," I say. "I guess it's kind of like you and anal sex. It's not really my thing."

To be honest, I don't know what my thing is. I've never found anything I was particularly good at or really wanted to do. Even my dream jobs are just that. Dreams. I don't expect them to come true. And even if they did, I don't know if I'd be all that happy managing a baseball team or playing professional golf or taking pictures of beautiful naked women.

Okay, yes, I'd probably enjoy that last one. But if you asked me what I'm *passionate* about, if you asked me what I want to do that would make me happy and fill me with a sense of satisfaction and personal enrichment, doing something that mattered to me and nurtured my soul? I couldn't give you more than a shrug and a blank expression.

I'm thirty years old and still trying to figure out what I want to be when I grow up.

"I realize working in a grocery store isn't your thing," Sophie says, attempting to guide me into adulthood. "But I wish you'd at least think about it. Putting all of these chemicals in your body can't be good for you. You don't know the possible long-term effects of all of these drugs you've been testing."

Over there, behind loving concern, is thinly disguised questioning of intelligence.

While I understand Sophie's anxiety, I've been a guinea pig for almost five years and I have a pretty good understanding of what I'm doing. And if any adverse side effects were going to manifest themselves, they probably would have done so by now.

"I like being a professional guinea pig," I say, which isn't an entirely factual statement. While I do enjoy the freedom and flexibility my lifestyle affords me, it's more like I've just grown used to the idea of doing what I do and I don't have the desire or motivation to change.

I'm a victim of my own inertia, having succumbed to the ennui of my existence.

But I don't think I'm alone. The American dream hasn't worked out the way a lot of people imagined, so they've settled into their lives, existing in a pervasive, low-level misery: commuting an hour to work; sitting in makeshift offices surrounded by false walls; sharing half-hour lunches and fifteen-minute breaks with office mates who have their own makeshift offices; spending nine hours a day in a garden of cubicles beneath a sky of fluorescent lights; taking another hour to get home, then waking up the next day and doing it all over again.

Somehow I doubt this is the life anyone dreamed about when they were kids.

"I know you like the freedom your job offers," Sophie says. "And I respect your choices, Lollipop . . ."

That's Sophie's pet name for me. I asked her once, why Lollipop? She told me it's because I'm sweeter than an apple pie.

". . . but don't you ever think about your future? Don't you think about your destiny?"

I've never been a big believer in fate or destiny, in the idea that there's some invisible, cosmic force planning out my life or guiding me to my inevitable doom.

I'm more of a *shit happens* kind of guy.

Good shit, bad shit. It doesn't matter. It's all shit and it either happens or it doesn't. I've had my share of both, though I don't have a Swiss bank account or a penthouse apartment on Central Park West. But it's kind of embarrassing to complain about your life when you're a white, heterosexual male living in the twenty-first century.

Sophie, on the other hand, believes everyone has a destiny and that we all need to figure out what that is, who we're meant to be, and what we're supposed to do. I don't think much about my future, because it makes it that much harder to live in the present. And I believe *destiny* is just a word people throw around to make themselves feel like they have some kind of special role to play when in reality, we're all just turds caught in the siphoning water of a giant toilet, our lives getting flushed down the drain one day at a time.

No one has ever suggested that I become a motivational speaker.

Rather than share my cynical analogy with Sophie, I just smile and say, "As far as I'm concerned, my destiny is right here with you."

Sophie doesn't return my false cheer. "I just don't think being a professional guinea pig is a long-term plan."

And straight ahead of us is a philosophical roadblock.

"Do we really have to talk about long-term plans?" I ask, realizing too late that was the wrong thing to say to someone I've been living with for five years. I try to come up with something to make it better, but when you're a man, sometimes it's best to just quit while you're behind.

Which brings us to the end of our tour.

We finish the rest of our meal in silence, then I do the dishes while Sophie straightens up the apartment and waters the plants, whispering to them before she sprinkles some of her pixie dust over their leaves and soil. I think that's the main reason plants don't tend to do very well in our apartment: pixie dust doesn't make good fertilizer. Sophie, on the other hand, blames their poor health on the lack of south-facing windows.

When I'm done in the kitchen, I turn on the television and flip from the Discovery Channel to Animal Planet, trying to entice Sophie to stop cleaning and come over and join me on the couch while hoping that I don't end up spending the night on it like I did when I moved in with Sophie five years ago.

For the first month or so I slept on the couch and continued to look for a full-time marketing job while keeping both of my part-time jobs. Sophie and I weren't dating or having sex. I was just a new friend crashing on her couch and she was just a kind and trusting person who gave me a place to live for cheap while I tried to get my life back in order.

Then one day, while riding the F train from one part-time gig to the next, I saw an ad inside the train, right above the emergency instructions and next to a Dr. Zizmor notice for beautiful, clear skin:

DO YOU HAVE A DRINKING PROBLEM AND BIPOLAR DISORDER?

The ad described a research study for men and women, age twenty-one to sixty, who were bipolar alcoholics and who would be willing to take medications or placebos for two weeks. The study offered to pay eligible participants up to $2,000.

I didn't have a drinking problem or bipolar disorder, but I was willing to have both of them if it would get me two grand for a couple of weeks of doing nothing but taking medications.

So I started searching the Internet for clinical trials and found a study in Brooklyn for the association between brain function and depression. They wanted healthy subjects as controls to be given PET scans and MRIs. It only paid $600, but it was the easiest $600 I'd ever made. And they told me I could come back to participate in two more studies.

At the time, I figured volunteering for clinical trials would just be a temporary solution to my financial situation and allow me more time to find a full-time job. But eventually I stopped looking for a marketing career and started looking for more clinical trials. And somewhere along the way, I stopped sleeping on the couch and started sleeping in Sophie's bed.

That's more or less the way my life has gone. I don't make decisions so much as I fall into things. But the problem with falling into things is that you don't think about having a plan. And the problem with not having a plan is that you don't learn how to follow through on anything.

This isn't the best blueprint for financial success.

Eventually Sophie finishes watering the plants and joins me on the couch, neither of us saying a word. After a few minutes of our silent standoff, she breaches the empty space between us and curls up next to me with a small sigh. I kiss her on the top of her head and put my arm around her and we watch TV for another half hour in silence before going to bed.

I'm not expecting makeup sex and don't make any overtures to that effect, but Sophie surprises me with her desire to get naked, and I don't argue. It's more or less the way we resolve our problems or disagreements. Physical intimacy is a great salve for emotional wounds. The problem is, the scabs often get pulled off before the wounds can properly heal.

When we're done, Sophie sprinkles pixie dust on my penis, blows the rest across my thighs and abdomen, then curls up next to me and kisses me good night. I want to get up and go into the bathroom and wash off the pixie dust before it gives me another rash, but I can't get up without disturbing Sophie, so instead I listen to her soft exhalations as she drifts off into sleep.

I stare at the ceiling for a few minutes before I close my eyes and wait for sleep to claim me, but thoughts keep racing inside my head, chasing each other around and around until they finally fall down, exhausted. A moment later, off in the distance, comes the pitter-patter of more thoughts.

Some of them are about clinical trials. Some are about the kid on the skateboard. Some are about black-and-white cookies and coconut cream–filled doughnuts.

But most of my thoughts are about Sophie.

Sometimes I think she deserves someone better than me. Someone with more ambition and the courage to think about his future. Someone who has his shit together and knows what he's doing and where he's going. Someone who has his life mapped out. Any map I may have once had of my life is good and lost.

This is not the kind of internal dialogue that is conducive to getting a good night's sleep.

I get like this sometimes after a trial, my head filled with thoughts that keep me up into the early morning. I've tried counting sheep. Counting backward. Meditating before going to bed. Taking valerian root. None of it works. Lately it's been getting worse, happening to me more often, resulting in a lot of unscheduled afternoon naps and stifled yawns. I'm hoping it's a phase and that it'll pass, sooner rather than later.

I'm still hoping this at three in the morning, when I finally drift off into a restless slumber.

From the New York *Daily News*, page 4:

FORGET-ME-NOWS:
MANHATTAN MUGGING VICTIMS DRAW BLANKS

A string of muggings in Lower Manhattan has victims and police scratching their heads.

"I don't remember what happened," Andrea Orozco said. She was robbed while walking along Grand Street after withdrawing money from a nearby Wells Fargo ATM. "I have a vague recollection of someone approaching me, but I don't remember what he looked like or what he said to me. The next thing I know, my purse is on the ground and the two hundred dollars in my billfold is gone."

She's not alone in her confusion. Over the past week, more than half a dozen people have reported being mugged after withdrawing money from ATM machines throughout Lower Manhattan. And none of them can recall who robbed them.

"It's not uncommon for people to get mugged after walking away from an ATM, especially at night," Sergeant Perry Lee of the NYPD Fifth Precinct said. "What *is* unusual is not having any eyewitness testimony to help us find out who's doing this."

While eyewitness accounts are often unreliable due to such factors as anxiety, stress, and false memories, the muggings are remarkably unique in that none of the victims can remember anything about the perpetrator.

"At first I wasn't sure I was mugged," Andrea Orozco said. "I thought maybe I'd just had some kind of a fugue or episode and dropped my purse. I wasn't even sure I'd taken any money out of my bank. Except I still had the receipt. It's baffling."

Six other victims have come forward to report what they believe was a mugging, with nothing for the police to go on other than hazy memories and blind guesses. About the only

constant is that no one knows for sure how the mugger is causing them to forget him.

"Maybe he's using some kind of gas," Andrea Orozco said.
"Or hypnosis. Or drugs. It's almost like someone gave me a roo-
fie."

The police are warning everyone in Lower Manhattan to
use extra caution and vigilance around banks and ATMs and to
report any suspicious persons or activity to their local precinct.

A few days later we're at Charlie's playing Texas Hold'em, seven of us crowded around a six-foot folding table decorated with bottles of cheap beer and stacks of poker chips—though Blaine's stack is by far the largest, which is unusual. Blaine rarely wins at poker.

"You guys better break out the plates and forks." Blaine lays down his cards and pulls in another pot of chips. "Because taking your money tonight is a piece of cake."

Blaine is a thirty-two-year-old know-it-all with a Brooklyn accent and a helmet of black hair that makes his head look one size too big.

"You better be careful." Vic runs a hand across his head, his bald dome the cosmetic yin to Blaine's abundance of hair. "You know what happens when you talk shit."

"I feel better about myself at the expense of others?" Blaine says.

"You end up tempting fate and getting kicked in the ass by karma," Randy says. "That's what."

"I think you're mixing your idioms about predestination and cause and effect," Blaine says.

Charlie looks around the table with his usual expression of confusion. "What does that mean?"

"It means that fate and karma are two entirely different things," Blaine says. "Karma is the sum of all that a human has done, is doing, and will do. The effects of all actions and deeds create past, present, and future experiences. So a particular action now doesn't condemn you to some predetermined fate. It simply leads to a karmic consequence."

"How do you know all that?" Charlie asks.

Blaine shrugs. "I read it in a book somewhere."

Four years ago, Blaine lost all of his money to an identity thief who cleaned out his bank accounts and charged thousands of dollars to Blaine's credit cards. While he didn't have to pay the credit card debt, he needed some quick cash to cover his rent and some of his other bills and got a payday advance from an instant-cash service, only to end up owing more in interest than the original loan when he kept getting charged cash-advance fees on the unpaid balance. He started guinea-pigging to pay off the fees and just never stopped.

"So then what's f-fate?" Isaac asks.

Isaac is a twenty-six-year-old wannabe actor with bleached-blond hair and a mild stutter, which might have something to do with his inability to land any roles.

"Fate predetermines and orders the course of a person's life," Blaine says. "If you're forced into your circumstances, then that's your fate."

"So my fate is being forced to play poker with you assholes in Charlie's rectum of an apartment," Frank says.

Charlie has a studio apartment one floor above the Original Chinatown Ice Cream Factory, complete with industrial-strength brown carpet and a postcard view of Bayard Street Obstetrics & Gynecology.

Most of the time we play poker at Randy's, Charlie's, or Frank's. We played at my and Sophie's apartment once, but Blaine's allergic to cats. We've never played at Vic's. As far as I know, no one has ever been to his apartment. For all I know, he could live in Queens.

"Blinds," Randy says as he deals the cards.

"Why do they call them blinds?" Charlie asks.

"We go over this every time," Vic says. "How do you not remember?"

"I have a problem with short-term memory," Charlie says, scratching his head. "Or is it long-term memory? I forget."

"They're called *blinds* because you make your bet without seeing any cards," Blaine says. "So you go into the hand blind."

That's kind of what we do every time we volunteer for a drug trial. We go in blind and lay down a bet that we'll come out healthy without knowing whether or not our cards are any good.

"Did you know when they started playing poker in saloons back in the 1860s, players took turns dealing to avoid cheating?" Blaine says. "Back then, a knife was used to identify the dealer and the marker became known as a *buck* in reference to the buck horn handle of knives. When the dealer finished, he would *pass the buck*, which is how the expression became a metaphor for avoiding responsibility."

"Who the fuck are you?" Frank says. "Professor Poker?"

"Hey, I'm just throwing down some knowledge," Blaine says. "I can't help it if you don't appreciate a little education."

"What I appreciate is proper poker etiquette," Frank says. "So why don't you stop vomiting useless information that needlessly stalls the action of the game and make a bet."

Blaine calls the big blind and I follow suit, then stifle a yawn.

"Past your bedtime, Sleeping Beauty?" Vic asks.

"Just tired," I say, trying to focus on the game, but my thoughts seem a little muddled. "And I sure hope you're not my Prince Charming."

"I always thought it would be awesome to be Prince Charming," Randy says. "Snow White. Cinderella. Sleeping Beauty. I bet he gets major booty calls all over Fairy Tale Land."

"Did you know that in the original version of *Sleeping Beauty*, the king who finds the sleeping beauty fails to wake her?" Blaine says. "So he rapes her instead."

"Well," Vic says, "there go my childhood memories."

"You been eating a lot of carbs?" Frank asks me.

Certain carbohydrates with a high glycemic index break down fast and cause a steep rise in blood sugar levels, causing an initial rush that's followed by periods of drowsiness.

I shake my head. "I've just had trouble sleeping lately."

"What kind of trouble?" Charlie asks, then calls.

"Trouble," I say. "You know, the kind that keeps me from falling asleep."

Isaac looks at me from across the table like he's getting ready to say something he finds amusing. He's easier to read than a Dr. Seuss primer.

Isaac's a lousy poker player.

"You sure it's not your girlfriend's p-pixie dust?" Isaac says, then lets out a snort of laughter.

Isaac was a bit of a thespian in high school and thought he had enough acting chops to make it big on Broadway. Apparently, he had a couple of minor roles in small theater productions and was waiting tables part-time but wasn't making enough to pay his bills, so he and a couple of other actors/waiters started volunteering for clinical trials to earn some extra cash. Somewhere along the way, he developed a stutter, which made it tough to land any roles. As far as I know, Isaac hasn't had an acting gig in over four years.

Every guinea pig has a story. Most of them don't end with *happily ever after*.

"I'm out." Frank throws down his cards and gets up from the table.

Randy and Isaac call and Vic checks the big blind, then Randy deals the flop and everyone checks to me.

"You been upping your caffeine intake, Lloyd?" Frank asks.

"Nothing more than usual," I say, not liking the look of my hand, so I check.

The check goes around the table as Frank opens the refrigerator to grab another beer. Outside on the street, some woman starts shouting at the top of her lungs.

"What's going on?" Charlie asks.

Frank glances out the window. "Just some homeless woman pushing a shopping cart down the street and shouting at everyone."

"What's she shouting?" Randy asks.

"Her Facebook status," Frank says. "How the fuck should I know?"

"Did you guys know that at least a third of all homeless are thought to suffer from severe mental illness?" Blaine says. "Many of them were released from state mental hospitals due to huge cuts in public mental-health spending and ended up on the streets."

"That's not cool," Randy says.

"A lot of homeless people apparently have mild to severe schizophrenia," Blaine says. "They're delusional and have trouble telling the difference between what's real and what isn't."

"You guys hear about how someone's been dosing people?" Charlie says.

"D-dosing them with what?" Isaac asks.

Charlie shakes his head. "They think it might be LSD, but no one knows for sure. Apparently it's happened a few times. People hallucinating and freaking out. I heard at least one person died."

"Douche bags," Vic says, shaking his head. "The world is full of douche bags."

Randy deals the turn and Isaac bets a dollar. The bet goes around the table, with Vic and me folding before Randy deals the river.

"Have you been d-d-dreaming?" Isaac asks.

Everyone looks around the table, wondering where Isaac's question is directed. He occasionally asks questions or makes comments that don't make any sense until you figure out he's referring to something someone said three conversation threads before.

"Dreaming?" I ask. "About what?"

"I d-don't know. Just . . . dreaming," Isaac says.

It takes me a moment before I realize he's asking me about the trouble I've had sleeping lately.

"Yeah," I say, nodding. "But they're just snippets. Like thirty-second commercials from my subconscious. I don't remember much about them."

"Your subconscious needs to work on its advertising campaign," Frank says, then sits back down and grabs a bag of potato chips.

"Have you gained weight?" Blaine asks and bets a dollar.

"Why is everyone so focused on my goddamned weight?" Frank says around a mouthful of Ruffles.

"Well, you're usually the one preaching moderation and diet," I say. "So it seems a little unusual."

"Plus there does seem to be a little more of Frank than usual," Vic says, cleaning his glasses. "Kind of like you've been supersized."

Charlie nods. "And you *have* been kind of cranky lately."

"Crankier than normal, anyway," Randy says.

"What is this?" Frank says. "A fucking intervention? I thought we were playing poker."

Randy scratches at his chest. "We're just expressing our concern, that's all."

"Well, all of you ladies can stop waving your tampons," Frank says. "Now can we speed things up? By the time this hand is finished I'll be wearing Depends."

Blaine ends up winning another hand, which turns the attention from Frank's weight to Blaine's run of luck, with Vic accusing him of cheating. I catch Isaac looking at me like he has something on his mind, something he wants to ask me, his head tilted like he's trying to figure something out. But then he just gives me a smile and cuts the cards and deals the next hand.

ew York always looks so romantic from here," Sophie says, her right arm hooked through my left and her head against my shoulder as we stand at the back of the Staten Island Ferry and watch Lower Manhattan recede beyond the wake, the buildings reflecting the late-afternoon sun and the blue sky painted with clouds. "It's beautiful and sad all at the same time."

Sophie loves to explore New York and do all of the fun, cheap, touristy things that most people who live in Manhattan never get around to doing. Like hanging out in Times Square or touring the art galleries in Chelsea or riding the Staten Island Ferry.

"How is it sad?" I ask.

"I don't know," she says, her head still against my shoulder. "It's like it wants to come with us, to tag along and see where we're going and share in our adventure, but it has to stay behind and watch us go."

Sophie is always attributing feelings and thoughts to inanimate objects. She believes there's a consciousness in everything and that we're all connected in one big, cosmic web, the way a flower is connected to the soil and to the sun and water that brought it into being.

It's one part Buddhism and one part quantum mechanics.

"See how the sun is reflecting off the glass of that building?" She points to the curved façade of 17 State Street, the windows reflecting the sun and the blue sky. "When the sun heats the glass, it changes the configuration of the electrons of the glass and the electrons shift their energies. That changes the electrons in the air around the glass, which causes all of the electrons in the universe to shift, since none of the electrons in the universe can share the same energy level. It's cause and effect, a ripple of cosmic activity, connecting everything."

"Well . . . when we get back, we'll be sure to tell Manhattan all about our trip."

She looks up at me. "Really?"

I look down at her face just inches from mine, her eyes so big and blue they seem like windows into another universe. The corny romantic in me thinks about seeing heaven in her eyes and starts to compose a haiku around the cosmic nature of love, while the sarcastic cynic in me thinks about blue wavelengths being scattered more widely than other colors and starts to write a limerick about atmospheric perspective.

Eventually, the corny romantic and sarcastic cynic both get writer's block.

"Absolutely," I say and kiss her.

Sophie and I watch Battery Park and the rest of Lower Manhattan continue to fall away, neither one of us saying a word. These are some of my favorite moments with Sophie. Neither one of us talking, just enjoying the simplicity of each other's company and knowing that words would just spoil the moment. Or at least my words would spoil the moment.

When it comes to Sophie, I think I'm at my best when my mouth is shut.

As we continue toward Staten Island, Sophie and I walk around the deck. The ferry is packed with tourists enjoying the ride, pointing at Ellis Island and the Statue of Liberty, taking pictures and talking to one another in a dozen different languages, their conversations mixing together to form a background of unintelligible linguistic babble.

When I was a kid, I used to attend Sunday school. This was before my father decided he'd rather spend his Sundays playing golf and my mother decided she'd rather spend them drinking gin and tonics. One of the stories I always found confusing in my religious schooling was the story of Babel. There humanity was, working together after the Great Flood, united in language and purpose, filled with the promise of peace and harmony, and God decided that was a bad thing. So he scattered humanity across the face of the earth and confounded the language of man so no one would be able to understand one another, thus helping to foster all of the suspicion and animosity and bloodshed that followed throughout the history of man.

When you think about it, God was kind of a dick.

"I love listening to other languages," Sophie says, pulling close to me and speaking just above a whisper. "It's like hearing all the different parts of an orchestra."

"An orchestra?"

"Romance languages are like strings, Slavic languages brass, Asian languages woodwinds, and Germanic languages percussion," she says. "And all of them blend together to play a beautiful, unrehearsed symphony."

Leave it to Sophie to make my worldview on humanity seem cold and cynical.

We walk along the deck, our faces warmed by the afternoon sun and the air filled with Sophie's symphony of languages, though I'm not sure if what we're listening to is more Bach, Beethoven, or Danny Elfman.

Ahead of us, a young teenage boy points and talks animatedly to his father in French. Next to them, a wispy girl of no more than ten or eleven leans against her mother, the girl's face pinched from apparent motion sickness. The mother runs a hand across her daughter's head and brushes the hair out of her face, then turns and says something to her husband in a flute solo. Or is it a cello? Or a French horn?

While I'm trying to remember which part of the orchestra the French language belongs to, Sophie squeezes my hand and leans into me, motioning toward the family of four with her head.

"I love that," she says. "I hope we can be like them when we're older."

"French tourists?"

"No silly." She squeezes my hand again. "A family."

While Sophie has hinted before at the idea of getting married, usually by asking me about long-term plans and talking about the future, this is the first time she's ever mentioned anything about wanting children.

When I think about having children, it's always more as an abstract concept. Like love and beauty. Or the existence of Bigfoot.

"I'll be right back." Sophie kisses me on the cheek. "I have to use the ladies' room."

She walks away through the crowd, then glances back over her shoulder and gives me a smile that melts my heart before she disappears into the cabin. And I'm reminded once again of how I wish I could be more the man that Sophie deserves, the man she would like me to be. But marriage and children just seem like more responsibility than I can handle. At least right now.

Who am I kidding? My idea of being an adult is taking out the trash. And when it comes to responsibility, I tend to think it's overrated.

I glance back at the French family of four and wonder if I can ever live up to Sophie's expectations and be like them: married with children.

The mother, who apparently noticed Sophie's affectionate departure, gives me a smile that says she remembers what it was like to have a little romance in her life before she had kids. Or at least that's my current frame of mind. Her daughter, her face still pinched, glances up at me, obviously not enjoying the ferry ride. I start to offer my own smile to let her know that I understand how she feels, when my lips suddenly go numb and an immediate pressure builds up in the back of my throat. My eyelids grow heavy, along with my arms and legs, like someone turned the gravity up to eleven. It's all I can do to keep from curling up on the deck to take a nap.

My mouth opens in a wide, jaw-popping yawn. I have to close my eyes just to get it out of me, my hand covering my mouth halfway through. When I'm done, I notice that the young French girl has stolen my idea and laid herself out across her mother's lap to take a nap. I also feel refreshed and realize that my lips are no longer numb.

"Danielle?" The mother caresses her daughter's face. "*Êtes-vous d'accord, miel?*"

I don't know what she said, but her husband looks over and says something else in French, to which the mother responds while shaking her head. Then the father gets off the bench and squats down in front of his wife and daughter.

"Danielle?" he says, shaking his daughter gently before saying her name again.

Danielle remains unresponsive, although she doesn't appear to be unconscious. She just looks like she's taking a nap. A moment later she curls up in a fetal position and puts both of her hands under her head.

And I can't help thinking about the kid on the skateboard.

"Hey." Sophie appears at my side as the French parents try to awaken their daughter. "There's a Spanish couple talking next to a group of Italian students and it sounds like a violin concerto. Come on."

As Sophie takes my hand and leads me away, I glance back at the sleeping French girl and wonder what the hell just happened.

chapter 10

In the movies, when people discover that they've developed, or think they've developed, some strange new ability that defies logic and reason, they spend about five minutes getting used to the idea and then incorporate this information and understanding into a brand-new paradigm.

Telekinesis. Invisibility. Superhuman strength.

X-ray vision. Animal mimicry. Mind control.

In real life, for instance, if you thought you'd developed the ability to make people fall asleep, you'd more likely spend several days yawning at people—on the street, on the subway, in Central Park—but the most you'd get is a reciprocal yawn and a mild case of TMJ. You'd even spend several accumulated hours pinching and biting your lips and sucking on ice cubes to try to make your lips go numb, and when nothing happened, you'd start to wonder if you'd suffered a psychotic break.

Characters in films who develop supernatural abilities don't tend to spend a lot of time questioning their mental health. Or at least if they do, that footage gets edited out because it doesn't test well with audiences.

I wish I had an editor. Someone to cut out all of the bad parts of my life and just leave the bits that make me look good. While we're at it, I could use a good musical score, too. Something fun and playful, like the soundtrack from *Pulp Fiction*. Or *The Blues Brothers*. But since I don't have a twenty-four-hour DJ and I'm stuck with the uncut version of my life, I just have to try to figure out what the hell is going on and hope I haven't been dosed with LSD or become delusional.

The rational part of me realizes I couldn't possibly have anything to do with what happened to the French girl on the Staten Island Ferry or the skateboarder in Central Park. Except the more I think about it, the more I wonder about the timing and my lips going numb and the uncompromising yawn that built up inside of me. Both the skate rat and the French girl seemed to fall asleep the moment I yawned, and immediately afterward I felt refreshed and reinvigorated.

Sophie's voice plays back in my head. She keeps waxing on about Buddhist philosophy and quantum mechanics, telling me how everything is connected to everything else in the universe and how a change in molecules here has repercussions and consequences there. A cosmic ripple effect of energy.

Cause and effect.

But it's not just the effect of two people falling asleep that's on my mind, along with the still-debatable idea that I may have caused their unexpected catnaps. It's the effect of my lips going numb and what caused me to feel tired and yawn in the first place that has me wondering about my life choices.

All sorts of prescription drugs can cause drowsiness. It's a common side effect and one I've experienced countless times. So while the idea is still something I'm not quite ready to embrace, I'm considering the possibility that all of these drugs I've tested over the past five years may have caused an unexpected and unusual effect.

True, it's only happened twice. And I remember reading that once is chance, twice is coincidence, and three times is a pattern. So I'm trying to see if there's a pattern here or if I'm just borderline schizophrenic.

"What are you doing?" Sophie asks.

She asks me this from the bathroom doorway while I'm leaning forward, staring at myself in the mirror and pinching my lower lip to try to make it go numb. Not as bad as getting caught masturbating, but it's still kind of awkward.

To make things worse, I noticed a few strands of gray in my hair.

I haven't said anything to Sophie. Not about the gray hair. But she already wants me to stop volunteering for clinical trials. If I tell her I think the drugs I've been testing for the past five years have affected me to the point where I believe I'm making people fall asleep, she'll make me stop for sure.

The fact that Sophie's reaction would be perfectly rational doesn't factor into my decision making.

"Just checking my gums," I say, still holding on to my lower lip like I'm trying to keep it from flying away.

"What's wrong with your gums?"

"Nothing. I was just making sure they looked healthy."

Sophie stands there in her Westerly Natural Market polo shirt and stares at me. For a moment, I think she knows I'm lying. Somehow her fairy powers allow her to see that my aura has changed from blue to red or orange or whatever color your aura turns when you're manipulating the truth.

"When was the last time you saw a dentist?" she asks.

"I don't know," I say, both relieved and ashamed. "At least two or three years."

"You should make an appointment, Lollipop," she says. "You need to take care of your teeth."

I know she's right, but I hate going to the dentist and having people stick things in my mouth. Some people are afraid of clowns. Others are afraid of snakes. I'm terrified of dentists.

The light over the chair that stares down at you like a giant, malevolent eyeball. The chalky substance they use to clean your teeth. The sound of the suction funnel. The high-pitched whine of the drill. The pinch of the needle as the dentist injects lidocaine into your gums and your lips turn to rubber. It's like a sadistic nightmare. Or torture porn.

As I'm thinking about sitting in the dentist's chair with my mouth open and a dental hygienist all up in my molars, a tingling starts in my lips, at first like they're being tickled by a feather and then as if a small jolt of electricity is being pumped through them. Before I know it, my lips turn numb.

"I'm going to work." Sophie walks up and gives me a kiss on the lips. "Can you feed Vegan his dinner?"

"Sure," I say, barely feeling her kiss.

"I love you, Lollipop," she says as she walks out of the bathroom.

"I love you, too," I say. Only it comes out sounding more like *I lub you, too.*

Once Sophie leaves, I close my eyes and force myself to imagine I'm at the dentist, lying in the chair with my mouth wide open and the light of doom shining down on me, the sound of the suction tube sucking saliva out of my mouth and threatening to take my uvula with it as the dentist pulls out a needle and syringe. I see the needle going into my mouth, disappearing into my lower gums, the contents of the syringe emptying as the plunger depresses and my lips go numb.

Exhaustion rolls over me, thick and heavy, like a dense fog blocking out the light of consciousness. A yawn builds up in the base of my throat, a tangible object with weight and mass, pushing up from my esophagus, through my larynx, and into the back of my throat—a fully formed fetal yawn about to be birthed into the world. My excitement at finally having achieved this is matched only by my exhaustion.

The only problem is, I don't have anyone to test it on.

When I open my eyes, Vegan is sitting on the toilet seat, staring at me with either disdain or impatience, I can't tell which. Probably it's a little of both.

"Meow," he says.

"Hold on," I say and let out a yawn that feels like the godfather of all yawns. When I'm done, I feel invigorated and refreshed, like I've just woken up from a long winter's nap.

"Oh shit," I say.

Vegan is on the bathroom floor, out cold.

chapter 11

"D oes this place serve anything edible?" Frank asks, looking over the menu.

Frank is wearing sweatpants and an oversize T-shirt, which makes it harder to guess his weight, but from the fullness in his cheeks, he seems to have put on a few more pounds since last week's poker game.

"They have a bunch of awesome sandwiches," Randy says. "I'm getting the chopped-egg-salad sandwich. Packed with protein. It's so Pink Floyd."

"Please don't tell me this has anything to do with going to the dark side of the moon," Vic says, looking over the top of his glasses at Randy.

Randy does a double-biceps pose. "It's money."

"What's the dark side of the moon?" Charlie asks.

The seven of us are grabbing lunch in the East Village, waiting to order while I look around at everyone, trying to figure out a way to tell my guinea pig comrades about this brand-new ability I've developed.

After giving Vegan an unplanned catnap, I made three humans fall asleep—not all at the same time, but spread out over a couple of days: a homeless man in Chinatown; a woman sitting on a bench by the Bethesda Fountain; and a guy reading Plato in the philosophy section at the Strand. Although to be honest, he was probably going to fall asleep without my help.

Still, this is most definitely a pattern.

My inner child is excited to tell my friends about what I discovered, while the adult Lloyd wonders if I should keep this to myself. I still haven't told Sophie. I'm waiting for the right moment. I just haven't figured out when that will be.

"I don't see any dishes with meat," Frank says.

"That's because this is a v-v-vegetarian restaurant," Isaac says.

"Vegetarian?" Frank turns the menu over. "Are you fucking kidding?"

"Mostly vegetarian," Randy says. "No pork, beef, or fowl."

"Why didn't we pick someplace that serves meat?" Frank asks.

"They have tuna burgers," Charlie says, trying to be helpful. "And fish and chips. And salmon croquettes."

"Fish isn't meat," Frank says. "In order to be meat, it has to have legs."

"Yeah," I say. "I think they have that listed on the FDA labels."

"Did you guys know that in addition to food and drugs, the FDA handles sanitation requirements on interstate travel and disease control on products from household pets to sperm donation?" Blaine says.

Randy nods toward a pair of twenty-something women who walk past our table. "I can get behind the idea of sperm donation."

"Well," Vic says. "I guess I won't be ordering the rice pudding."

"Can we please have a meal where you don't talk about anal sex or body fluids?" Frank says.

"What about s-s-snakes?" Isaac says.

Everyone looks at Isaac, who doesn't provide any additional information.

"Is that supposed to be a metaphor for something?" I ask.

Isaac looks at Frank and tilts his head. "S-snakes don't have l-legs."

It takes us a moment to realize he's referring to Frank's definition about what constitutes something being meat.

"When was the last time you saw me eat a fucking snake?" Frank asks.

"Hey Frank, have you considered anger-management classes?" Randy says. "Or maybe meditation?"

"Have you considered kissing my ass?" Frank says.

"There's a lot of it to kiss lately," Vic says. "Can you narrow it down to a longitude and latitude?"

The waiter approaches our table. "Are you gentlemen ready to order?"

Everyone looks at Frank, who stares at the menu like it's written in Hatfield and he's a McCoy. "Goddamn it!"

The rest of us place our orders while Frank tries to make up his mind. He finally decides on the smoked-whitefish sandwich with a bowl of vegetarian chili, but isn't happy about it. When the waiter leaves, I figure this is my chance to bring up my newly discovered ability to make people fall asleep, but Charlie starts asking questions about his upcoming clinical trial for an experimental drug to combat seizures and the conversation inevitably turns to business.

"What are some of the side effects?" Blaine asks.

Charlie reads off the list of more serious ones, which include mood and behavior changes, depression, thoughts of suicide, muscle pain, weakness, tenderness, easy bruising or bleeding, swelling in the hands or feet, and rapid weight gain.

"Hey Frank," Vic says. "Did you take this medication?"

Isaac lets out a snort and Frank silences him with a glare.

We spend the next fifteen minutes talking about other up-coming clinical trials and sharing information about which ones to volunteer for and which ones to avoid; then our food arrives and we all dig in. Even Frank, though he complains the whole time about how he was in the mood for a bacon cheeseburger.

While we're eating lunch, a fat guy in a Hawaiian shirt who weighs at least two-eighty walks past us and sits down at a table with his buddy, who's wearing a Sex Pistols T-shirt and playing Laurel to the other one's Hardy. The skinny one lets out a yawn that I catch, which prompts Frank to ask if I'm still having trouble sleeping.

"Not lately," I say. "But I think I've figured out what was causing it."

"Sorry to eat and run." Blaine tosses his napkin on his plate and a twenty on the table. "I've got a two o'clock in the Bronx."

"Is that the trial for the West Nile virus vaccine?" Charlie asks.

"Irritable bowel syndrome," Blaine says.

"Well, I'm done." Frank pushes the last of his vegetarian chili away.

I pick up Blaine's twenty. "How much change you want?"

"Don't worry about it." Blaine flashes a smile and dual peace signs like Richard Nixon before he leaves, walking past the table where the obese guy in a Hawaiian shirt is ordering half the menu while his skinny companion sits slouched so far down in his chair it looks like he's taking a nap.

And I decide that's my cue.

"Anybody have anything weird happen to them lately?" I say.

"Weird?" Isaac asks. "What k-kind of weird?"

"The kind of weird that makes you wonder if there's something going on that you don't know about," I say.

"I get that all the time," Charlie says. "It's called *women*."

Randy claps Charlie on the shoulder. "I can help you with that."

"When you say *weird*," Vic says, "are you talking about with you or with other people?"

"A little of both," I say.

"Does it have anything to do with body spasms or convulsions?" Charlie asks, running a hand through his disheveled red hair.

"No," I say. "Why? Did something like that happen to you?"

Charlie looks around the table like he just farted and doesn't want to own up to it. "Maybe."

"Did you report it?" Frank asks.

Charlie shakes his head and Frank launches into lecture mode about personal responsibility and the Guinea Pig Code, which we're all pretty sure is something Frank made up.

Isaac stares at me and cocks his head, as if waiting for me to continue.

Outside the restaurant, a homeless man starts shouting something about being impregnated by aliens and pounds on the window a couple of times before he runs off down the street.

Never a dull moment in Manhattan.

"Can we get back to Lloyd's question about things being weird?" Vic says.

"Yeah." Randy scratches at his chest, which is something he's been doing a lot lately. "What do you mean by *weird*?"

I look around at everyone, then lower my voice and fess up, telling them everything about the girl on the Staten Island Ferry and the kid on the skateboard in Central Park.

"And they both passed out right after your lips went numb?" Vic asks. "At the same moment you yawned?"

I nod.

"Are you s-s-sure it wasn't just a c-coincidence?" Isaac asks.

"I don't think so," I say. Then I tell them about the others I've made fall asleep over the past few days.

"That *is* weird," Randy says.

Everyone looks around the table, but it seems like we're all trying to avoid eye contact. Like we're hiding something.

"Any of you feel nauseous?" Vic asks. "Not right now, but I mean in general?"

"No," I say.

"Only when I'm forced to eat vegetarian food," Frank says. "Or contemplate Blaine's IBS study."

Charlie and Isaac both shake their heads.

"I haven't been feeling nauseous," Randy says, scratching the back of his head. "But I *have* been getting these rashes."

Frank, who is sitting next to Randy, scoots farther away.

The thought occurs to me that Randy might have had something to do with what happened to that punk on the subway a few weeks ago. I'm about to ask him when Vic leans forward so only we can hear him and says:

"I think I'm making other people throw up."

PORCELAIN GODS WORSHIPPED HERE

Vic stands in line at the Deluxe Food Market, waiting to pay for three boxes of pork dumplings and a couple of steamed buns. As usual, the market is crowded with a mixture of young and old, Asian and Caucasian—with the Asians in the majority. Mandarin- and Cantonese-speaking voices dominate the conversation, a cacophony of *shee*s and *tong*s and *aiya*s, people shouting or talking loud, and everyone sounds angry. As far as Vic is concerned, Chinese people are always pissed off. They could be making dinner plans or discussing classical music and still sound like they're about to beat the shit out of each other.

But in the Deluxe Food Market, getting angry is easy to understand.

Everywhere up and down the narrow aisles people elbow and shove their way between each other and cut in line, violating everyone else's personal space with complete disregard. About every thirty seconds, one of the Chinese workers shouts out *Hello!*

at anyone who isn't paying attention, usually some white person who is so overwhelmed that they don't know whether to laugh or run out the door screaming. Inevitably some douche bag tries to navigate his way down the aisles with one of those folding shopping carts, running into people's knees or up the backs of everyone's legs.

It's barely controlled chaos, a banana republic teetering on the verge of anarchy, hot and humid and thick with the smell of greasy food and human perspiration. To quote Charlton Heston, it's a madhouse. And to Vic, the place doesn't smell a whole lot different than a holding cell for unwashed carcasses. But the prices are cheap and the food is worth fighting for, so long as you stay away from the deep-fried stuff.

The checkout line is running long (typical) and Vic's patience is running short (also typical). He lets out an exasperated sigh, looks around, and considers giving up, except he's been craving the steamed buns all day long, almost since the moment he woke up. But now, standing in line, surrounded by crowds of shouting, shoving, unapologetic douche bags, he wonders if it's worth the trouble.

Actually, that's been the running question for Vic lately: Is it worth the trouble? Not just for the steamed buns, but for his life in general.

As far as Vic can tell, his life has no purpose anymore. It used to be the opposite. In spite of the occasional politics and bullshit and pain-in-the-ass students or, more often, pain-in-the-ass administrators, Vic loved to teach. He felt like he was doing something that mattered, offering guidance and knowledge and tools that his students could use to help them become better humans and find success in life.

But then in a single moment of bad judgment and lack of self-discipline, he screwed up and has been paying the price ever since.

Now, instead of being filled with self-confidence because he's doing something worthwhile, Vic is filled with self-loathing over the wasted opportunity of his life. Sometimes it feels like the self-loathing is something he's eaten, this constant weight sitting in his stomach, waiting to be digested, and he wishes he could find a way to get it out of his system.

"Hello!" the man shouts from behind the meat counter. "Hello! Next!"

An elderly Chinese woman with a small box in her hands approaches Vic, elbows him in the ribs without so much as a glance or a gesture of acknowledgment, and pushes her way past him to get to a display of uncooked noodles. Once she gets what she wants, she stays where she is, right in front of him, looking straight ahead like she hasn't done anything wrong and he was holding her place. Vic considers poking her in the shoulder and asking her to go to the back of the line, but he doesn't speak Mandarin or Cantonese and even if he did, she would probably just ignore him or else yell at him in a language he doesn't understand.

Instead he stands there holding his boxes of pork dumplings and steamed buns, now one customer farther away from the cashier than he was just a few moments ago, staring at the back of the old woman's head—which doesn't appear to have seen a bottle of shampoo in at least a week. Vic swears he can smell her—the odor of her unwashed hair mixed with a concoction of late-afternoon sweat, greasy fried duck, and barbecued pork. It's like a cloud of stink, a fog of pungent, sweaty, greasy funk swirling around him, permeating his skin and seeping into his pores.

The queasiness starts in his stomach and works its way up to his diaphragm, spreading out across his entire lower torso, accompanied by a cold sweat and a slight bout of light-headedness. He hopes it's just a temporary reaction to the crowd and the odors, but he's never felt this sick this suddenly before. So he blinks his eyes and takes a deep breath, which he realizes too late was a bad idea.

The stench of the place—it has now moved from odor to stench and could never in any possible way be described as a scent—flows into his nostrils and down the back of his throat, nearly causing him to gag. He tastes the barbecued pork getting spooned into a takeaway box mixed with the cooked alligator tail hanging on display and the raw chicken getting chopped up on the meat counter, along with the oniony breath of the twenty-something hipster in line behind him and the ripe funk of sweat rolling off the middle-aged bearded guy who just walked past.

Vic looks at the back of the head of the old Chinese woman who cut in front of him, her scalp at the perfect height for him to notice the strands of black woven in with the predominance of gray, all held together and matted into a uniform clump. He can smell the buildup of dirt on her scalp and can almost feel the greasy fibers of her hair brushing against his lips.

Before Vic can help himself, he gags and thinks he's going to throw up, but instead he burps. Fortunately it's not accompanied by any surprise juice. He makes a face just the same as he lets out a single explosion of rancid breath.

And just like that, Vic feels better. More than that, he feels clean, as if he's purged himself of something that needed to get out. A bug or a virus or a parasite. It's as if he just spent three days on some kind of cleanse to purify his body.

Vic has never meditated before. He always thought that was something monks or hippies did to keep from having to do a good day's work. But standing in line at the Deluxe Food Market, he experiences something similar to enlightenment, as if he's floating and grounded at the same time. He's not even bothered by the crowd or the noise or the smells anymore.

The old woman in front of him drops her dried noodles and her box of what Vic presumes are either dumplings or sponge cake. In spite of the rudeness she exhibited by cutting in line, Vic is in a forgiving mood and decides to help the old woman pick up her groceries. Then she bends over and throws up.

At first there's just a series of several coughs and wheezes accompanied by a short, controlled expulsion of vomit that reminds Vic of a cat coughing up a hairball. She even convulses like a cat. When she's done, the old woman takes a deep breath, her hands on her knees, and for a moment it seems like that's it. She just needed to get something out and now she's done. Then she lets out a loud groan and somewhere inside of her a valve opens and the vomit starts pouring out of her as if someone turned on a faucet.

The people near her move away faster than you can say *jook*, which is apparently what the old woman had for lunch. Nobody offers to help her or to see if she's okay. Instead, everyone gets out of the splatter zone before they can get contaminated.

The aroma of fresh vomit mingles with the bouquet of cooked meats and the smell of human sweat. Some of the customers cover their mouths and noses with their hands as others look away and gag. Cries of disgust mix with shouts of *Aiya!* while some of the Deluxe Food staff let loose with a steady stream of color commentary and emphatic hand gestures. Vic doesn't need to speak Chinese to know that they're not happy about someone throwing up in their store.

In less than a minute the old woman is done, a pool of vomit spreading out across the floor like a Rorschach test. But rather than stick around to clean up her mess or get a psychological interpretation of her regurgitated lunch, she elbows her way through the customers, who get out of her way like she's Patient Zero, and escapes onto Mott Street, with the shouts of more than one employee following her out the door.

Vic stays put for a few moments, trying to make sense of what just happened; then he steps over the discarded contents of the old woman's stomach and stands in line to pay for his pork dumplings and steamed buns.

chapter 12

Thinking I'd caused other people to fall asleep was one thing. Now I find out Vic made an old woman throw up and Randy apparently makes people break out in rashes.

"That's called herpes," Vic says, sitting on Randy's couch with a beer in his hand. "You might want to get yourself checked out."

While there are certain medications that may lead to an outbreak of genital hives or blisters, you're not going to get herpes from any of them. Still, there are hundreds of prescription drugs that can cause rashes. Antibiotics and diuretics and laxatives. Medications for diabetes and seizures and high blood pressure. Drugs that people are prescribed on a daily basis.

"It's not herpes," Randy says, scratching the back of his head. "But sometimes my nuts itch."

Frank, Charlie, Randy, Vic, Isaac, and I are at Randy's studio apartment in the Bowery, which comes with an around-the-clock homeless person on the front doorstep and a view of someone's hanging laundry. If you want a twenty-four-hour doorman and a view of Central Park, you're in the wrong neighborhood.

"Is that what happened with the punks on the subway a few weeks ago?" I ask Randy.

Randy nods. "I think that's when I popped my cherry."

"What punks?" Vic asks.

Randy and I fill the others in on our close encounter on the way back from Queens.

"I read something about that," Vic says. "They thought it might have been some kind of viral contagion that had been released in the subway."

Leave it to the news to make everything sound like a possible terrorist attack.

"What's happening to us?" Charlie asks, his face filled with concern. Even his freckles look worried.

Charlie confessed to having moments where he gets the chills and right after they go away, someone around him suddenly drops to the ground and starts going into convulsions.

"I have a theory," I say.

Vic puts his feet up on Randy's coffee table. "Let's hear it."

I look around the room and wonder if this will sound as rational out loud as it does in my head. "I think that, through the course of volunteering for clinical trials and taking all of these pharmaceutical drugs over the past five years or so, we've developed some kind of mutated side effects that we're able to project onto other people."

No one says anything. If I were a stand-up comic, someone would start heckling me. Then Vic says, "Makes sense."

"That's ridiculous," Frank says.

"What is?" Randy asks.

"All of it." Frank gestures around the room. "Everything you're suggesting."

"What's so ridiculous about it?" I ask. "We've all been volunteering for clinical trials for what? Five years? Six years? And how many of those trials have involved some experimental drug that caused a bunch of side effects like vomiting or rashes or drowsiness?"

"Or seizures," Charlie says.

"Yeah, and what about that study we all took part in last month?" Randy says. "The one where we were given multiple drugs to see how they interacted with one another? Maybe that triggered something."

I hadn't thought about that, but considering we all started to experience these side effects not long after that study ended, it might have been a factor. After all, when you take multiple medications at the same time, you never know what can happen.

"I give p-people erections," Isaac says, as if making a confession, his face turning red. "Not w-w-women, but, you know, men. I cause them to get b-boners."

"Seriously?" Vic asks.

Isaac nods.

"That's awesome," Randy says.

In addition to the popular medications taken to help manage erectile dysfunction, priapism is a possible side effect of numerous drugs, including antidepressants, anticoagulants, and medications to treat post-traumatic stress disorder.

"But what you're talking about aren't just side effects," Frank says. "Making people fall asleep or throw up or go into convulsions? That's not possible."

"Then why don't we put that to a test?" Vic says, standing up. "You didn't like your lunch anyway. How about you let me see if I can help you get rid of it? Shed some of those extra pounds you've been putting on."

"No way," Randy says. "Not in my place."

"Why not?" Vic gestures to the floor, which is about 350 square feet of patterned vinyl flooring. "It's just linoleum."

"For your information, this is luxury vinyl," Randy says. "And I don't want Frank or anyone else throwing up all over it. You want to make someone puke, go outside."

"Well, since I doubt anyone wants to go into a seizure or have Isaac hand out hard-ons, how about we have Lloyd cast his fairy tale sleeping magic on one of us," Vic says. "That way we won't make a mess on Randy's luxury vinyl or cause anyone to question their sexuality."

Isaac lets out a laugh, while I wonder if I can perform under pressure. Over the past couple of days, I've become better at making my lips go numb, but doing it on command in front of an audience makes me wonder if I need a fluffer.

Vic turns to me. "How about it, Lloyd?"

"Sure," I say, even though I'm not.

"This is bullshit," Frank says.

"Why is it bullshit?" Randy asks.

Frank looks around at all of us and folds his arms across his chest like a petulant child. "It just is."

"You know what I think?" Vic says.

"No," Frank says. "But I'm sure you're going to tell me anyway."

"I think Frank doth protest too much," Vic says.

"What does that mean?" Charlie asks.

Vic grins a humorless little smile. "It means I think Frank's hiding something."

"I'm not hiding anything," Frank says.

"Really?" Vic says. "Randy's having itching attacks. Lloyd's developed insomnia. I've been nauseous. Charlie's got the shakes. And Isaac . . ."

Vic looks at Isaac, who shrugs and gives a sheepish smile.

"Well, I don't think I want to know what precipitates Isaac's ability to dispense woodies," Vic says. "But the point is, everyone here has something going on, some physical manifestation that reflects these side effects we've developed. And we've all noticed you've been eating for two lately. Since you're not pregnant, I'm guessing there must be some reason for your increased appetite."

"No reason," Frank says, though he doesn't sound convincing. "I've just been hungry."

"Then why are you so reluctant to believe that the rest of us have developed these abilities?" Vic asks. "Is it because you haven't developed your own unique talent and you're feeling left out?"

Frank doesn't say anything but instead just stares at Vic.

Vic takes a couple of steps closer to Frank. "Or is there something else going on?"

"I'm done with this." Frank steps around Vic and walks to the front door. "You can finish your ridiculous conversation without me."

"Come on, Frank," Vic says. "What are you hiding?"

Frank throws his left hand up in the air without looking back and extends his middle finger, then walks out of the apartment, slamming the door behind him.

No one says anything. Vic looks at me and shrugs while Isaac clears his throat and hums an unrecognizable tune. Randy drops to the floor and starts doing push-ups.

"Do you guys think we should tell someone about this?" Charlie asks.

"Tell who?" I ask.

"I don't know," Charlie says. "Someone who might know what's going on. Someone who's in charge."

"In charge?" Vic says with a sarcastic laugh. "In charge of what? The only ones in charge of this are *us*."

"What about G-God?" Isaac says.

Vic gives a Bronx cheer and waves off Isaac's comment as if someone just farted.

"I was thinking more like the people who run the clinical trials," Charlie says. "If the drugs we tested caused this, maybe they can figure out why it happened and how to reverse it."

"I don't care why it happened," Vic says. "And I don't want to reverse this. I like having this ability to make people throw up. It gives me the chance to teach all of the douche bags of the world a lesson."

Randy stands up. "I agree with Vic. Not about the douche bag thing, but I'm okay with this. It's kind of Kool and the Gang. Once you get used to the itching."

While there's a voice inside of me that echoes Charlie's concerns, it's muffled behind a closed door at the end of a long corridor. The other voice, the one whispering encouragement in my ear, makes me feel special and empowered, which is a new experience. So I'm not in any rush to risk giving that up.

Plus, if anyone knew what I could do, what *any* of us could do, we'd probably end up in a lab somewhere, forced to endure a bunch of tests, and no one would ever see us again. We'd go from being volunteer guinea pigs to imprisoned lab rats.

"I think we should keep this to ourselves," I say. "You never know what could happen to us if word of this got out."

"Yeah," Charlie says. "You're probably right."

Charlie's easily persuaded. He'd make a lousy politician.

"Isaac?" Vic says. "You have any concerns you'd like to share?"

Isaac looks around as if he's trying to find a concern; then he smiles and shakes his head.

"All right then." Vic rubs his hands together. "Now that we've got the existential crisis out of the way, who's up for a little scientific research?"

R andy, Vic, Charlie, Isaac, and I are near the corner of Forsyth and Broome in Sara D. Roosevelt Park, where teams of thirty-something men play soccer on the fenced-in synthetic turf field in an effort to extend their sporting youth. Right now, in the mid-August heat, the only ones out on the field are a couple of teenagers throwing around a Frisbee, but there are plenty of other targets for us to choose from walking past on the sidewalks and sitting on benches, enjoying a normal Manhattan summer afternoon.

"Okay," Vic says, taking out a handkerchief and wiping the sweat from his chrome dome. "Who wants to go first?"

"Me, me!" Charlie waves his hand in the air like a student who never gets called on.

"Let's try to tone down the enthusiasm," Vic says. "The last thing we want is for anyone to know what we're doing."

"Oh, right." Charlie puts his hand down. "Sorry."

"It's okay," Vic says. "But since you're such an eager beaver, let's see what you've got."

Charlie smiles and takes a couple of deep breaths, then closes his eyes a moment before opening them again. "Okay. I'm ready."

He looks around for a target and appears to settle on one of the two teenagers tossing around the Frisbee.

I watch them making backhand throws and acrobatic catches, having fun and showing off, and it occurs to me that the five of us are not so different. Beneath the veneer of adulthood, we're just five kids who got new toys and we want to take them out for show-and-tell. It just so happens that Charlie's new toy makes people go into convulsions.

Lots of prescription drugs list seizures as one of their possible side effects. There are even anti-epileptic drugs that can make seizures worse, so taking them is kind of like going on a diet to lose weight so you can get fatter.

For several minutes Charlie stares at the teenagers, his face tight with concentration, doing his best to make something happen. He reminds me of the hulking mute sidekick to General Zod in *Superman II*, trying to blow something up with his laser vision and not being able to do much more than cause a cigarette burn.

After another minute, Charlie turns back to us. "I can't do it while you guys are watching."

He says the same thing in public restrooms when he refuses to use the urinals.

"Isaac?" Vic says. "You want to give one of them a boner?"

Isaac laughs and looks around like a kid in a spelling bee who can't remember how to spell *bacon*.

"I d-don't think I can right n-now," he says. "It just d-doesn't feel right."

"I'll give it a shot." Randy stands up and looks around and

picks out a fiftyish woman sitting on a nearby bench, reading a paperback.

Rashes caused by prescription drugs can come in a variety of flavors, including hives, purpuric eruptions, and Stevens-Johnson syndrome—which is a hive-like rash on the lining of the mouth. Not something you'd want to list on your Match.com profile.

While Randy tries to make the woman break out in a rash or hives or seborrheic dermatitis, I turn to Vic. "So how many people have you made throw up?"

"I don't know," Vic says. "Three or four."

I get the impression he's lowballing me. "Is that all?"

"Maybe more," he says with a shrug and a smile.

"How many more?" I ask.

"Let's not focus on numbers," Vic says. "Instead, let's focus on Randy's attempt to give that woman herpes."

"Is he really going to give her herpes?" Charlie asks.

"Not if he wears a condom," Vic says.

Isaac laughs while Charlie gets a puzzled expression on his face and looks at me for help.

"He's kidding," I say.

"Oh," Charlie says, then laughs. "I get it."

He doesn't.

Randy, meanwhile, isn't having any more luck than Charlie, so he gives up and sits back down. "I can't get it to work."

"That's because you haven't learned how to develop your trigger," Vic says.

"What's that?" Charlie asks.

"Just before I make someone throw up, I get nauseous," Vic

says. "Then this pressure builds up inside of me until I think I'm about to throw up, which is when I project my side effect. But the nausea is where everything starts."

Nausea and vomiting are listed as possible reactions for nearly every prescription drug on the market, from antidepressants to sleeping pills to opioids. They're like the Starbucks of side effects. They're everywhere.

"For me, my lips go numb," I say.

"I get cold," Charlie says. "Like my stomach fills up with ice."

"I feel like someone rubbed Bengay all over my balls," Randy says, a little too loud, and several people walking past get treated to the out-of-context statement of the day.

"How about you, Isaac?" I ask.

"It's kind of like R-Randy," he says. "Only d-different."

"Whatever it is," Vic says, "the trick is to access that trigger on your own rather than having it just happen. You need to re-create the circumstances that exist just before your lips go numb or your stomach fills with ice or your nuts start to burn. That's the key to success."

The keynote speaker at my college graduation said the key to success was hard work, ingenuity, and perseverance.

"I want to see you d-do it," Isaac says. "I want to see you m-m-make someone throw up."

"All right," Vic says. "I don't think you'll learn anything by watching me, but let's pick out a target."

"How about one of them?" Charlie points to the two teenagers still playing Frisbee.

Vic shakes his head. "They're not doing anything to deserve having me make them blow chunks."

"I didn't realize there were rules," Randy says.

"There are always rules," Vic says. "Of course, rules are made to be broken."

At the moment, it seems like we're breaking all sorts of rules. Rules of biology. Rules of physics. Rules of nature. Eventually we'll probably have to consider the philosophical implications of what's happening to us, but right now we're just having some fun.

We all look around, trying to find a target for Vic so he can make them throw up—not exactly how I thought I'd spend my afternoon when I got out of bed this morning, but sometimes life takes you places you never thought you'd go.

"Bingo." Vic points to a slick-looking guy in a light gray suit a block away, smoking a cigarette and talking on his cell phone loud enough for us to hear him.

"Why him?" Randy asks.

"Because he's a self-absorbed douche bag," Vic says, as if the answer should be obvious.

Vic doesn't own a cell phone. Mostly, he says, it's because he doesn't want the obligation of having to answer phone calls when he's not home. He doesn't have voice mail or an answering machine for the same reason.

He's not the easiest person to get hold of in an emergency.

We all watch the self-absorbed douche bag as he gets closer, talking so loud you'd think the person on the other end of the conversation was hearing impaired. "No, no, no. It's like I told you. He doesn't give a shit. And as far as I'm concerned, he can go fuck himself."

When he reaches the corner less than five feet from us, he

stops and takes a drag on his cigarette, then flicks the butt onto the sidewalk, his cell phone to his ear, no regard for anyone around him as he swears and walks away.

I glance over at Vic, waiting for him to do his thing, and I notice that his eyes are closed and he's taking several deep breaths. His face has grown pale, his lips look thin and colorless, and he appears to have come down with the flu. Just as I'm about to ask him if he's okay, he opens his eyes and gives me a weak smile.

"You might want to get out of the way," he says, the suggestion coming out in a rough whisper.

I move aside and Vic takes a deep breath, then makes a face as if he's just bitten into a rotten tomato before he lets out a burp, deep and guttural, like Darth Vader with indigestion.

For a moment nothing happens and I think this was all just some silly game of pretend we were all playing. Then the guy in the suit stops talking, leans over, and starts throwing up. And when I say *throwing up*, I don't mean like your garden-variety street drunk spewing on the sidewalk at two on a Saturday morning. This is more like a busted water pipe. Or a fire hydrant.

Vomit pours out of his mouth across the sidewalk. He doesn't even have time to make any noise until the first wave is out of him. Then he sucks in a long gasp of air and wipes his mouth before he lets out a groan that's followed by another stream of vomit. For whatever reason, the entire time, he keeps the cell phone pressed to his ear.

"Holy shit!" Randy says.

Charlie and I watch in silence while Isaac lets out a machine-gun burst of laughter. None of the other people in the vicinity seem to notice Isaac's reaction since they're all too busy watching the suit lose his lunch and his breakfast and whatever he ate for dinner last night. After it goes on for another ten or fifteen seconds, I start to wonder if he might need some help.

I turn to Vic. "Do you think we should call an ambulance?"

The color has returned to Vic's face and he no longer looks like a candidate for a blood transfusion. Instead he's shaking his head slowly back and forth as the suit drops down on all fours and starts dry heaving.

"Fucking smokers," Vic says. "It's like they think the entire planet is their goddamned ashtray."

From the *New York Post*, page 5:

GOT MEDS? PRESCRIPTION DRUG THEFTS
ON THE RISE

A wave of prescription drug thefts has swept across Upper Manhattan, with thieves posing as potential buyers while targeting open houses and then raiding the medicine cabinets. Last weekend alone, three separate homes on the Upper East Side were hit while hosting open houses.

"We don't know who the culprits are," Detective Sergeant Steve Moura said. "By the time the owners realized their prescriptions were missing, the thieves were long gone. Sometimes the homeowners didn't even realize they'd been robbed until several days later."

One real estate agent, who asked not to be named, said she didn't remember anyone who looked suspicious or who appeared to leave with any prescription bottles.

When asked if they had any suspects, Detective Moura said, "While we do have some video surveillance footage from a couple of homes, unfortunately there's not much to go on."

Prescription drug thefts are nothing new in the criminal landscape and have been on the rise in recent years. Various crimes—from home invasions and muggings to homicides and assaults—have been committed in the name of prescription drugs. Frequently the victims are those least able to defend themselves.

Addicts often prey on the sick or the elderly in order to get their fix. Some, rather than using the drugs themselves, will resell them. Opioids such as Vicodin, OxyContin, and Percocet tend to be the drug of choice for getting high and can command a premium price on the street.

But the recent rash of drug thefts in Upper Manhattan has a decidedly different prescription.

Antianxiety drugs like Valium, Xanax, and Ativan have been reported missing or stolen, along with the pharmaceutical sleep aids Lunesta, Sonata, and Ambien. In addition, statins like Lipitor and Zocor, which are used to lower high cholesterol, have gone missing.

"It's a bit of a change from the usual prescription drug thefts we see," Detective Moura said. "High-quality pain relievers tend to be the drug of choice, but I guess if you've got a craving, a drug's a drug. So long as it gets you high or puts you in an altered state of mind, that's all that matters."

When asked if this was the work of a single person or several different thieves, Detective Moura said he thought they were looking at a single group of maybe three or four individuals who are selling the drugs on the street.

"The volume of pharmaceuticals that's been stolen is more than the average addict would consume," he said. "So it's unlikely to be the work of a single individual."

'm home on the couch, surfing the Internet for clinical trials and watching television, flipping from Adult Swim to *The Daily Show* while I try to figure out how to tell Sophie that I've developed the ability to make people fall asleep. It's not the kind of thing you ever expect to have to explain to your girlfriend.

Coming home late after drinking with your buddies? Sure.

Getting caught watching Internet porn? You bet.

Receiving drunk texts from an ex-girlfriend? Absolutely.

Men have been justifying and explaining themselves to women for centuries, and we've learned to talk our way out of a myriad of awkward situations, but there aren't any guidelines on how to spin the fact that you cause others to experience spontaneous narcolepsy.

The clock on the wall says it's almost time for Sophie to get home from work, and I still haven't decided how to tell her. I suppose the truth would be the easiest way, but I keep thinking about how she'll react. My guess is she won't be happy about it, and that's the problem. Because I *am* happy about it. I like what's happening to me. It's fun and exciting and it's all I can manage to think about.

Vegan sits on the floor in the corner behind some golden pothos and English ivy, staring at me. Ever since The Incident in the Bathroom, Vegan has kept his distance, refusing to let me near him and only eating his meals once I've left the kitchen. Whenever I open my mouth to yawn, he disappears and hides under the bed.

I just hope he doesn't rat me out to Sophie.

"Vegan," I say in a soothing voice, trying to coax him over, but he's not buying it. The fact that I have to stifle a yawn doesn't help. The next moment he's gone in a cloud of cat hair and dust bunnies.

On *The Daily Show*, there's a commercial for a new drug called Bifixaprin.

Are you talking too fast? Flying off the handle? Spending out of control? You just might have bipolar disorder. We can help!

Drug companies are always trying to make you think that you're sicker than you are by giving psychiatric labels to everyday personality problems. And ever since 1997, when the U.S. government legalized direct-to-consumer marketing of pharmaceutical drugs, you can't watch a show anymore without thinking that you need the latest prescription medication to help you lead a better, more fulfilling life.

Half the time you're watching a commercial with these people scuba diving or going on African safaris or catching a space shuttle and you think, *Hey, that looks like fun.* Then it turns out it's an advertisement for some drug and you feel like your life sucks because you've never been scuba diving or on an African safari or to outer space, so maybe if you take the drug then your life will be as exciting as the lives of the people in the commercial.

The United States and New Zealand are the only industrialized countries on the planet that allow direct-to-consumer marketing of prescription drugs. All the other first-world countries have banned it. And while pharmaceutical companies are allowed to advertise drugs that may cause heart failure, memory loss, and increased risk of death, manufacturers of natural supplements can't make any claims that their products help to prevent diseases or have any curative properties without facing substantial fines and possible incarceration.

The term *double standard* comes to mind.

This is a sore point for Sophie and one of the other reasons why she has a problem with how I make a living. She feels that by volunteering for clinical trials, I'm not only helping to empower the pharmaceutical companies, I'm also helping to perpetuate the culture of prescription drug use that encourages people to treat their problems with medications first and ask questions later.

A recent study found that seven in ten Americans are on at least one prescription drug and more than half take two or more—with antibiotics, antidepressants, antianxiety drugs, opioids, high blood pressure medications, and vaccines making up the bulk of the prescriptions. According to that same study, a third of all prescription drugs are toxic to humans, with the side effects of the medications often worse than the affliction being medicated.

Your average person will take their doctor-prescribed prescriptions without giving much thought to what long-term effects those drugs might have on them. At least we guinea pigs understand what we're getting into, even if it's not a smart career move. But for people who have normal jobs, taking a drug to cure one problem can lead to additional side effects that require more drugs until you wind up in a never-ending pharmaceutical loop, medicating your medications.

In a way, we've turned into human smartphones, only instead of apps, we're downloading prescriptions.

You've got high blood pressure? There's a pill for that.

You're anxious and stressed out? There's a pill for that.

You can't get an erection? There's a pill for that.

We're gradually becoming more and more dependent on pharmaceutical drugs in order to survive. Whether we have problems with sleeping, depression, or gaining weight, there's a prescription answer waiting for us at the drugstore. So it seems reasonable that it's only a matter of time before evolution makes a leap forward and humans start being born with a dependency on pharmaceutical drugs. Or exhibiting permanent side effects.

Apparently, some of us have already made Darwin's short list.

I've met up with Randy, Vic, Isaac, and Charlie several times to test out our newfound abilities on random people we catch littering or swearing in public or texting on their cell phones in movie theaters. I never realized how many people are failures when it comes to common courtesy, displaying a lack of social grace and exhibiting inappropriate behavior, existing in their own little cocoons of self-absorption with complete disregard for how their actions affect other human beings.

So we've taken it upon ourselves to give them a little payback.

Sometimes before we go out, we get together at Charlie's or Randy's, and Vic shows us some meditation and relaxation techniques to help us calm our minds and channel our triggers. While Charlie and Isaac don't mind taking power naps and let me practice on them, we don't do any pairing up or applications because no one wants to vomit or have a seizure or sport some wood in a room full of guys.

On Adult Swim is a commercial for erectile dysfunction.

Are you lacking that old spontaneity? Having trouble with your performance? Unable to be the man you'd like to be? You just might have ED. We can help!

In addition to improving my newly acquired skill, I've discovered that I'm not as tired as I used to be. It's like I've cured my insomnia by making other people fall asleep. And I have a lot more energy and stamina.

"Are you sure this doesn't have anything to do with the drugs you're taking?" Sophie asked the other night after a ninety-minute sex marathon, which isn't normal for me. When it comes to sex, I usually abide by the Andy Warhol Rule: I get my fifteen minutes and that's about it.

I assured Sophie I'm not testing any form of sexual-performance-enhancement drugs, but I know she senses something different about me. Not just in bed, but in general. I notice it too. It's not one specific thing, but I just feel good about myself, and that's not a place I've spent a lot of time over the course of my adult life. Even when I was a kid, I never thought of myself as unique or special. And Mom and Dad didn't exactly guide me in that direction. They were usually too busy with their own lives to worry about mine.

We all have our baggage. For some of us it's a small carry-on, while for others, it's a couple of oversize duffel bags held together with duct tape.

I switch over to one of the local news channels, where the news anchor is talking about the tragic death of two high school students from the Bronx who overdosed on their parents' prescription drugs.

In the United States alone, nearly two million people are addicted to prescription painkillers, most of those opioids like oxycodone and hydrocodone, which have been shown to be just as addictive as their illegal cousin, heroin.

While recreational overdose from prescription drugs is a growing problem, it's not the only one. Last year alone, more than a hundred thousand people died after taking properly prescribed and administered pharmaceuticals. When you throw in overdoses, improperly prescribed medications, and debacles like Vioxx and Baycol, prescription drug use is the fifth leading cause of death in the United States, right behind heart disease, cancer, chronic lower respiratory disease, and strokes.

Considering that drugs like heroin, cocaine, and ecstasy account for fewer than twenty thousand annual deaths, it seems like the DEA's war on drugs needs to shift its focus from MDMA to the FDA.

"I'm home!" Sophie says as she walks through the front door.

Vegan appears like a magic trick, running up to her and meowing up a storm. While he's probably just happy to see his female human, I can't help but think that he's trying to tell Sophie that her boyfriend is some kind of asshole wizard.

Fortunately, I don't think Sophie speaks fluent Cat.

While Sophie showers Vegan with love and hugs and affection, I run through all of the different ways in which I can break the news about my newfound ability, trying to pick the best one. But I was never good at multiple-choice problems. So instead I decide to see where the conversation goes and try to work my confession in organically.

After sprinkling some pixie dust on Vegan and blowing the rest into the air, Sophie sits down on the couch and curls up next to me like we used to be conjoined twins and she's trying to reattach. I reciprocate by putting my arm around her and sinking into the couch to watch the news, where one of the anchors is talking about the ongoing investigation into reports that someone has been spiking food and drinks in Manhattan restaurants with acid or mushrooms. Over the past couple of weeks, more than two dozen people have experienced hallucinations ranging from mild to severe, but so far neither the authorities nor the Health Department have been able to isolate a single source of the outbreak.

"I don't understand why you watch the news," Sophie says.

"I like to stay informed," I say. "I like to know about what's going on in the world around me."

"But it's only about all of the bad stuff," Sophie says. "Murders and kidnappings and spectacles of destruction. People taking advantage of other people. How does that help anyone feel better? How does that make the world a better place?"

"It's the news," I say. "It's not supposed to make you feel better."

Sophie purses her lips and gets this serious look on her face that she wears whenever she's trying to save the world.

"Well, it should make you feel better," she says. "The news

should focus on inspirational stories and people who commit random acts of kindness rather than on horrific stories and people who steal from their neighbors. Then everyone would feel more positive about the world in which they live."

Sophie believes that the reason so many people are unhappy and afraid and mistrustful is because that's what the news shows them: acts of terror and tragedy and crime. That's the culture the news has created. That's the societal paradigm we've all been led to believe exists.

"I know bad news sells," she says. "But only because that's what we've been conditioned to buy."

So far the conversation isn't giving me much of an organic segue into telling Sophie about what's going on with me, so I decide to tell her and get it over with before I lose my nerve.

"I have some news," I say.

"Is it good news?" she asks, looking up at me.

I look down at her curled up next to me, her face inches from mine, her eyes big and blue—feminine Kryptonite to any sense of masculine resolve. "I think so."

"Tell me something good," she says, pressing tighter against me and talking into my chest. "Tell me something that will make me happy."

Her body pressed against me like this—her face in my chest and her voice vibrating in my bones—isn't helping matters. I'm pretty sure telling Sophie I've developed a genetic mutation that allows me to make people fall asleep isn't going to make her happy. And as much as I want to tell her the truth, right now I'd rather give her some good news.

"I got an interview for a marketing job," I say.

For some reason, this little white lie seemed like a good idea before I actually said it.

"Really?" Sophie sits up and looks at me with an expression of surprise and delight. "When?"

"Monday," I say without thinking.

"With who?"

"Starbucks," I say because it's the first thing I can think of without hesitating. "It's a corporate job."

Never mind that Starbucks' corporate headquarters is located in Seattle. At this point, I don't know what I'm saying or why I'm saying it, but it just keeps coming out of my mouth like verbal vomit.

"Lollipop, that's great!" Sophie gives me a kiss and a hug, followed by another kiss.

"I take it this makes you happy," I say.

"Happy?" she says. "I'm thrilled!"

Apparently I overshot the target.

"I don't have the job yet," I say. "It's just an interview. And I haven't done any marketing in five years."

"I know," she says, curling up against me again. "But I'm sure they'll love you. And even if they don't, I appreciate that you're looking. Just promise me we won't have to move to Seattle."

The two of us continue to sit and watch the news as I try to figure out how to get myself out of this one. While I know I can always tell Sophie that I didn't get the job and she'll believe me, the fact that I just told her a string of lies makes me feel like I cheated on her. Only in this case, the other woman is false hope.

On the television, a reporter is talking about a married couple from Michigan who discovered all of their money and valuables stolen with no memory of what happened. Before the reporter can continue, Sophie grabs the remote control and switches to Animal Planet to watch something more uplifting.

'm hanging with Randy and Charlie at a Starbucks on Broadway outside Columbia University, where the three of us are in the middle of a one-week trial for an experimental treatment to combat ADHD—which is appropriate, considering that lately we've all been easily distracted. Though when it comes to controlling our behavior, we're not the ones who seem to be having a problem.

A couple of tables away from us a cell phone rings, loud and obnoxious—Beethoven's Fifth Symphony on steroids. A woman fishes the phone out of her purse and starts talking like she's hearing impaired.

"Do you think we should be drinking coffee right now?" Charlie asks.

"Sure," Randy says. "Why shouldn't we?"

"Because of the ADHD trial," Charlie says. "Won't caffeine make it worse?"

"We don't have ADHD," I say. "We're just taking the medication to test its side effects."

"Oh," Charlie says. "Right."

While Charlie may not be the smartest monkey in the jungle, he's got a heart the size of King Kong.

At the pickup counter, a monkey with an advanced case of male-pattern baldness flings his poo at the barista, who apparently put whipped cream on his mocha when he clearly asked for no whip and he doesn't have the behavioral skills to explain this without belittling her.

"I went out with this barista once who loved using whipped cream," Randy says.

"Did she make a lot of ice cream sundaes?" Charlie asks.

"More like banana splits," Randy says.

"You know," I say, "I could have gone without that visual for the rest of my life."

A mother with a baby in a stroller in one hand and a venti in the other prepares to negotiate her way out the front door when a guy with short hair and sunglasses enters Starbucks and walks past without bothering to hold the door open for her.

"Does everything with you have to revolve around sex?" I ask.

"It doesn't *have* to." Randy gives a nod and an appreciative glance to a shapely redhead standing in line. "But that's what life is about, man."

"Life's about sex?" Charlie says.

"Absolutely," Randy says. "Sex is everywhere. It's all around us. All you have to do is look."

Charlie looks around the coffee shop and appears disappointed with the results.

"Sex is the reason we go to bars and join online dating services," Randy says. "It's the reason we start up conversations with people we find attractive. It's in the clothes we wear and the time we spend in front of the mirror and the perfume or cologne we dab behind our ears. It's on billboards and in magazines and on TV, selling everything from beer to sports cars to fast food. You ever see a Carl's Jr. commercial? You can't even think about eating one of their burgers without wanting a hot woman with large breasts slathered in barbecue sauce."

"Is that on the menu?" Charlie asks.

"Everything is on the menu," Randy says. "You just have to know how to order."

The poo-flinging monkey is now screeching at the barista for taking too long to get him his replacement mocha.

"Sex is why we were put on this planet," Randy says. "Not to sit in front of a computer or watch TV or play video games, but to connect with each other physically and enjoy the carnal pleasures of life. To copulate and populate. It's biology and evolution all rolled into one awesome package."

"What about connecting with someone on more than just a physical level?" I say. "What about emotional intimacy and developing a meaningful relationship?"

"Not everyone wants a relationship," Randy says. "Or even knows how to be in one. The fact is that there are two kinds of people: marionettes and hand puppets."

"What does that mean?" Charlie asks.

"I think he means that some of us prefer not to have any strings attached," I say.

Randy taps the end of his nose with his index finger and grins.

Two tables over, Beethoven's Fifth Symphony starts up again, flexing its ringtone muscles.

"When it comes to sex and romance," Randy says, "some of us are early Beatles and some of us are Rolling Stones."

"Well, thanks for enlightening us on our primal nature, Mick," I say. "But I think it's time the three of us got down to business."

"Can I pick first this time?" Charlie asks, looking back and forth from me to Randy like an obedient dog.

"Be my guest," I say.

Charlie purses his lips and looks around, then nods toward the counter, where the courtesy thug who couldn't be bothered to hold the door open for the mother with the stroller is placing his order. "Him."

"Randy?" I say. "Whipped cream or Beethoven?"

"Definitely whipped cream," he says.

"All right," I say. "Let's teach these douche bags some manners."

Randy takes a deep breath, Charlie closes his eyes, and I think about Steve Martin as the sadistic dentist in *Little Shop of Horrors*. Then we all take aim.

The hearing-impaired woman talking on her cell phone slumps over on the table and starts snoring; the monkey drops his mocha and scratches at himself like he has a flea infestation; and a middle-aged woman standing near the counter drops to the ground and goes into convulsions while the courtesy thug stands a few feet away, unaffected.

"Oops," Charlie says.

When it comes to Charlie's ability, it's often *oops*.

Randy shakes his head. "You really need to improve your aim."

"I know, I know," Charlie says. "I'm working on it."

INTERLUDE #2

⬤▭

Little Seizures (Pizza Pizza)

Charlie sits on the subway facing the opposite side of the train and watching the darkness of the subway tunnel flash by in the windows. He's on the number 1 train uptown on his way to Zabar's for some chocolate rugelach before heading out to the Hudson River to watch the sun set over New Jersey. He does this a couple of times a week, always by himself. If he ever got up the nerve to create an online dating account, he would list *watching sunsets on the Hudson while eating chocolate rugelach from Zabar's* as one of his favorite things to do. Maybe he would find someone who liked to do the same thing.

He's thinking about this while sitting next to an attractive brunette who smells like vanilla. Charlie catches her scent every time he inhales and he wants to say something about how good she smells, that she reminds him of fresh-baked cookies, but even in his head that sounds creepy. Maybe he could say it another way, ask her what she's wearing, but he can't seem to come up with the nerve to talk to her.

Women have always confused and flustered Charlie, with their smiles and their breasts and their long hair pulled back in ponytails. If only he could figure out how to approach them, but he's never known what to say or when to say it. They're a mystery to Charlie. A language he doesn't understand. An algebra problem he can't solve. A riddle to which he doesn't know the answer.

Take the woman sitting next to him. She's pretty but not in an intimidating kind of way. Still, there's something about her long hair and smooth skin and feminine figure that causes Charlie's brain to short-circuit, preventing him from speaking. It's like her breasts have cast a spell over him, causing him to lose the ability to form a complete sentence.

But even if Charlie could summon the courage to speak to her, he doubts she would be interested in having a conversation with him. She seems more interested in the guy sitting across from her wearing a Boston Red Sox cap and a T-shirt that says FUCK NEW YORK. Charlie keeps expecting someone to say something to him, to give him some shit or maybe tell him that the Red Sox suck, but no one says anything.

So Charlie sits there smelling the woman next to him, becoming more intoxicated by her scent and her presence, trying to find the courage to talk to her, to let her know he's interested, to let her know he exists. But his courage remains buried beneath a steaming pile of self-doubt and insecurity. Instead he remains silent and imagines how things would be different if he was more confident and charismatic, like Randy.

Even though his father and stepmother loved Charlie and appreciated everything he did for them, Charlie never felt like he mattered much. But then, you tend to feel that way when most of the other kids in school call you a pathetic loser and make you feel less important just because you're not attractive or popular or smart.

Dropping out of high school wasn't so much a personal sacrifice for Charlie as it was a much-needed vacation.

Over the past few years, Charlie has finally begun to feel like he matters. Part of that has to do with volunteering to help test drugs. Even though he's getting paid for it, he's doing something to help others. And that gives Charlie a sense of self-worth that working in a fast-food restaurant or delivering pizzas can't.

But the biggest reason Charlie feels more important is because of Lloyd, Vic, Randy, Frank, Isaac, and Blaine.

Growing up, Charlie never had much in the way of friends. No one to go to the movies with or read comic books with or pal around with during summer vacations. The most social interaction Charlie had was going to Forbidden Planet and Bergen Street Comics and talking to the staff or other customers about their favorite superheroes.

Then he met Randy and Vic and Lloyd a few years ago, and for the first time in his life Charlie had a group of guys he could hang out with and joke around with and count on if he needed help. Even though they make fun of him sometimes, he still knows they're his friends. And that makes him happy.

More than that, it makes him feel like he matters.

Now if only he could figure out how to get a girlfriend.

When they reach Times Square, the brunette gets up and joins the group of passengers getting off. Just before she exits, she turns and looks back. For a second Charlie imagines she's going to smile at him, to let him know that she noticed him sitting there and understands. Instead she glances at the guy in the Red Sox cap and gives *him* a smile. Then she's gone and the doors close and the train continues uptown.

Charlie sits and thinks about the brunette as the train continues to Fiftieth Street, then Fifty-Ninth, stealing glances at the guy sitting across from him wearing his FUCK NEW YORK T-shirt and his smug expression and his carefree attitude that the woman who smelled like vanilla found appealing. Someone needs to say something to him, tell him that he should go back to Boston if he doesn't like it here. So Charlie decides that if no one else is going to do anything, he will.

As the train pulls out of the Fifty-Ninth Street station, Charlie closes his eyes and starts to cultivate his trigger, imagining his stomach full of ice, the blood flowing through his veins as cold as a winter stream, and every breath he takes expanding his lungs with freezing Arctic air. He feels himself growing colder as goose bumps break out on his arms and the back of his neck and a shiver builds up inside of him like an orgasm, waiting to release.

When it comes to his new ability, Charlie knows he has a problem with self-control, which is another reason he's never been good with women. And right now he can feel the ability inside of him reaching the point of no return. But then Charlie thinks about what he's doing and why, and he realizes that his problem with the guy sitting across from him has less to do with his T-shirt and more to do with the brunette who found him attractive.

Charlie's not a spiteful or petty person, nor the type to hold grudges or keep score. He's always considered himself easygoing and agreeable, which is probably why people have a tendency to take advantage of him. He also knows he's not exactly the sharpest tack in the drawer, but he's smart enough to know what's right and what's wrong. And making the guy in the FUCK NEW YORK T-shirt pay for being more attractive than Charlie isn't right. Besides, he'd probably miss and make someone else go into convulsions.

So for the first time since he discovered his new ability, Charlie tries to stop it by taking a deep breath and imagining hot air melting the ice in his stomach. At first nothing happens, but then he takes another deep breath and the ice begins to melt, his internal temperature slowly rises, and the blood in his veins turns from a winter stream to a tropical river.

Charlie takes one more deep breath and lets it out, the inevitable release of his ability receding, then he smiles and opens his eyes. But his elation is replaced by confusion when he sees a sexy redhead sitting across from him, dressed all in crimson and listening to her iPod, her red, leather-clad legs crossed and her right foot bouncing up and down to the beat of some unheard tune.

Charlie looks around, wondering what happened to the guy in the FUCK NEW YORK T-shirt, and notices that not only is he no longer here but some of the other people who were on the train before are gone, too. And in addition to the redhead, there are new people sharing his car who weren't here a minute ago. When the train pulls into the Seventy-Second Street station rather than Sixty-Sixth Street, Charlie realizes that he somehow missed a stop.

He looks around the car, trying to figure out what happened, giving a nervous smile to the redhead because when it comes to women, that's the only thing he can manage. She smiles back, but Charlie's too insecure to do anything about it. Plus he's still trying to figure out what happened to the two minutes he lost and the subway stop he doesn't remember.

By the time the train reaches the Seventy-Ninth Street station, Charlie decides he must have been so focused on what he was doing that he just lost track of time. No big deal. Nothing he needs to worry about. If anything, he feels a sense of confidence and empowerment at being able to focus and control his ability. Maybe even confident enough to say something to the redhead, but when he looks at her and she gives him another smile, Charlie chickens out and exits the train without looking back.

One step at a time, Charlie thinks. *One step at a time.*

chapter 16

Y ou can make people fall asleep?" Blaine says, the lenses of his black sunglasses reflecting the chessboard as he takes one of my remaining pawns with his bishop.

I nod and take his bishop with my knight. "I know. It's weird, right?"

"*Weird* is an understatement."

Blaine and I are sitting at one of the stone chess tables in Tompkins Square Park beneath a green canopy of American elms. The sun is out, the sky is blue, and a wino is throwing up behind a garbage can. Two skinny white guys who haven't bathed since the Clinton administration share a forty on a nearby bench while somewhere unseen, a saxophone serenades us with "Over the Rainbow."

There's no place like home.

Blaine moves one of his knights to threaten both my king and my remaining rook. "Check."

I look for a way to save my rook, but he's done for, so I move my king to safety.

"So can you make me fall asleep right now?" Blaine asks, taking my rook.

"My lips have to go numb first," I say. "It's my trigger."

Blaine looks at me over the top of his sunglasses. "Your trigger?"

"It's what causes this ability I have to come out and play," I say, moving my knight to protect my king.

"And everyone else has some kind of side effect they're able to project onto others?" Blaine moves his queen. "Check."

"Everyone but Frank. But Vic thinks he's not telling us something."

Blaine nods and glances at an overweight black woman in dirty sweatpants who walks past us, mumbling while waving one hand in the air and scratching her ass with the other.

While handfuls of locals and tourists and dogs help to balance out the number of homeless and drug addicts, Tompkins Square still has a higher quotient of crazy than most of Manhattan's other parks. But it has character and free chess tables and its own unique smell. However, I wouldn't recommend using the public restrooms. Not without a good health plan.

"And nothing's been happening to you?" I ask as the black woman starts shouting at her invisible friend.

Blaine watches the woman a moment, then returns his attention to the board. "Like what?"

"Like anything strange or out of the ordinary?"

"You mean, have I been making people throw up or fall asleep or get hard-ons? No. Not that I know of." Blaine takes my knight with his queen. "Checkmate."

I study the chessboard for a few moments, trying to see my way out of losing. Blaine rarely beats me at chess. At best, he usually gets a draw one out of three games. But he's right. It's checkmate.

Blaine and I meet up once or twice a month to play chess—sometimes here, sometimes in Central Park, sometimes in Union Square. But none of those places have crackheads getting into arguments every ten minutes or an army of rats that comes out at dusk.

"Another game?" Blaine asks.

"Sure."

"How about we play for lunch," he says. "Loser buys."

"You're on," I say and start putting my pieces back in place.

"Did you know that the term *checkmate* originates from the Persian phrase *shāh māt*?" Blaine says. "Which literally means *the king is helpless*, not *the king is dead*."

"Thanks for clarifying. I'll sleep better now."

In addition to the etymology of *checkmate*, Blaine has also explained that chess is a descendant of the ancient Indian game of *chaturanga*, which is apparently named for something having to do with infantry and cavalry and elephants. I think my knights are supposed to be the cavalry and my bishops the elephants, but I can't remember.

My thoughts seem kind of muddled today and I'm having trouble focusing. I wonder if it has anything to do with this whole making-people-fall-asleep thing. And if I should be worried.

"So what are you guys doing with these newfound abilities of yours?" Blaine asks.

I tell him about the smokers and litterbugs and people talking on cell phones in restaurants whom we've been teaching lessons.

"Sounds like you guys are cleaning up the city," he says.

I can't tell if he's being serious or sarcastic, but I move the white pawn in front of my queen out two squares to start a new game. Blaine counters with the pawn in front of his king to threaten me, so I protect my pawn with my knight.

"What does Sophie think about all this?" he asks.

"She doesn't. I haven't told her yet."

"Why not?"

I shrug. "I'm not sure she'll understand."

"I'm not sure I understand," Blaine says. "And you told me."

"It's different with you. You're a guinea pig. You're one of us."

"That I am," he says. "That I am."

After a handful of moves, I've brought out my knights and bishops and castled my king. Blaine has done the same and aggressively taken out two of my pawns and one of my knights, countering each of my moves in half the time it takes me to make mine, like he knows what I'm going to do the moment before I do it.

A blonde in a sundress walks past us with a pair of shapely legs and some kind of dog on a leash. She glances at us as she passes and Blaine returns her glance with one of his own, lowering his shades to watch her go.

"You ever wish that instead of making people fall asleep, you could read their minds?" Blaine watches the blonde walk away before he turns back to the game and takes one of my bishops.

"You mean like a psychic?" I look at the board, trying to remember where I was going with my last move.

"No, I mean really read people's minds," he says. "Not just flip over some cards or look at someone's palms and come up with some hocus pocus about their future, but actually *know* what they're thinking. Know what they know."

"I don't think I'd want to know what other people are thinking," I say, threatening one of his rooks. "People keep a lot of secrets and the last thing I want to do is go into their closets and start sifting through their skeletons. You never know when you might find something you wish had remained buried."

"I don't know." Blaine moves his queen across the board with seeming indifference. "I think the more you know about someone, the easier it is for you to gain the upper hand."

"Is that how you beat me last game?" I say, kidding around. "By reading my mind?"

"Just playing to your tendencies, Lloyd."

"I don't have tendencies."

"Sure you do," he says. "Everyone has tendencies."

The overweight black woman suddenly starts shouting and waving her hands in the air, as if fending off some invisible attacker. The two white guys sitting on the nearby bench decide they don't want anything to do with her and slink away in search of another forty while the woman continues to play Crack Addict Charades.

In the background, the saxophone plays "Still Crazy After All These Years."

"Did you know *Still Crazy After All These Years* was Paul Simon's fourth studio album?" Blaine says.

"No. I did not know that."

"It produced four Top 40 hits and won a Grammy for Album of the Year."

"Did you get all of that off the Wikipedia page?"

"Just something I picked up."

Blaine and I continue to play, maneuvering and jockeying for position, though it seems like Blaine is no longer interested in the game but is just playing recklessly, taking my pieces without worrying about losing his own.

"So you think you guys have started to exhibit these abilities because of all the drugs you've tested?" he asks.

"That's the theory," I say.

"What happens if you stop volunteering? If you stop taking all of those drugs?" Blaine asks. "Will the abilities go away?"

"I don't know," I say. "I hadn't thought about it. Maybe."

Blaine nods, then takes my last bishop with his queen. "You know those tendencies I mentioned?"

"What about them?" I study the board and see that I almost have the match won.

"I've noticed that you're afraid to sacrifice your higher-valued pieces to get one of mine," he says. "You position yourself but you never make the first move. You always let me attack first."

"Is this going somewhere?" I ask, taking his queen with my rook and putting myself one move away from a free lunch.

"Sometimes you have to be willing to make sacrifices, Lloyd. You have to be willing to take a risk and lose something of value if you want to win." Blaine takes my rook with his bishop and smiles. "That's checkmate. So where are you taking me for lunch?"

've always wanted to go here with you." Sophie squeezes my hand and pulls tight against me as we walk along Canal Street toward the Mahayana Buddhist Temple. "Thank you for indulging me."

While I'm not as excited about today's field trip as Sophie, her enthusiasm is contagious. Such as when she gets excited about going to the movies. Or the way she laughs when we're running to catch the ferry back to Manhattan. Or how she claps at parades and throws her arms around me after I come home from a three-day lockdown.

These are the little things that make me realize how much Sophie matters to me, and how much I enjoy being with her. They're also a reminder of what I would miss if I lost her. And I'm afraid that when I tell her about this ability I have and that I don't want it to go away, she isn't going to stick around.

"It's so beautiful," Sophie says as we approach the bright red doors that mark the entrance to the temple. "So spiritual."

I smile and nod, though I can't help but think how the Mahayana Buddhist Temple hasn't always been a place of religious mediation and spiritual connection. In its previous life, before it was reborn as its current incarnation, it was an adult movie house called the Rosemary Theater. Back then, people came here to worship Ron Jeremy and Jenna Jameson and to pray at the temple of the almighty orgasm.

I just hope they did a good job of sterilizing this place.

Once we step past the gilded lions and through the doors into the faux pagoda, the scent of incense hits us from a large urn that sits in front of a small shrine with red columns and golden dragons and a small statue of Buddha.

I've never been a big believer in any kind of higher power or purpose, be it Buddha, God, or the Flying Spaghetti Monster. I'm not what you would call an atheist. I just don't believe in *anything*. Plus, when you have the newfound ability to make other people fall asleep in an instant, the idea of worshipping someone or something else feels a bit like slumming.

Sophie presses her palms together in front of her and bows slightly toward the statue of Buddha, then she takes a pinch of incense and throws it into the urn. She turns to me and I know she wants me to do the same, so I do, but more to make her happy than to show my respect. Plus the incense is making my eyes water.

"Welcome." A monk in a rich saffron robe greets us with a smile and a bow and an air of complete calm that immediately sets me at ease. He's like a human antianxiety drug, but more like Librium or Elavil than Ativan.

As the monk welcomes more worshippers and tourists who enter the temple, I keep thinking about how people used to masturbate in here.

Past the monk and the giant urn of tear-inducing incense is a red sign with gold letters that says:

PICK YOUR FORTUNE AND DONATE $1.00

Next to the sign is a basket of small individual scrolls rolled up in rubber bands. Sophie and I each donate a dollar and receive our fortunes as another monk gives us a smile.

"May you receive the words you long to hear," he says, then gives a slight bow and stands there emanating a sense of calm similar to that radiated by the first monk—though this time I'm getting more of a Paxil vibe.

Sophie opens up her fortune and reads it and gives a little smile.

"What?" I say. "Tell me."

"I can't." She reads the fortune again, then rolls it back up and puts it in her pocket. "It's a secret. If I tell you, then it won't come true."

"Is that right?" I ask the monk.

He just gives me the same noncommittal smile, like he's taken too much Valium and he can't remember.

"So I can't tell you my fortune, either?" I say.

"Not if you want it to come true," Sophie says.

"What about fortune cookies?" I say. "We always share those."

"Fortune cookies are just for fun," she says. "They don't mean anything. This is different."

I'm not sure if Sophie is kidding around or if she really believes that these fortunes are any different than the ones that come at the end of a meal of Mandarin eggplant and vegetarian kung pao with tofu, but I'm intent on making her happy and don't want to spoil her good mood.

I unroll my fortune and make a big show of not letting Sophie see it, then I read what future has been foretold for Lloyd Prescott:

IN TRUE LOVE, DESTINY AWAITS.

I look up at Sophie, who raises a single eyebrow at me, then puts an index finger to her lips, so I give my fortune one more glance before I fold it up and put it in my wallet.

Sophie takes my hand and we continue into the temple, which is simple in appearance, with wooden floors and red chairs and red paper lanterns hanging from the walls. There's so much red in here it's like Valentine's Day threw up. The centerpiece of the temple at the back of the main room is the sixteen-foot gold Buddha resting on a lotus flower with an ethereal neon blue halo around its head.

"Isn't it beautiful?" Sophie says.

Personally I think it's a little Indiana Jones meets Burning Man, but I hold my tongue as well as Sophie's hand and just nod, the two of us contemplating the enormous gold sculpture in silence. Prints depicting Buddha's life line the walls on either side of us, while tables in front of the statue are covered with oranges and grapes and provide a place for offerings in memory of loved ones.

And I can't help but wonder what part of the movie theater this place used to be.

"Can we sit and meditate for a little bit?" Sophie asks.

"Define *a little bit*."

Sophie gives me a look that lets me know I'm not being a supportive boyfriend.

"Sure," I say. "Let's sit and meditate. For as long as you'd like."

Sophie has always encouraged me to develop a regular practice of meditation as part of a well-balanced life. While I've sat with her numerous times and tried my best to clear my mind and focus on my breath and repeat some kind of silent mantra over and over, I've just never been able to make it a priority. Plus it's kind of difficult to keep your focus when you're testing drugs that make you anxious or restless or agitated. Or that cause cramping and explosive diarrhea.

So while Sophie meditates in the lotus position with her back straight and her eyes closed, I sit in the half-lotus and sneak glances at the tourists and worshippers who approach the Buddha, leaving offerings or taking pictures. Knowing that I could make any of them fall asleep makes me think about what I could get away with. Practical jokes. Revenge. Stealing people's wallets and purses while they're out cold.

I wonder if deities ever struggle with their own inner demons.

I also wonder if there's something more I should be doing with this ability rather than teaching a bunch of courtesy criminals a lesson on social etiquette. I just don't know what that something is.

As I pretend to meditate in front of the statue of Buddha, contemplating my purpose and my own omnipotence, there's a muffled crash from down the hallway toward the front of the temple, followed by a single shout of surprise.

"Hey! Stop that!"

"What's going on?" Sophie asks.

"I don't know," I say, then stand up.

"Where are you going?" she asks.

"I just want to check it out," I say. "I'll be right back."

While getting involved has never been my thing, for some reason I'm compelled to find out what happened, maybe see if there's something I can do to help.

I walk down the hallway to the front entrance, where I find the donation box near the basket of fortunes smashed open and one-dollar bills scattered across the floor. A crowd of about a dozen people watch as two monks roll around on the dollar bills, grappling with one another—their earlier sense of calm nowhere to be found.

"What happened?" I ask a young woman with a backpack.

"The one on the bottom smashed open the donation box," she says with a German accent, which is either percussion or brass, I can't remember. "The one on top tried to stop him, then they started fighting."

The men and women stand around and watch the show, but no one does anything to help. I consider using my ability to solve the problem and make one or both of them fall asleep but figure that might be too conspicuous, so instead I step in to break them up. A burly guy with sideburns and a ponytail follows my lead and together we separate the two monks.

"Are you okay?" I ask one of them after I help him to his feet.

He has a bloody nose and what looks like a welt forming above his left eye. He doesn't answer but just looks down at the other monk, who remains on the floor, thrashing around like he's still fighting with someone. At first I think maybe he's having a seizure, then he stops and sits up and says, "Did you see that?" before he scrambles back against the wall and looks around wearing a wild expression.

"What's wrong with him?" I ask.

The first monk only shakes his head and wipes the blood from his nose. "He has never done anything like this."

"Maybe it's one of those random dosings," the guy with the ponytail and sideburns says. "Maybe someone slipped a tab of acid or some mushrooms into his food."

I glance around at the dozen or so men and women watching us and wonder if one of them might have dosed the monk. Except other than the food left out as an offering to Buddha, there's nothing edible or drinkable in here that could have been spiked.

As the monk continues to have what appears to be some kind of hallucinatory episode, another possibility occurs to me: What if what happened here was due to something other than a prank involving recreational psychedelic drugs? Not just here, but throughout Manhattan?

What if the people who have been experiencing these reported hallucinations haven't been the unwitting marks of a gastrointestinal terrorist, but the victims of a pharmaceutical guinea pig?

A host of prescription drugs have been known to cause hallucinations in volunteers and patients. Antipsychotics and anticonvulsants and antidepressants. Medications for insomnia and obesity and Parkinson's disease. Drugs that are advertised during news programs and soap operas and prime-time TV shows.

It never occurred to me that this might be happening to anyone else. I presumed it was unique to our group. Or maybe that's the way I wanted it to be. Just the five of us. Our own little club. But for all I know, there could be dozens of other guinea pigs out there discovering that they've developed strange new abilities.

chapter 18

I'm walking through Little Italy with Randy, Vic, and Charlie after eleven o'clock on a school night, the four of us on our way back from Veselka, where we just finished off some tasty pierogi. The moon is out, the sky is clear, and a homeless guy is talking to himself in front of the Church of the Nativity.

"You think there are other guinea pigs out there able to do what we do?" Randy asks.

"I don't know if anyone's making people throw up or break out in rashes," I say.

"Or go into convulsions," Charlie says.

"Or go into convulsions," I say. "But yeah, I think there might be someone who's developed abilities like us who's responsible for all of the hallucinations that have been happening lately. I mean, we're not the only guinea pigs who live in New York City."

"What about those people who got mugged and can't remember a thing?" Charlie says. "Do you think that might have been done by a guinea pig?"

There are a lot of prescription drugs on the market known to cause memory loss. Sleeping pills and narcotics and statins. Medications for anxiety and depression and seizures. Drugs prescribed by hospital nurses and handed out by primary-care physicians like breath mints.

"I don't know," I say. "It's possible."

"What about Frank?" Vic asks.

"What about him?" Randy says.

"He didn't show up to the last meeting," Vic says. "Or to poker night."

"You think Frank is doing this?" Charlie asks.

"I don't think anything," Vic says. "I'm just spitballing here. But when was the last time anyone saw Frank?"

No one says anything, but we all know the answer. No one's seen Frank since he stormed out of Randy's nearly three weeks ago. We all just assumed he'd show up for the next meeting and when he didn't, no one thought twice about it. We've all missed meetings before. It happens. But apparently we were all so caught up in the excitement of our new abilities that no one bothered to call to see if he was okay.

Still, the idea that Frank might be the one behind the hallucinations or the muggings strikes me as wrong—both as an unpalatable option and an impossibility. From the silence that seems to have engulfed our quartet, I'm guessing I'm not the only one struggling with this possibility.

We walk along Bowery toward Chinatown in pensive silence, the stores closed and the roll-up doors pulled down, some late-night stragglers on their way to or from somewhere. The shine seems to have been rubbed off the evening and it's approaching quitting time for Sophie, so I'm about to peel off and head for home when someone starts shouting.

A block down Bowery in front of the Royal Jewelry Center, a couple of punks are harassing a homeless man who appears to be trying to protect his worldly possessions. His protests only seem to escalate their abuse and laughter.

"Stop it!" he shouts. "Get lost, you fuckers!"

Being a hero has never been my strong suit. It's never even been a suit, or a sports coat, for that matter. But something inside of me clicks and I feel compelled to act.

I look at Randy, who looks at me with an expression that seems to mirror my thoughts. Charlie says, "We should do something," and Vic nods. "Then let's do it."

The four of us jog down the sidewalk, side by side, preparing to do battle like Eliot Ness and the Untouchables. Except we're not carrying shotguns or badges. And we have no idea what we're doing.

One of the punks shoves the homeless man to the ground, eliciting a "Hey!" from Randy, who gets out in front as we arrive at the scene. The two punks turn and notice us and I expect one of them to develop a sudden and severe case of poison oak. Instead, Randy drops to the ground, rolls over once, and starts convulsing.

"Shit," Charlie says.

"Goddamn it, Charlie!" Vic says. "What the hell are you doing?"

"I'm sorry," Charlie says. "It was an accident."

"Everything you do is an accident," Vic says. "You're a walking disaster."

"I said I was sorry!"

"Yeah." One of the punks walks up to Charlie and flashes a knife, waving it in the air. "You're gonna be fuckin' sorry."

It takes a moment before I realize it's none other than Cornrows from the J train.

"Hey asshole!" I shout, and start to access my trigger.

He looks at me over Charlie's shoulder and narrows his eyes before opening them wider and smiling. "Hey Deke, guess who—"

Before he can get any more out, Cornrows drops his knife and projectile vomits all over Charlie's chest and face. Two seconds later, Charlie returns the favor. Whether out of disgust or because he's collateral damage from Vic's efforts I don't know, but both of them start puking like a couple of fraternity pledges.

"Yo Billy," the other punk says, who turns out to be Soul Patch. "What the fuck, man?"

Cornrows/Billy throws up all over the sidewalk like someone turned on a faucet in order to empty his stomach while Charlie vomits in short staccato bursts. A few feet away, Randy continues to convulse and spasm like a fish on the deck of a boat.

"Hey, man!" Soul Patch says. "What the fuck you bitches do to Billy?"

Soul Patch doesn't wait for an answer but takes out his own switchblade and flips it open, the blade glinting in the glow of the streetlight. On the sidewalk nearby I see Billy's knife, but I've never been in a fistfight let alone a knife fight, so I use the only weapon I have at my disposal.

I take a deep breath and summon my trigger, imagining Steve Martin from *Little Shop of Horrors* shoving a needle into my gums, lidocaine flowing out of the syringe and turning my lips numb, channeling all of my focus and energy into my lips, turning them numb.

"Yo man!" Soul Patch says. "You're that fucker from the subway!"

He comes at me with the knife as my eyes grow heavy and the pressure builds up in the back of my throat.

"I'm gonna cut you open like a fuckin' pig!" he says.

My mouth opens and I yawn, my lips stretching wide like I'm Steven Tyler or Mick Jagger mugging for a music video. Before I can get out of the way, Soul Patch stumbles into me and we tumble to the sidewalk in a heap of arms and legs, the deadweight of Soul Patch pinning me to the sidewalk. The next moment, Vic is shoving the punk aside and into the gutter and reaching down with his hand to help me up.

"You okay, Lloyd?" he says.

I nod, relieved not to have a knife sticking out of any part of my body, then I stand up and look around.

Cornrows/Billy is on his hands and knees dry heaving while Charlie sits on the sidewalk in front of the Chinatown Health Castle, groaning. Soul Patch is out cold in the gutter, flat on his back, sleeping like a baby—his knife on the ground next to him like a forgotten pacifier. The homeless guy who was getting attacked when we showed up has gathered his possessions and is shuffling off as fast as he can down the street.

I guess a thank-you would be too much to ask for.

Randy stops convulsing, sits up, and holds his head in his hands like he's trying to keep it from cracking open.

"Jesus," Randy says. "I'm totally Led Zeppelined right now."

I'm presuming Randy means he's dazed and confused and not

going in through the out door, but we don't have time to play classic-rock roulette. A few bystanders have noticed the commotion and are walking toward us while somewhere in the distance, a siren wails. Whether it's headed this way or to another scene I don't know, but it's probably not a good idea for us to stick around and have to explain what happened.

"Let's get out of here," I say.

chapter 19

You got any Tylenol?" Randy asks as we walk into Charlie's apartment.

"In the kitchen," Charlie says. "Above the sink."

Randy opens the cupboard. "You really need to work on your aim."

"Yeah, you're not the only one." Charlie burps and makes a face, then puts a hand over his mouth and runs to the bathroom.

"It's not my fault you were standing right next to my target," Vic says, sitting down on the couch. "I was trying to keep you from getting stabbed!"

While Randy chases three Tylenol with a glass of water and Charlie dry heaves in the bathroom, I can't stop thinking about what just happened and how good it felt to take down those two punks. It's not exactly the Yankees or *Playboy* or *National Geographic*, and you'd think if I'd been born to make people fall asleep, then I would have just become a politician or an art-film director. But there's something undeniable about the importance of what we just did.

"Hey, have you guys thought about why this happened?" I say.

"Yeah," Vic says. "It happened because Charlie needs to work on his aim."

"I'm not talking about tonight," I say. "I'm talking about what we were meant to do with these new abilities of ours."

"You mean like our destiny?" Randy says.

"Yeah," I say. "Something like that."

"I didn't think you believed in all that crap," Vic says.

"I believe in destiny," Randy says, sitting down next to Vic. "I think we're all born with some specific purpose and that things happen for a reason."

"Well," Vic says, "then I believe this happened so that I can teach all the douche bags in Manhattan a lesson."

"Don't you think there should be more to this than just dishing out our own form of karmic justice to the douche bags of the world?" I say. "Something more fulfilling? Something that gives our lives a little more meaning?"

"What are you guys talking about?" Charlie asks, returning from the bathroom.

"Lloyd is waxing on about predestination," Vic says.

"What does that mean?" Charlie asks.

"It means that I've been thinking about why this happened to us," I say. "Or at least why this happened to me. I don't know if it's destiny or God or some random act of weirdness, but I'm starting to think that we're supposed to do something more with these abilities than just teach lessons to litterbugs and smokers and people who read their e-mail in the movie theater."

"Like what?" Charlie asks.

"Yeah," Vic says. "What could be more important than that?"

When you don't have health insurance or paid sick days, putting yourself at risk for a complete stranger is more often a matter of economics than doing the right thing. Heroism doesn't stand much of a chance when common sense is in charge. But once you've accepted the fact that the drugs you've been testing for five years have affected you on a genetic level and you've decided to avoid seeking medical help because you like yourself better this way, common sense isn't really part of the equation.

"Like tonight," I say. "Like that homeless man we just helped. Like the asshole Randy took care of on the subway. I think we're meant to use our supernatural powers to help people."

Randy stands up and pumps his fist in the air. "Right on!"

"Hold on a minute," Vic says. "Did you just say *supernatural powers?*"

"Wouldn't you call what we can do supernatural?" I say. "Or even superhuman? Causing people to fall asleep and throw up and break out in rashes?"

"And go into seizures," Charlie says.

"I just think calling them *supernatural powers* is taking it a little far," Vic says. "They're more like freakish genetic mutations."

"A lot of supernatural powers are genetic mutations," Charlie says. "Spider-Man. The Hulk. Mister Fantastic. The Invisible Woman. The Human Torch. The Thing."

"The X-Men are all mutants, too," Randy says.

"Yeah," Charlie says. "But they were all born that way."

"They're still genetic mutants," Randy says. "And the X-Men could totally take the Fantastic Four."

Vic looks back and forth from Randy to Charlie. "You two

both got the shit kicked out of you in high school on a regular basis, didn't you?"

While I'm not a huge comic book geek, I'm familiar enough to know that we have something in common with a lot of comic book superheroes who gained their powers due to mutations after exposure to some scientific experiment or anomaly. While we can't make ourselves invisible or engulf our entire bodies in flames or turn into green, humanoid monsters with anger-management issues, we're not that dissimilar from the Fantastic Four or the Incredible Hulk.

"If we have superpowers," Randy says, raising his eyebrows, "doesn't that kind of make *us* superheroes?"

"Here we go." Vic points to his watch. "Delusions of grandeur, right on schedule."

"Hey, there's a superhero supply company in Brooklyn," Charlie says. "They have capes and secret-identity kits and all sorts of gear and supplies for fighting crime. They even have mechanical web shooters and invisibility-detection goggles. We could totally pimp out!"

Vic throws up his hands. "Great. We've now left the country of the Silly and have entered the country of the Absurd."

"I don't know," I say. "It doesn't seem absurd to me."

"Yeah," Charlie says. "New York is superhero central. The Fantastic Four live in New York."

"So does Iron Man," Randy says.

"Spider-Man grew up in Queens," Charlie says. "Daredevil was raised in Hell's Kitchen. And Captain America was born on the Lower East Side."

"It's unanimous," I say. "We're genetic mutants living in New York City. We don't have a choice but to become superheroes."

"It is our destiny," Randy says in his best James Earl Jones impersonation.

Randy and I high five each other while Charlie grabs some beers from the refrigerator.

"Not to play Eeyore to you three Tiggers," Vic says, "but I don't think we can just start fighting crime without thinking about the consequences."

"Like what?" Randy asks.

"Oh, I don't know. Like getting shot or stabbed," Vic says. "We're not exactly impervious to bullets or knives, you know."

"That doesn't mean we can't use our powers to help people," I say.

"Yeah," Charlie says. "Just because we're not from the planet Krypton and we weren't bitten by a radioactive spider doesn't mean we can't be superheroes."

"Whatever's happened to us," I say. "*However* it's happened, I don't think we developed these abilities for our own personal amusement."

"'With great power comes great responsibility,'" Charlie says, looking pleased with himself. "That's from *Spider-Man*."

Vic looks at Charlie and shakes his head. "No wonder you never get laid."

"So what do you guys think?" I say. "Are you in or out?"

"I'm in." Charlie says with a smile and thrusts his hand high into the air like an exclamation point.

Randy raises his bottle of Budweiser. "Me, too."

Vic looks at the two of them, then over at me for a moment before he lets out a sigh and puts his hand up like he's giving a lazy Heil Hitler.

"Okay. So now that we've decided we're all idiots, what's next?" Vic says. "How do we go about cleaning up the city?"

Before I can come up with an answer, the intercom by the front door buzzes. Charlie walks over to the intercom and presses the TALK button.

"Hello?" he says, like he's used to getting visitors after midnight.

"It's Frank," says the voice out of the intercom.

Charlie buzzes him in.

"What's Frank doing here?" I ask.

"I texted him while I was in the bathroom and asked him to come over," Charlie says.

"Why?" Vic asks.

"Because I was worried about him," Charlie says. "And I don't believe he's mugging people or making them have hallucinations."

Thirty seconds later there's a knock at the door. Charlie goes over and opens it to reveal Frank standing there with a Big Mac in one hand and a large fountain drink in the other, dressed in sweatpants and a generous V-neck sweater.

"Charlie," Frank says and walks in.

Charlie closes the door behind him and we all just stand there, not saying anything, looking around at one another like guilty teenagers.

"So Frank," Vic says. "What have you been up to?"

While I'm with Charlie and don't believe Frank has been

behind the hallucinations or muggings, Vic's apparently not so convinced.

"Oh, you know." Frank takes a bite of his Big Mac. "A little bit of this. A little bit of that."

From the looks of it, Frank has been up to a little bit of this, a little bit of that, *and* a lot of the other. If he hasn't gained another ten pounds, then Charlie doesn't have an inferiority complex.

"I see you're still storing up for winter," Vic says.

I'm expecting Frank to counter with some angry comment about his weight. Instead, he sucks down the last of his drink and belches. "Not exactly."

Supersize Me

Frank sits at a table at a Dunkin' Donuts on Tenth and West Forty-Fourth, eating half a dozen Double Cocoa Kreme doughnuts for breakfast and washing them down with a large Dunkaccino. He was going to order an extra-large Dunkaccino, but he didn't want to be a glutton.

Up until about a month ago, Frank hadn't stepped inside a Dunkin' Donuts in years, not even for coffee. At first it was a matter of avoiding temptation. He didn't want to end up overweight and depressed like he was for the first six months after his divorce. Once he started guinea-pigging, he laid off sweets and empty carbs that might increase his risk of being disqualified from a trial. Not to mention that a diet high in sugar, trans fats, and salt can lead to type 2 diabetes, hypertension, and heart disease.

Frank has always found it kind of ironic that pharmaceutical companies make prescription drugs to help treat humans for their poor lifestyle choices.

But over the last few weeks, Frank has given in to his temptation more often than not. In the last week alone, he's been to Dunkin' Donuts three times, including this one. While he knows how easy it is to become addicted to sweet foods and to the rush of a sugar high, the brain telling him that he's still hungry even though he's already eaten three doughnuts, Frank can't seem to help himself.

It's not that the doughnuts are so yummy, which they are. It's more like he's eating to stock up on resources, like his body knows he's going to need them but isn't letting his brain in on the plan.

So he finishes off Double Cocoa Kreme number three, knowing that he's had more than enough but unable to stop himself from picking up number four and biting into it. The fried cake and the creamy center fill his mouth with sugary goodness, which he washes down with a long pull on his large Dunkaccino. Frank realizes with a sense of despair there's not enough of his drink left to complement the rest of his half-dozen deep-fried confections.

While Frank is bemoaning his decision not to order the extra-large version of his beverage, a couple of frat boys walk in, one with dark hair and the other blond and both of them fit and trim and barely out of their college diapers. They order up matching bacon, egg, and cheese bagels with medium coffees, then sit down with their fourteen ounces of caffeine apiece and wait until their bagels are ready. One of them looks Frank's way and gets a smirk on his face like he's about to make a wisecrack, which he does after he turns back to his friend. Then they both look at Frank and start laughing.

Frank knows he's packed on extra weight. The other guinea

pigs remind him of it every chance they get, so it's kind of hard to pretend that it doesn't bother him—not the questions and the ribbing, but the fact that he can't seem to keep the pounds off.

He doesn't know why he's been so hungry, craving pastries and fast food and milk shakes and wanting seconds of everything when he knows he should be full. It baffles him, because he's made a point of taking care of himself and watching his weight, especially when he's getting ready for a trial. He prides himself on his preparation, on being able to trim down and get himself in shape, on having better discipline than the other guinea pigs. But lately, his discipline has been taken hostage by his appetite.

Frank finishes off his fourth doughnut and the last of his drink as the two frat boys continue to look his way and laugh. If Vic were here, he would start in on his talk about how the two of them were douche bags. And for once, Frank would be inclined to agree.

Anger and resentment build inside of Frank. He's always had a problem with anger, ever since he was a kid. Tantrums and bursts of vitriol were just part of his daily existence. Most children go through the Terrible Twos, but for Frank the Terrible Twos lasted until he was eleven. That's when he discovered girls, or at least discovered that he was interested in them and wondered what it would be like to kiss one without being worried about cooties. For some reason, that caused him to turn into a more pleasant human being.

But ever since the divorce, Frank's anger has been surfacing more often, making guest appearances and cameos whenever he gets frustrated or annoyed or when he can't figure out why he can't stop eating.

While he knows he's not hungry and he should just get up and go home, maybe take a walk to get some exercise, Frank grabs doughnut number five and takes a bite, the cream squishing out around the sides of his mouth and a glob of it dropping onto his T-shirt.

The blond frat boy makes a sound reminiscent of a pig squealing while his dark-haired doppelgänger brays laughter like a donkey; then the guy behind the counter calls out their order.

As Blondie walks past him to the pickup counter, Frank's anger flares up and he gets this feeling inside of him, a bloating in his stomach, like he's suffering from indigestion or gas. Except it feels stronger. More intense. And it's not just his stomach. Frank feels as if his entire body is expanding, growing larger. When he looks down he half expects to see himself inflating, like Violet Beauregarde in *Willy Wonka & the Chocolate Factory*. Except his body remains the same size. And his skin hasn't turned a deep shade of blue. And there aren't any Oompa Loompas singing and getting ready to roll him away.

Even though Frank feels like he's about to burst, he also feels as if he's floating, suspended in air—though in his current state of mind he feels less like a kite and more like a balloon in the Macy's Thanksgiving Day Parade.

Oh no, he thinks. *Not again.*

Frank closes his eyes and takes several deep breaths, trying to calm down and relax before it's too late. But the sound of laughter distracts him and he opens his eyes and sees the two frat boys sitting at their table, biting into their bacon, egg, and cheese bagels, glancing over at him, laughing.

So much for calm and relaxed.

Frank stares at Blondie and imagines himself floating, a big inflatable Frank going higher and higher into the atmosphere—the pressure outside of him decreasing while the volume of gas inside of him continues to expand until, inevitably, he pops.

Blondie drops his bagel then opens his mouth and lets out a strange sound, a cross between a strangled cry and a squeak. An instant later, Blondie starts to expand, his hands and arms and torso swelling up.

"Oh shit!" His buddy pushes away from the table and stands up. "Hey! I think he's having an allergic reaction or something!"

Or something is right.

Blondie continues to inflate, his shirt stretching and tearing at the seams. He lets out a strangled cry as the top button pops on his pants and the inseam starts to rip.

"Help," he squeaks.

One of the customers is calling 911, while another is performing his civic duty by taking a video with his cell phone. Several people come over to see if they can help, but everyone else has stopped what they're doing to watch the spectacle. Some of them move farther away, apparently afraid that whatever is happening might be contagious.

Frank realizes he's not hungry anymore. Not only that, he feels lighter. When he looks down he hopes to discover that he's lost some weight, but other than his sweatpants feeling a little looser around the waist, he's the same goddamn size he was when he sat down to eat his half dozen doughnuts. Blondie, on the other hand, has popped every stitch and seam on his clothes and looks like he's gained more than thirty pounds.

This isn't the first time this has happened. There was the steroid monkey at McDonald's, the NYU coeds at Shake Shack, and the snarky tourists at Papaya Dog. But Frank doesn't want to admit he had anything to do with what happened to them. The idea is ridiculous and unreasonable and beyond the laws of biology and physics. The problem is, Frank's beginning to think that those laws might not apply to him anymore.

Frank gets up from his table, takes one final look at the inflated frat boy, and walks out of Dunkin' Donuts, leaving the last of his Double Cocoa Kremes behind.

chapter 20

Two days later, the six of us (Frank, Charlie, Vic, Randy, Isaac, and I) are in lower Manhattan after 10:00 p.m. on a Saturday night, on our way to help some of the homeless who have been getting mugged in Battery Park. It's our first official foray as superheroes. Our own little band of Mystery Men. The Super Six.

Or, as Vic likes to call us: the Mutant Squad.

We're all wearing hoodies or baseball hats to help conceal our identities and keep a low profile. Charlie, on the other hand, thinks we should have worn capes.

"They come in five colors," he says. "Red, blue, yellow, black, and green. They even have silver and gold lamé. And they're only thirty bucks!"

"What part of 'keeping a low profile' do you not understand?" Vic says.

"Let him have his fun," Frank says around a mouthful of the turkey sandwich he bought at Duane Reade. "It makes him happy."

Frank's a lot more easygoing since he's accepted what's happening to him.

When Frank told us about his ability, we were sure he'd want to adhere to his bullshit Guinea Pig Code and report his mutation to the proper authorities. But like the rest of us, he was more concerned about the possibility of ending up in a research lab than he was about any potential long-term effects.

Some people might say we're being stupid and risking our health in order to live out some childish comic book fantasy. Maybe they're right. Maybe they're smarter than we are. Or maybe they've never felt lost or useless, as if their existence didn't matter.

Common sense doesn't stand much of a chance when you've been given the opportunity to be something greater than you ever imagined.

When we walk past the Staten Island Ferry terminal, I glance up at the curved glass façade of 17 State Street stretching forty-two stories into the sky and I think about quantum mechanics and cause and effect and Sophie, and I wonder how much longer I'm going to be able to keep this from her. It's a good thing she works nights or I'd have a lot of explaining to do.

Now I understand why most superheroes are single.

As we walk into Battery Park, Frank pulls out a two-pack of Little Debbie cupcakes and starts eating one.

"I hope you brought enough to share," Vic says.

A number of drugs are associated with weight gain or increased appetite. The irony is that a lot of medications used to treat obesity-related conditions like diabetes, hypertension, and depression can cause those who are taking the drugs to gain weight.

Frank finishes the first of his Little Debbie cupcakes before starting in on the second.

"Is that healthy?" Randy asks, then takes a drag on his cigarette.

Frank looks at Randy. "Are you kidding?"

Randy used to smoke in high school but quit once he got hooked on cardio and weightlifting. Lately, however, he's become fidgety and says smoking an occasional cigarette helps to calm his nerves and keep him focused.

"Everyone ready?" I ask.

Charlie, Vic, and Isaac nod, while Frank answers in the affirmative around a mouthful of cupcake.

The plan calls for one of us to act as a decoy in order to draw the attention of any would-be muggers. The idea is to isolate our targets without causing any innocent homeless people to projectile vomit or break out in purpuric eruptions.

We're still getting the hang of this superhero thing.

"Randy?" I say.

Randy volunteered to be the decoy and dressed up in some old clothes and a knit beanie and brought along a forty of Olde English 800 in a brown paper bag.

"Ready," Randy says, then grinds out his cigarette before putting the dead soldier in a cigarette case. "This is so Lynyrd Skynyrd."

"I hope that doesn't mean we're all about to die in a plane crash," Vic says.

"'Saturday Night Special.'" Randy looks around at our blank faces. "Because it's Saturday night and this is a special moment. Am I the only one who gets this?"

"Yes," everyone says.

"Okay," I say. "Let's go."

Frank, Isaac, and I keep to the shadows of the trees on one side of the pedestrian path while Vic and Charlie take the other side. Randy stumbles along the path, weaving his way toward the water and the Statue of Liberty Ferry terminal, drinking his Olde English 800 and singing in a drunken slur. At first I can't quite make out the song, but then I recognize the melody as "New York State of Mind."

"I'm drinking a forty, on the Olde English brewery line. I'm in a fucked up state of mind."

The three of us walk along in silence as Frank opens a small bag of Cheetos, which he offers to me and Isaac.

"No thanks," I say, while Isaac accepts.

"I love Cheetos," Isaac says. "They're yummy."

"Your stutter seems to be improving," I say.

Isaac shrugs and stuffs some Cheetos into his mouth. "It c-c-comes and goes."

I listen to Randy channel Billy Joel while the three of us walk along in the shadows and I think about how the six of us have been living in the shadows, existing on the margins of society, doing whatever it takes to find a way to survive: selling ourselves to research labs and panhandling in Central Park or working menial, low-wage jobs in order to pay our rent and buy groceries and afford minor modern-day luxuries like cable TV or a wireless data plan.

Now here we are, doing something to help others, and even though we're just getting started and haven't really proved our-

selves yet, it feels rewarding. More than that, it feels like a valida-
tion of my existence.

There comes a moment in everyone's life when you realize
your true purpose. Sometimes that moment takes years to arrive,
moving like a glacier until it starts to nudge you in the right direction. Other times it arrives like a slap in the face. Or a kick in
the nuts. Either one gets your attention. One just hurts more than
the other.

"Hey man," Randy says, his voice slurred with false drunken-
ness. "What are you guys doin'?"

"None of your business," a voice says, deep and threatening.

"Stop it!" a second voice shouts, high-pitched and indignant.
"Those aren't yours! I found them!"

"Shut up," a third voice says, the menacing twin to the first.

Frank, Isaac, and I move closer until we see a big black guy
with a scraggly beard and dreadlocks rifling through a couple of
rolling suitcases. A homeless man with wild gray hair is on his
back, pinned to an adjacent bench by another black guy. This one
doesn't have dreads or a beard like his buddy, but he's nearly as
big.

"Hey!" The homeless guy shouts in frustration and thrashes his
arms and legs, making a futile attempt to get free. "That's mine!"

"Not anymore." The dreadlocked giant continues to pull items
from the suitcase, tossing most of the contents aside.

I get Frank's attention and point from me to the dreadlocked
guy, then motion for Frank to take the guy on the bench. He
nods once before tossing a few more Cheetos in his mouth and
starts moving.

"What about m-me?" Isaac whispers.

I don't think giving one of these guys an erection is in our best interest. The last thing they need is more testosterone. But I don't want Isaac to feel left out, so I motion for him to follow me.

"I'm giving you one last chance," Randy says, while Isaac and I circle around the two muggers.

As I get into position to sing the dreadlocked giant his own personal lullaby, someone shouts, "Bah bah dah dah!" like a trumpet fanfare. Before I can act, Charlie emerges from the trees, says, "Unhand him!" then runs right out in front of Randy, stops, shivers, and goes into a full body spasm.

When it comes to being a superhero, Charlie has as much self-control as a teenager who just discovered masturbation. But you have to give him points for enthusiasm.

The black behemoth stumbles back, his arms flailing and his legs twitching and jerking, a marionette controlled by a puppeteer with cerebral palsy. Then he starts to go into convulsions, like someone plugged his spine into an electric socket. His mouth opens in a silent scream and a big pink tongue flops out across his lower lip an instant before his teeth snap shut. The tip of his tongue, a quarter-inch of pink, shiny muscle glistening with saliva and blood, tumbles from between his lips, turning over in the air before landing on the ground and bouncing once, then coming to rest on the pedestrian path like a paralyzed slug.

A moment later, he drops to the ground, twitching and convulsing, his fists clenched and blood foaming out between his closed lips as Randy shouts, "Goddamn it!"

I don't have time to see what's wrong, because the other guy says "What the fuck?!" in a deep, menacing voice before he gets up off the homeless man and heads toward Charlie.

My lips grow numb and I feel myself getting sleepy, the pressure of a yawn building up in my throat. Before I can open my mouth, the guy stops walking and lets out an incongruent high-pitched squeak, his eyes opening wide before he suddenly starts to inflate.

His arms and torso and legs expand and for a moment I think he's actually a giant who is revealing his true identity. In a matter of seconds, he looks like he's gained more than twenty pounds. Or maybe it's thirty. I never was good at guessing anyone's weight. But the baggy clothes he's wearing are now a good two sizes too small. I half-expect him to pop, but instead he just screams in agony as he splits his pants and tidy-whities.

I can't hold back any longer, so I let loose with a yawn and the inflated mugger topples over in a heap of fat and ripped clothing next to his convulsing partner. A moment later, Frank appears out of the shadows, licking Cheeto dust off his fingers.

"Well," Frank says. "That was fun."

The homeless guy scrambles over to his suitcases, zips them up, and then gives us a crazed, wide-eyed look before he hurries off with his prized possessions rolling along behind him.

No one knows how to say thank you in this city.

"What were you doing?" Vic says from behind me.

"I was just trying to help!" Charlie shouts.

When I turn around, Randy and Vic are standing next to Charlie, who is scratching at himself as if he has spiders crawling all over him.

"What's wrong with him?" I ask.

"Genius here ran right out in front of Randy," Vic says.

When I get closer I see that Charlie has hives all over his face and neck.

"Stop scratching," Frank says, then he removes a Snickers bar from his jacket and takes a bite. "You'll only make it worse."

Isaac stands there looking forlorn, like the last kid picked for kickball.

"You okay?" I ask.

Isaac nods. "Yeah, but no one could t-tell I gave that guy a b-b-boner."

"I could tell." Randy puts his hand up for a high five, which Isaac reciprocates with an enthusiastic smile. "That was awesome!"

I'm guessing Randy's just trying to make Isaac feel better. If he does have the ability to tell if Isaac gave one of those guys an erection, I don't want to know.

Vic walks over and looks down at the would-be muggers. "So what should we do with these two?"

"Why don't we tie them up?" Randy says.

"With what?" Frank asks as he finishes off his Snickers.

"Did anyone think to bring any rope or zip ties?" Vic asks.

No one did.

"You g-got any Twinkies?" Isaac asks.

"I don't think they have enough tensile strength," I say.

It takes us a moment before we realize Isaac is talking to Frank.

"No," Frank says. "I don't have any Twinkies."

"What a surprise," Vic says.

We leave the two incapacitated muggers behind and make our way out of Battery Park, our first mission as superheroes a relative success.

"How long does this last?" Charlie asks, his skin covered with red, angry hives.

"Twenty minutes," Randy says. "Maybe half an hour."

"Half an hour!" Charlie says.

Randy shrugs. "Maybe longer."

Charlie groans and scratches his chest and back. "Does anyone have any calamine lotion?"

From the New York *Daily News*, page 2:

JUST SUPER! UNIQUE COLLECTION
OF HEROES TAKES MANHATTAN

Vomiting and seizures and rashes, oh my!

What sounds like a musical number for an Off-Broadway mash-up of *The Wizard of Oz* and *Rent* is, instead, the aftermath of a series of bizarre incidents involving a group of individuals who have interfered to stop crimes against New York's elderly and homeless.

Ramona (no last name given), a homeless woman who lives at the Neighborhood Coalition for Shelter, claims to have witnessed them in action.

"There were three of them . . . maybe four." Ramona said. "I saw them one night in Central Park. They helped a friend of mine. Made one of the men attacking her throw up and the other one fall asleep, just like a baby. Like they sung him some kind of a lullaby."

Over the past several weeks, there have been increasing reports of anonymous strangers who have come to the rescue of people in distress—which isn't all that unusual in New York. In recent years, Manhattan has been home to superheroes such as Squeegeeman, who wields his squeegee of justice to fight crime, and Dark Guardian, who employs his martial art skills against drug dealers in Washington Square Park.

So while New York has a history of ordinary people taking extraordinary measures to try to make a difference and help clean up their neighborhoods, these new crime fighters appear to have somewhat unique methods of dispensing justice by allegedly causing their victims to vomit uncontrollably or break out in full-body rashes.

The police have so far refused to comment other than to

say that crime fighting should be left to the proper authorities, but there have even been reports of would-be criminals allegedly suffering bouts of narcolepsy, going into epileptic seizures, and experiencing extreme and sudden weight gain.

"One of the men who attacked me inflated like a balloon," Carolyn Vecchio said. Vecchio, a 72-year-old woman, was mugged in Columbus Park. "I thought he was going to pop."

As is often the case in eyewitness accounts, it's not always easy to separate fact from fiction. However, according to medical reports, the rashes and seizures and vomiting are apparently real. And while the effects suffered by the criminals appear to be temporary, how these vigilantes are able to cause others to experience such reactions is unknown.

However, some people, like Kyle DeWolfe, one of the homeless helped by the group of heroes, have their own theories.

"I bet they're some kind of army experiment," DeWolfe said. "Soldiers in training for some new kind of covert warfare."

Could they be part of some kind of government experiment? It's a conspiracy theorist's wet dream, and not without precedent.

In addition to these crime-fighting vigilantes, there are continuing reports of people throughout the city suffering from memory loss and hallucinations, the latter of which call to mind Project MKUltra—a Cold War CIA project that involved dosing unsuspecting citizens in several U.S. cities with LSD, mescaline, and other hallucinogens in an effort to develop mind control.

"I'm telling you," DeWolfe said. "It's the government. You mark my word."

So are these mystery vigilantes for real? Agents of a covert government operation? Or simply part of an elaborate hoax?

While the answer remains to be seen, Captain Glenn Cotter of the Ninth Precinct shared the NYPD's company line.

"Whoever these vigilantes are, they're operating outside of the law," Captain Cotter said. "Criminals are best left to those who have been trained to deal with them, and we do not encourage or support their assistance in fighting crime."

In spite of the NYPD's unenthusiastic embrace of the vigilantes, New York's latest superheroes are sending a message to those who would take advantage of the disadvantaged—a noble endeavor in a city often plagued by apathy and inhabited by those who frequently turn a blind eye rather than lend a helping hand.

So how's the job search going?" Sophie asks while we're eating a dinner of quinoa pasta with organic tomato sauce and a fresh spinach salad with cranberries and walnuts.

"Good," I say, almost choking on a walnut. "It's good."

Though when you think about it, a job search is only *good* if you find a job. Otherwise your job search is, by definition, a failure. That's presuming, of course, that you're actually seeking employment. If not, then I guess technically your job search is a success.

This is the circular logic I use to justify my answers.

The problem is, it's becoming easier to lie to Sophie and harder to tell her the truth. But I keep managing to convince myself that eventually I'll figure out the best way to tell her that I'm now a superhero half the city is talking about and that when I do confess, everything will be fine.

Apparently, delusions aren't limited to prescription-drug side effects.

"I know you're disappointed that you didn't get the job with Starbucks," Sophie says. "But I appreciate that you're out there looking."

I wonder if guilt can ooze out of your pores when you perspire.

"And I know you're doing it more for me than for you," she says. "But I want you to do this because *you* want to do it."

"I do," I say, with a smile so counterfeit you could buy it out of a suitcase on Canal Street.

"I hope so," Sophie says. "Because as much as I'd like you to find a way to earn a living that doesn't involve taking prescription medications, I just want you to be happy."

"I am," I reply, this time with a genuine smile. Except I'm not happy for the reasons Sophie imagines.

Several nights a week, at least three of us get together to help those who can't help themselves, fighting crime all across Manhattan.

Turtle Bay. The Meatpacking District. Central Park.

Tompkins Square. Stuyvesant Square. East River Park.

It feels good to be doing our part to clean up the parks and neighborhoods, teaching would-be thugs a lesson. More than that, it feels good to have a purpose that doesn't involve getting injected with radioactive tracers or wearing a twenty-four-hour rectal probe.

Mom and Dad would be so proud.

Sophie looks around like she's lost something. "There you are," she says to Vegan, who's watching us from behind the corner of the bedroom doorway, staring at me like he's trying to make my head explode.

"Come here, sweetheart," Sophie says, trying to coax Vegan over without success. She walks over and picks him up and brings him back to the table, where he claws and fights and yowls until

Sophie finally puts him down and watches as he runs off and disappears into the bedroom.

Sophie shakes her head. "I don't know what's wrong with him. He's been acting so odd lately."

"Beats me," I say, staring at my dinner as if it's the most fascinating thing I've ever seen.

"So what movie do you want to watch tonight?" Sophie asks.

"You pick," I say.

Tonight is Movie Night, one of the few evenings Sophie doesn't have to work at Westerly. Since I missed our last Movie Night while out fighting crime, I'm letting her make the decisions.

"How about *WALL-E*?"

Sophie's always been a sucker for animated films and environmentally themed movies.

After dinner, we put on our coats and head out into the cool October evening to rent a movie. Halloween is still a couple weeks away, but I'm on the lookout for goblins and trolls and other mischievous creatures, especially with Sophie at my side. It's almost to the point where I can't set foot outside without assessing any potential danger. When it comes to fighting crime, superheroes can't afford to take days off. Especially with someone out there stealing memories and causing hallucinations.

More and more news reports and articles are popping up about people suffering amnesia and having delusional episodes. While some of the latter are homeless, most are average Dicks and Janes who suddenly suffer psychotic breaks from reality.

So far the police don't seem to have any leads, and neither the authorities nor the media have indicated they believe the crimes are related to us. I don't know if the people responsible for the amnesia and hallucinations are working together or going into business for themselves but whoever they are, I'm pretty sure they're guinea pigs. Otherwise, if they're just average American citizens on meds for anxiety or depression or insomnia, then we're going to end up with a country of mutants, considering fifty percent of Americans take two or more prescription drugs on a daily basis.

In the meantime, I'll keep my shields up and my bad-guy radar on to make sure nothing happens to Sophie.

"There's something different about you, Lollipop," Sophie says, her left arm hooked around my right elbow.

"How am I different?" I say, hoping she doesn't notice that my heart has started playing a drum solo.

"I don't know." She remains silent for several moments before continuing. "It's like the Lloyd I've known for the past couple of years has taken a trip somewhere."

I know what she means, although I think of it more as having been upgraded to a new version. The Lloyd 2.0.

"Is that a good thing?" I say.

"I wouldn't say it's good or bad," she says, stopping and turning to face me. "But there's definitely something new that wasn't there before."

"So you like it?" I say.

"Yes," she says. "I like it. I just wish I understood where it came from."

That's not exactly the answer I was hoping for, but I'll take it.

She reaches up and brushes the hair from my forehead, then traces her fingers along the side of my head. "I think you've got some more gray, Lollipop."

"Thanks for noticing," I say.

She smiles and runs her fingers behind my ear. If I were a dog, my tail would be wagging.

"I like it," she says. "It makes you look distinguished."

"Great," I say. "That's just the look I'm going for. Now can we go get the movie?"

Just before Delancey Street, we pass a couple of trolls hanging out with their hands stuffed in their jackets and their eyes all over Sophie. It's probably nothing more than appreciative appraisal and isn't anything I haven't seen before. Sophie's an attractive woman. Even when she's not dressed up in her fairy outfit, she still exudes a certain something that men find appealing. But as we cross the street, I glance back and notice the two trolls still watching us.

Sophie and I go into the Duane Reade and rent *WALL-E* from Redbox. Since I'm in the mood, I suggest we get two movies and pick out *Mystery Men*, thinking maybe it'll be a good lead-in to having a conversation about my secret identity.

"Okay," she says. "But I'm not a big fan of superhero films. They're kind of silly."

Or maybe not.

On the way back, we cross Delancey again and the two trolls are still hanging out on the corner. As we continue down the street, I glance back and see that they've fallen in behind us.

"Something wrong?" Sophie asks.

"Nope," I say as I summon my trigger and my lips go numb. "Everything's ducky."

I've never used my superpower in front of Sophie or anywhere in her general vicinity, and that's not the way I want her to learn the truth about me. But I'm not going to risk her safety for my ideal confession scenario.

Up ahead of us there's scaffolding erected in front of Eisner Brothers. Other than the two of us and the trolls, there's no one else around, so once we get under the shadows of the scaffolding, I step in front of Sophie and face her and tell her to close her eyes.

"Why?" she asks.

"It's a surprise."

Sophie's always been one to play along, and she loves surprises, so as soon as she closes her eyes, I step to one side and let out a yawn. Before the two trolls reach the scaffolding, both of them fall to the ground in unconscious heaps.

In a normal world, the one in which I used to exist, I never would have had the confidence to believe I could protect Sophie. Or even considered it. So Sophie and I might have been mugged. Or worse. But now I have the courage. Now I have the power.

"What's going on?" she says. "Where's my surprise?"

"Hold on," I say, then search through my pockets to see if I can find a good cover story, but all I come up with are my apartment keys, some lint, and a half pack of Mentos. Sophie already has a set of keys and probably wouldn't appreciate the lint, so I tell her to hold out her hands and give her the Mentos.

"You can open your eyes," I say.

Sophie looks down into her hands. "Mentos?"

I just look at her and smile.

"But I don't eat Mentos," she says.

"I know," I say. "That's the surprise."

Sophie stares at the half pack of Mentos, then looks back at me and cocks her head. "I don't know who's acting odder: you or Vegan."

"Come on." I take Sophie's hand and lead her away from the two trolls slumbering behind us on the sidewalk. "Let's go watch a movie."

chapter 22

Frank, Vic, Charlie, Randy, Blaine, and I are upstairs having lunch at Curry in a Hurry, which is packed with the weekday lunchtime crowd. Hanging plants and watercolor paintings of snake charmers and Indian romance adorn the walls. In the back, next to the bathrooms, a flat-screen television plays something from Bollywood.

"Did you know that a lot of Bollywood films are just remakes of Hollywood films?" Blaine says. "And not remade with permission, but plagiarized?"

"Like what?" Charlie asks.

"*The Godfather. It Happened One Night. Mrs. Doubtfire*," Blaine says, ticking them off on his fingers. "There are hundreds of films that have been plagiarized. Some of them scene for scene."

"Please don't ask him to list all of them," Vic says. "Otherwise he won't shut up."

"Another one of these!" shouts some obnoxious guy sitting with a friend three tables away, waving an empty Kingfisher Lager bottle, trying to get the waiter's attention.

I glance over at Vic. "Don't even think about it."

"What?" Vic says, wearing his innocent face.

In spite of the fact that we all agreed to not use our abilities to teach douche bags a lesson, Vic seems to have a problem staying on message. More than once we've been out to the movies or to lunch or walking down the street and some man or woman smoking or swearing or blabbing away on a cell phone has suddenly started vomiting.

At another table, a Japanese woman answers her iPhone.

"Not her, either," I say.

Vic pouts as he digs into his beef curry. "Cell phones shouldn't be allowed in restaurants."

"What about for emergencies?" Charlie asks.

"Emergencies existed before cell phones," Vic says. "And we got along just fine without them."

"More than seventy-five percent of nine-one-one calls come from cell phones now," Blaine says. "The problem is, since cell phones don't have a fixed address, police and fire departments and paramedics aren't able to respond as quickly as if the call originated from a landline."

"Speaking of emergencies, there was a four-alarm fire in my bedroom last night," Randy says. "Total Talking Heads."

"Can we please have one meal without you discussing your sexual escapades?" Frank asks.

I notice Charlie isn't joining the conversation and looks kind of spaced out, staring at his food as if in some kind of a trance. I'm about to ask him if he's okay when Blaine says, "Hey, check it out."

The obnoxious guy has climbed on top of his table and is sitting down in his plate of half-eaten food.

"I like to think of myself as a scale," he says, striking a pose with his legs crossed in the lotus position and his arms held out to the sides, palms up.

"How about now?" Vic asks.

Charlie laughs and takes a bite of his aloo gobi instead of staring at it, so apparently he's fine.

"I am Karma," the guy on the table says in a loud, commanding voice. "I weigh the outcome of your decisions. Heed my wisdom."

"Heed this," a balding man says, displaying his middle finger. A few seconds later, he trips and falls into another table.

"Now that's some instant karma," Vic says.

"I don't know." I watch the guy who is still sitting on the table and wonder if he might have had anything to do with Baldy falling face-first into someone else's lunch. "Maybe it's more than that."

"What do you mean?" Randy asks.

I nod toward the guy sitting on the table. "Maybe he's like us."

"You think so?" Charlie says, his eyes wide like those of a star-struck teenager.

All of us turn to look at the self-proclaimed Karma.

"Couldn't it be a coincidence?" Blaine asks.

"As far as I'm concerned," Frank says, "nothing's a coincidence."

At the back of the restaurant, the manager points his finger at Karma and yells, "Get off the table! Get off the table and get out or I'll call the police!"

Karma doesn't appear overly concerned about the manager's threats, because he's not moving.

"If you do good things, good things will happen to you," he says, then lowers his right hand and raises his left. "If you do bad things, yada yada yada."

"Do you think we should go talk to him?" Charlie asks.

"And say what?" Frank says, his mouth full of chicken masala.

"Maybe we could recruit him," Charlie says. "See if he wants to join up with us."

"I don't know," Vic says. "He seems like a huge douche bag to me."

The man who would be Karma remains on the table, espousing various Buddhist teachings to the lunchtime crowd about wholesome actions and kindness and truth. The strange thing is, a lot of the customers are actually paying attention. At one point, his lunch companion, who looks like the offspring of Brad Pitt and Ryan Reynolds, asks him a question about the path of destiny.

"Man creates his own destiny," Karma says. "The path you seek is your own."

While the manager calls the police and Karma continues to dispense his wisdom, a twenty-something man holding a baseball hat approaches him.

"If I apologize to my girlfriend, will she forgive me?" he asks.

"Deeds, not words, define the man," Karma says. "Apologize with actions and you will reap the rewards."

The young man gives his thanks and leaves the restaurant.

"Is it too late to make something right?" a young woman asks.

"It's never too late to atone for one's offenses," he answers.

She starts to cry and then leaves.

"Oh, come on," Vic says. "You have got to be kidding me."

Charlie stands up. "Will I be able to find happiness?"

"Happiness is found within," comes the reply.

"What the hell are you doing?" Vic says.

Charlie shrugs and sits back down. "I was just curious."

As the sound of sirens approaches and several other customers stand up and ask Karma for his advice, one of his answers plays back in my head:

Man creates his own destiny. The path you seek is your own.

Whenever Sophie talks about destiny, I always resist the idea, because the concept makes it seem like someone or something else is in control of my life. Not that I've done such a great job of managing things to date, but I like to think I have some say in the decision-making process rather than being bound by some cosmic decree written in the stars. But maybe I've been thinking about destiny all wrong. Maybe it's not so permanent.

Man creates his own destiny. The path you seek is your own.

Maybe our future isn't written in the stars. Maybe it's right here in our own hands, waiting for us to do something with it.

Then the police come in and arrest Karma and drag him out in handcuffs.

chapter 23

I'm standing across from the Flatiron Building just after midnight, my hoodie pulled up as ghosts of breath disappear into the chill of the early-November morning. The homeless who sleep in and around Madison Square Park have been getting attacked, assaulted, and beaten up. Since the police haven't managed to solve the problem, we thought we'd see if we could lend a hand.

Inside the park, Vic and Charlie wander around pretending to be drunk, while Randy waits across the street by the Twenty-Third Street subway entrance smoking, which he seems to be doing more often lately. Frank stands next to me, eating an apple fritter. For a few weeks, Frank kept exercising in an effort to keep off some of the extra weight, but eventually he decided it was a losing battle, so his wardrobe now consists almost entirely of sweats and loose-fitting clothing with elastic and Velcro.

"Mmmmm," he says, licking his fingers, then holding the apple fritter out to me. "You want a bite?"

"No thanks," I say.

I've already had my fill of pretzels and jellybeans, which are high on the glycemic index. Not as high as sourdough bread or instant rice, but they're easier to carry around and they help to up my glucose levels so I can improve the strength of my superpower. I just have to make sure I don't become diabetic. Even if I could afford to take something for type 2 diabetes, I wouldn't want to deal with possible side effects like jaundice or suffering from a severe skin rash. If I want that, I can always hit up Randy.

Isaac is enrolled in a four-day lockdown for an experimental drug to treat dementia and psychosis, so he's not here. While Isaac enjoys going out with us, I know he gets frustrated since no one can tell when he gives someone an erection.

Laughter drifts to us from inside the park by the Shake Shack, loud and boisterous, followed by the sound of a bottle breaking. That's the signal. Frank gobbles down the rest of his apple fritter and I pocket my jellybeans. Out by the subway entrance, Randy takes one last drag on his cigarette, then stubs it out and disposes of it properly and jogs across the street to join us before we head into the park.

During the day, the Shake Shack is the scene of long lines of men and women waiting to order burgers, hot dogs, fries, frozen custard, and of course, milk shakes. But after midnight, this is just another place for trouble.

When we get to the Shake Shack, two punks are hassling Vic by the closed pickup windows while Charlie backs away from a third out behind the hamburger stand. Two more punks terrorize a homeless woman by the southern fountain. Frank peels off from me and heads that way with Randy while I stand point and watch to make sure no one gets blindsided or outnumbered. Or in case someone pulls a gun.

Over the past couple of weeks, we've all worked on honing our skills and improving our teamwork. I don't know if we're ready yet to take on Doctor Doom or Magneto, but at least we're able to make a difference for those who can't stand up for themselves or who don't have anyone to fight for them. And we've learned how to fight for each other.

Since Vic's got his hands full with double the fun, I keep an eye on him in case he needs a hand. But as soon as he burps, the two punks start clutching their stomachs and stumble away, falling to their hands and knees before spraying vomit across the sidewalk.

While the local authorities have issued multiple statements saying that we're vigilantes acting outside of the law and are not to be encouraged, the local press hasn't helped matters by turning us into heroes and glorifying our exploits. They've even given us superhero names.

The two punks crawl around on the ground, moaning and puking, as Vic lets out a laugh and another burp and makes them throw up again.

Vic is known as Captain Vomit.

Out behind the Shake Shack, Charlie tries to reason with his would-be assailant. This is part of Charlie's new attempt to maintain his self-control when channeling his ability. But the punk isn't listening. So Charlie shivers in the early-November morning and the next instant the guy drops to the ground, shaking and convulsing like an epileptic having an orgasm.

Charlie's been dubbed Convulsion Boy.

At first Charlie was disappointed that Vic was given the rank of Captain while he was relegated to the status of sidekick, like Robin or Kato, but eventually we convinced Charlie that it didn't matter what everyone else thought. As far as we're concerned, he's a leading man.

None of us ever expected this to become our lives, but it's who we are now. We've become drug-reaction crime fighters. Side-effect superheroes, using our pharmaceutically enhanced abilities to teach criminals a lesson.

Over by the southern fountain, Randy lights up another cigarette and takes a deep drag as one of the thugs starts scratching at himself and whimpering, his skin blistered and covered with angry red splotches.

Randy is called the Rash.

While it's not the most glamorous of superhero names, Randy has embraced his new identity. We all have. We're genetic mutants. Freaks of science. A product of our profession. The modern prescription for an overmedicated society.

The last of the criminals cries out as his waist expands and his arms and thighs grow to twice their thickness. Before he has a chance to run away from Frank, he busts through the seams of his clothes and falls down, incapacitated, his frame unable to support the extra weight.

Frank is known as Big Fatty.

Two more punks show up late to the party. When they see what's happening to their buddies, they turn and run toward the subway entrance, so I take off after them.

In the four months since the skateboarder in Central Park, I've learned to direct my yawns at a single individual in a crowd with a range of up to fifty feet. I can even hit moving targets while running at full speed.

Just before the two punks reach Twenty-Third Street, I yawn and they collapse, sliding along the sidewalk and coming to rest next to each other by the park entrance, their eyes closed in deep, unexpected slumber.

They call me Dr. Lullaby.

Some people still get confused about my name, though I guess I shouldn't take it personally. After all, it's not like I've ever done any interviews or tried to set the matter straight. But apparently some people think I'm some kind of serenading physician or academic pedophile.

I think I need to hire a good publicist.

Since Isaac's ability to hand out boners has largely gone unnoticed, none of the tabloids have given him a pseudonym, so to make him feel better we all call him Professor Priapism.

Vic walks up to me and slaps me on the back. "Nice shooting, Doc."

"Thanks," I say. "Now let's wrap 'em up and call it a night."

Using zip ties and duct tape, we tie up the assholes and leave them gift wrapped for the NYPD, then split up and make our way to our respective homes.

It used to be that after a session of fighting crime we would go out and celebrate. But with our exploits being chronicled in the papers and on the local news, it's become risky for us to be seen together late at night grabbing a beer at the KGB Bar or pierogi at Veselka.

I guess that's the price of being a superhero with a secret identity. Sometimes you have to be willing to make a few sacrifices.

Vic and Frank head for the subway while Charlie, Randy, and I venture home on foot, heading down Broadway. We don't talk about what happened. Now it's just business as usual. When we do talk about it later, we'll discuss it in the privacy of Charlie's or Randy's or Vic's apartment, breaking down what went right and what went wrong and how to do it better next time.

I never thought being a crime fighter would require troubleshooting.

The three of us walk past a bank of newspaper-vending kiosks, most of them empty, but there's still a copy of yesterday's *Wall Street Journal* in the display window as well as a copy of the *New York Post*, the headline announcing:

BAD APPLES IN THE BIG APPLE:
SUPERVILLAINS SUCK

Much as they've done with us, the media has given names to the two villains who have terrorized New York with their supernatural ability to steal people's memories and give them hallucinations: Mr. Blank and Illusion Man.

Over the past few weeks their exploits have become notorious, leading to a lot of political finger-pointing and a demand for beefed-up police patrols. There have even been reports of the FBI and CIA getting involved.

The problem is, no one knows who Mr. Blank and Illusion Man are, what they look like, or where to find them. Not even us.

"I read that some people have had hallucinations that lasted for several days," Charlie says. "And that everyone who's encountered Mr. Blank has suffered permanent memory loss."

I don't know about anyone else's personal best, but the longest I've been able to make anyone take a nap has been thirty-seven minutes.

"Illusion Man and Mr. Blank are awesome names," Randy says. "A hell of a lot better than the Rash."

Randy's not real fond of his nom de plume.

"I hope we never run into either of them," Charlie says.

"Why not?" Randy asks.

"Because they're too powerful," Charlie says.

"Come on," Randy says. "You can't believe everything you read in the daily rags. What kind of superhero are you?"

Charlie looks down at the ground and answers quietly into his chest. "The practical kind."

Randy's cell phone goes off, his ringtone playing "You Shook Me All Night Long" by AC/DC. He pulls out his phone and checks it, a grin spreading across his face. "Looks like I've got some late-night booty to call on in Chelsea, boys. Hallelujah! Can I get a Jim Morrison?"

I don't know if that means he's going to love her madly or be her back door man, and I don't want to know.

"Catch you superheroes later," Randy says, then runs off down Nineteenth Street.

"How does he do that?" Charlie asks.

"Do what?"

"Get laid all the time?" Charlie says. "It's like a superpower or something."

"Hopefully he doesn't get his two superpowers mixed up," I say.

Charlie and I continue down Broadway to Union Square. My lullaby radar sweeps back and forth, checking out the homeless camped out on the benches and the drunks stumbling out of the nearby bars and the late-night crowd gathered in front of the subway entrance.

"Hey Lloyd," Charlie says once we're through Union Square and heading down Fourth Avenue. "Do you think I have what it takes to be a superhero?"

"You *are* a superhero," I say. "We all are."

"I know," he says. "But I want to be like the superheroes in the movies and comic books. Smart and brave and heroic. Someone like Spider-Man or Batman. Superheroes kids look up to and want to be when they grow up."

"Spider-Man and Batman aren't real," I say. "While kids may idolize them, they're just fictional characters. You're real, Charlie. And people do look up to you."

He nods. "I guess I just wish I had a real superpower. Like I could fly or become invisible or bend steel with my bare hands."

"You do have a real superpower," I say. "And you use it to help a lot of people. That's the true meaning of a superhero. Not whether or not you have superhuman speed or can leap tall buildings in a single bound."

After a moment, Charlie nods his head a couple of times and says, "Okay."

"And for what it's worth, you're one of the bravest people I know."

"Thanks," he says, a smile brightening his face.

We continue to walk along in silence, our breath pluming out in the cold November air, the city crouched and lurking, hiding in shadows.

"Hey Lloyd. Do you think I'd look better in a red cape or a yellow one?"

'm in Washington Square Park, sitting in the shade of the Arch—not preparing to fight crime but trying to score some charitable donations from marks walking into and out of the park via Fifth Avenue.

I don't usually panhandle outside of Central Park, but Thoth the Spiritual Prayformer booked the Bethesda Terrace Arcade for the afternoon, and my other favorite pitches were taken by an assortment of jugglers, magicians, and balloon-animal artists, which is how I ended up here, trying to appeal to the denizens of Greenwich Village.

"Chunky Monkey, dude!" some NYU student on a skateboard says as he rides past and flashes the peace sign. All I know is he's not flashing any green to help pay my rent.

My sign today reads:

ALL YOU NEED IS LOVE . . . AND AN OCCASIONAL PINT OF BEN & JERRY'S.

Not one of my top ten signs, but you can't expect a superhero to put a lot of energy into holding down a day job. I don't know how Clark Kent and Peter Parker do it. I bet in real life, they'd hate punching a clock at the *Daily Planet* or *Daily Bugle*. Or else they'd get fired for missing work because they were out fighting crime.

Maybe if I had a billionaire alter ego like Bruce Wayne I wouldn't have to panhandle, but since I don't have inexhaustible accounts to fund my weapons research and my last couple of clinical-trial checks have been less than fifteen hundred combined, I need to find a way to supplement my income.

Something tells me the Green Lantern doesn't have to worry about making rent.

I watch the NYU student ride away without contributing to my cause and I think about making him fall asleep, but I don't want to attract the wrong kind of attention. And making skateboarders fall asleep is yesterday's news. Besides, I need to conserve my energy for more important endeavors.

Being a superhero is a lot more work than I expected. It takes tremendous energy and commitment and attention to detail. You have to hone your skills. You have to maintain your focus and concentration. Otherwise you might end up making the wrong person break out in a rash or throw up.

I wonder if Superman ever has this kind of internal monologue.

But in spite of all the effort it takes to be a superhero, this is the most fun I've had in years. I wake up every morning and I can't wait for nightfall. During the day I walk around checking out people, sizing them up, wondering how fast I could take them down if the situation called for it. Still, sometimes I ask myself how I ended up with this superpower rather than someone else. Someone more deserving. Someone who didn't sleepwalk through the first thirty years of his life.

When it comes to self-worth, I've never made much of an investment in my own stock value.

I read somewhere that human beings are made up of thirty elements: mostly oxygen, carbon, hydrogen, and nitrogen, with a little calcium, phosphorus, potassium, and sulfur thrown in for seasoning. Boiled down into a consumer product, we're not worth much more than a foot-long sandwich from Subway. But when you add up all of the intangible qualities that make us human—things like courage and integrity and compassion—the overall value of the individual shoots up dramatically. Some more so than others.

Most of my life, I've considered my own market value closer to penny stocks than to precious metals. But over the past few weeks, I've developed a newfound confidence to go with my supernatural ability, and my self-worth has soared.

Now if only I could parlay that into rent money.

So I sit behind my sign, thinking about stock prices and scientific elements and cold-cut combos while trying to project some pre–Thanksgiving holiday cheer. But Washington Square Park isn't the best location to capitalize on the spirit of the season.

This time of year, Rockefeller Center and Times Square are the prime busking locations, where holiday crowds are in abundance wearing their festive Santa Claus red, their pockets filled with *Tannenbaum* green. Peace on Earth, goodwill toward men still strikes the right note when everyone's in a cheerful mood and possessed with the spirit of giving.

Maybe I should have used a holiday-themed sign, except every Joe Panhandler in the five boroughs plays that angle. I prefer to stand out in a crowd. The problem is, there's not much of a crowd. Still, after four hours I've made thirty-seven dollars and change, which is more than I could make behind a register at Pret A Manger or the Food Emporium. So I pocket my dollars and quarters and other loose change and head for the subway.

On my way out of the park, I pass the chess tables and stop to watch a handful of matches in progress. I consider sitting down and playing a little competitive chess for cash, see if I can turn my thirty-seven bucks into seventy-four, but I don't want to risk losing my hard-earned money. You never know when you might get hustled. Plus the last couple of times I played against Blaine he won every match, so it's not like I'm at the top of my game. I suppose I could always make Blaine fall asleep and take whatever money he has in his wallet, but that would be an abuse of my power.

Being a superhero is so complicated.

As I'm watching the chess matches and debating my morality, a black homeless woman walks past, pushing a shopping cart filled with her belongings and shouting at some invisible antagonist, giving him a piece of her fractured mind and waving a hand in the air as if dismissing him.

While it's not the same woman I saw in Tompkins Square when I was playing chess with Blaine, there's something about her that makes me think about how the other woman started shouting and waving her arms around like she was fighting off some attacker, much like this one.

At the time I figured the woman at Tompkins Square was just a broken-down homeless woman with a few spark plugs missing, but what if it was something else? What if she wasn't just cracked out or mentally ill? What if she was hallucinating? And what if someone with a supernatural ability was responsible for causing those hallucinations?

This train of thought continues through my head and when I look out the windows, I see Blaine leaving lunch early in the East Village just before a homeless guy starts screaming about being impregnated by aliens.

I see the two of us playing chess in Tompkins Square as the homeless woman walks past. I see Blaine watching her, staring at her, then turning back to the chessboard after she starts shouting at some invisible companion.

I hear him ask me if our abilities will go away if we stop volunteering for clinical trials, and I hear him tell me nothing unusual has been happening to him.

I could be imagining things or jumping to conclusions, connecting dots that aren't really there, but I can't help thinking there's something going on with Blaine.

Maybe he lied. Maybe he's developed abilities and he's not telling us. Maybe he's the one responsible for all the hallucinations.

Y ou think Blaine is Illusion Man?" Charlie asks.

Vic, Frank, Randy, Charlie, and I are at Randy's for poker night. I don't know if the Fantastic Four or the X-Men get together and play Trivial Pursuit or Guitar Hero to decompress from fighting the forces of evil, but we're all looking forward to a night of hanging out and playing cards.

Or at least we were.

"She could have just been a mentally unstable homeless person," Frank says after I tell them about the homeless woman at Tompkins Square. "It's not like there's a shortage of them in Manhattan."

"Maybe," I say. "But that wasn't the only instance where something weird happened when Blaine was around. There was also that guy who freaked out during lunch the day we figured out what was going on."

"What guy?" Charlie asks.

"It happened just after Blaine left," I say. "He started shouting about being impregnated by aliens."

"I remember that," Randy says.

"Then there was that guy at Curry in a Hurry," I say.

"You mean the douche bag who thought he was Karma?" Vic says.

I nod. "That's the one."

"I thought you said he might be like us," Frank says around a mouthful of pastrami sandwich from Katz's.

Frank's pushing 225 pounds now, which is a good forty pounds more than he used to carry. I'm a little worried about him, but right now, I'm more worried about Blaine.

"Maybe," I say. "Maybe I was wrong about him. Maybe he was mentally disturbed. Or maybe . . ."

"Maybe he was hallucinating and he thought he was Karma," Charlie says.

I touch my nose and point to him.

"So that's three times," I say, holding up three fingers for emphasis. "Now, we've all been guinea pigs for the past five years, and we've all participated in a lot of the same clinical trials. Including the one in August where we took all of those drugs to see how they interacted."

"That was right before this all started," Randy says.

"Right," I say. "So if we all developed these abilities not long after that, doesn't it seem likely that Blaine would have developed one, too?"

This last question is met with a silence so thick Frank could probably eat it with a fork.

"Son of a bitch," Vic says. "He's been playing us."

"We don't know that for sure," Frank says. "Everything Lloyd mentioned could just be coincidence."

"I thought you said there's no such thing as coincidence," Randy says.

"Yeah, Big Fatty," Vic says. "Are you eating your words now, too?"

While the three of them discuss Frank's new diet, I glance over at Charlie, who is staring out the back window. When I follow his gaze to see what he's looking at, I don't see anything.

"What is it, Charlie?" I ask.

He just keeps staring.

"Charlie?" I say, then reach out and put my hand on his shoulder.

He blinks and looks at me. "What?"

"You kind of spaced out there for a minute," I say.

"I did?" He looks around, confused, and then stares at me with this odd expression, as if trying to figure out a riddle. "When did you start going gray?"

"I don't know," I say. "A couple months ago. Why?"

He shrugs and smiles. "It makes you look distinguished."

"So what do we do about Blaine?" Randy asks.

"I say we gang up on him," Vic says. "He can't take us all."

"Maybe we should talk to Blaine first," Frank says, attempting to be the voice of reason.

"You mean like an intervention?" I say.

"A supervillain intervention," Vic says. "Great idea. 'Thank you for all that you've done to enlighten us with your boundless knowledge of trivia, Blaine, but your decision to cause people to hallucinate is hurting all of us. We all care about you. But please stop or else we'll have to make you throw up and turn into Fat Bastard.'"

"I don't know," Randy says, scratching the back of his head. "That could work."

"One way or another," I say. "We'll get our chance to talk to him tonight."

"He's coming here?" Charlie looks around as if he just found out the boogeyman is waiting outside. "What happens if you're right and he *is* Illusion Man? What do we do then?"

"I don't know," I say. "I guess we'll just have to find out."

"Find out what?"

We all turn to see Blaine standing in Randy's open doorway holding a six-pack of Corona. I don't know how he snuck up on us without anyone noticing but we all just stare at him without saying anything. This goes on for about ten seconds. It's so quiet you can hear Frank's waistline expanding.

"Did I interrupt something?" Blaine asks.

Charlie lets out a nervous laugh.

"We were just talking," I say, wondering how much he heard.

"About what?" he says.

I'm thinking it's probably best to suggest our suspicions with prudence and diplomacy, just in case I'm right about him being Illusion Man. Then Randy says, "About the fact that you're a supervillain."

So much for prudence and diplomacy.

Blaine looks around the room at everyone, then lets out a theatrical sigh. "I guess that means we're not playing poker."

"So you're not denying it?" Vic says.

"Why deny what's obvious?" Blaine says. "I'm a firm believer in embracing the truth, which is something you should really take to heart, Lloyd."

The last thing I need is relationship advice from a supervillain, but that doesn't mean it doesn't strike a nerve. So just in case, I decide we should probably go with Vic's approach and all gang up on Blaine. The problem is, I can't seem to remember how to make my lips go numb.

"What do you want?" Frank asks.

"Well, I wanted to drink some cold Coronas and take all of your money," Blaine says. "But since that's not happening, I guess I want what any supervillain wants."

"And what's that?" I say.

Blaine smiles and spreads his arms wide. "Everything."

"Well, you can't always get what you want," Frank says.

"Rolling Stones," Randy says. "Nice."

"Will you shut up?" Vic says.

Blaine lets out a laugh befitting a supervillain. More the Joker than Dr. Evil or Emperor Palpatine. "How anyone can mistake the five of you for superheroes amuses me. You're more like Keystone Kops."

"You don't know anything about us," Charlie says.

"Really?" Blaine says, briefly scanning the five of us. "Well, to prove you wrong, it just so happens I know that you're all trying to call up your superpowers right now and wondering why you can't."

We look around at one another. Apparently I'm not the only one having trouble accessing my trigger.

"How do you know that?" Randy says.

"You really have no idea who you're dealing with, do you?" Blaine says.

"Yes we do," I say. "You're Illusion Man."

Blaine laughs again, this time as if someone just told him a funny joke.

"You're not Illusion Man?" Vic says.

Everyone looks at me.

Uh oh.

"Christ," Blaine says. "You really are Keystone Kops."

"We're not Keystone Kops," Charlie says, his voice low and serious and filled with surprising resolve. "We're superheroes."

"You say tomato . . ." Blaine says.

Charlie's face turns red, like he's concentrating on something important. Or trying to call up his trigger. I join in and do the same but it's just not there. From the looks on their faces I'm guessing Frank, Vic, and Randy are doing the same, but nothing's happening and Blaine's still standing there—not throwing up or gaining weight or going into a seizure.

Charlie closes his eyes, his face turning a deeper red, the veins standing out on his forehead, his fists clenched against his sides. The next moment he shivers—a long, drawn-out convulsion that seems more intense than anything I've ever seen him experience before. When he opens his eyes and smiles, I think he's found his trigger. Then his smile falls away and the color drains from his face.

"Vanilla," Charlie says an instant before his eyes roll back in his head and he drops to the floor.

"Charlie!" Vic kneels down next to him and cradles his head while Randy checks Charlie's eyes and pulse.

"Well, it's been fun," Blaine says. "But I've got people to see and memories to steal."

"You can't get away, you son of a bitch," Vic says, looking up from Charlie. "We know who you are."

"Do you?" Blaine looks at Vic as if trying to win a staring contest. And I realize how Blaine might have blocked the memories to access our triggers.

"Vic, look away," I say.

Blaine lets out another laugh, then holds his finger and his thumb up to his forehead in the shape of an *L* before he turns and walks out the door. "Catch you later, super zeroes."

His laughter follows him down the stairs.

Vic stares at the open doorway a moment longer before he looks at me with a bewildered expression. "Who the hell was that?"

INTERLUDE #4

⬭▬

Memory Lane Is Closed for Repairs

Blaine sits in the lobby of the Waldorf-Astoria, dressed in a tailored navy blue Hugo Boss suit, a black Hugo Boss shirt, no tie, and a pair of black leather Roberto Cavalli wingtips that are so shiny they reflect the lights of the ornate crystal chandelier hovering beneath the ceiling like an alien spaceship. Tourists and guests sit in lavish lounge chairs or walk through the lobby, taking pictures of the murals and mosaics and the chandelier, while assistant managers and other hotel employees canvass the area, unaware that Mr. Blank is in the house.

After a few moments, Blaine stands up and walks across the lobby and into Sir Harry's lounge with its plush red armchairs and checkerboard tables and a polished mahogany bar lined with red-cushioned, low-backed bar stools. "Say It Isn't So" by Billie Holiday plays in the background. Blaine never used to know Billie Holiday from Etta James, but now he knows more about jazz than he ever imagined.

He eyes a pair of empty stools halfway down the bar. An older couple wearing jeans and smiles sits on one side while a brunette in a sleeveless black dress and a bored expression sits on the other. He picks the bar stool next to the happy couple and makes himself comfortable.

"Fresh nuts?" the bow-tied bartender asks with a Disney smile as he scoops some nuts from a silver bucket and places a small bowl down on the bar in front of Blaine.

"Thanks," Blaine says, flashing his own smile.

"What can I get you to wash those down?" the bartender asks.

"Can you make a mojito?"

"Absolutely," the bartender says. "Dirty or traditional?"

Blaine looks into the bartender's eyes and gets a flash of a thought that's not his own, another voice speaking in his head, then the moment is gone. But the thought remains.

"Dirty." Blaine takes a small handful of nuts and pops them into his mouth. "And a glass of water, if you don't mind."

The bartender gets Blaine his water, then starts preparing his drink.

When he first discovered he had the ability to steal people's memories, Blaine was clumsy in wielding his power and would ransack people's minds like an undisciplined thief. But after several months of practice, he's learned how to use finesse and a light touch so he can now access memories without anyone even knowing he was there.

"I didn't know they made dirty mojitos," the bored brunette in the black dress says from two stools over, swirling the remains of her drink around the bottom of her rock glass. "What's the difference?"

"A dirty mojito is made with spiced rum instead of white rum and brown-sugar syrup rather than white sugar," Blaine says, the synapses in his brain firing, incorporating the information into his memory.

The best thing about being Mr. Blank isn't just having the ability to make people forget him, but having the power to make all of their memories his own.

"Sounds yummy." The brunette drains the last of her drink and sets her empty glass on the bar.

"Make that two," Blaine says to the bartender, then turns back to the brunette. "I don't think anyone should sit at a bar with an empty glass."

"Thank you," she says.

Blaine smiles and looks into her eyes, thoughts and images from her mind drifting through his head. "Hemingway drank mojitos during the winters he spent in Key West."

"I *love* Hemingway," she says. "He's my favorite author."

Blaine smiles. "Imagine that."

"Have you ever been to Key West?" she asks.

"Never exactly made it on my list of Top Ten Travel Destinations," Blaine says, as more of the brunette's thoughts invade his mind, talking to him, telling him things. "But I'm planning a trip to Greece this fall."

The brunette leans one elbow on the bar, her chin in the palm of her hand. "I love Greece. It's my idea of paradise."

Blaine just smiles.

"Annabelle," she says, offering her right hand across the empty bar stool. "But my friends call me Bella."

"Pleasure to meet you, Bella," Blaine says, taking her hand. "You can call me Rick."

"Like in *Casablanca*. That was Humphrey Bogart's character."

"'I remember every detail,'" Blaine says. "'The Germans wore gray, you wore blue.'"

Bella smiles and laughs, then runs a hand along her neck. "I don't run across many men who appreciate old movies. I'm a sucker for them. *Casablanca* is my favorite film of all time."

"Small world," Blaine says, his synapses firing again. "Or, as they say in French: *Le monde est petit.*"

"Je n'en reviens pas," she says, looking surprised. *"Parlez-vous français?"*

"Oui." Blaine holds his thumb and forefinger an inch apart. *"Je parle un peu."*

Bella slides over into the seat next to Blaine and proceeds to speak to him in French, occasionally touching him on the arm or the knee. He responds in French with the proper inflection, pausing occasionally as if searching for just the right way to say something, but it's just a ruse to give him more of a vulnerable side. Even though he never studied French in school or had the opportunity to travel abroad, Blaine can speak the language as if he'd been born and raised in Paris.

In addition to French, he can speak Spanish, German, and Italian. Sometimes he even thinks in other languages. Plus he's absorbed more information about science, mathematics, history, sports, cooking, finance, marketing, stock trading, electrical engineering, medicine, animal behavior, filmmaking, feminine hygiene, mixology, and a lonely brunette's favorite movies and travel destinations than he ever imagined possible.

It's amazing how much you can learn by stealing other people's memories.

When the mojitos arrive, Blaine raises his glass to Bella and she reciprocates.

"We'll always have Paris," he says in his best Bogart impersonation.

She gives him another smile and looks at him over the rim of her glass and he knows it's only a matter of time before she asks him back to her room.

Another benefit to having backstage passes and VIP access to people's thoughts and minds is that Blaine has learned how to manipulate the inevitable.

"Will you excuse me?" Bella sets her drink down and stands up, touching Blaine on the shoulder with her hand. "I'll be right back."

"Mais bien sûr," he says.

She gives him another smile and saunters away, her hips swaying like an invitation beneath the clinging black fabric of her dress. Blaine watches her go, then he looks around at the other people inhabiting Sir Harry's on a Sunday afternoon and contemplates the information in their heads, just waiting to be his. All it takes is a moment of eye contact and he sees inside their minds, the windows to their souls, or at least to their thoughts and memories—which he makes his own, adding to his exponentially increasing amount of knowledge.

He wonders if this is how it feels to be God.

Except he doubts the creator of the universe would use his omniscience to take advantage of people. Or remove any memory of his existence.

When Blaine first became aware of his new ability, he thought he'd simply learned to read others people's minds, to see into their thoughts and memories, which he used to his advantage by guessing where people were from and what they did for a living. Or by beating his guinea-pig buddies at poker and chess.

But Blaine soon discovered that in addition to winning bets and impressing women, he could also cause people to suffer from memory loss. Specifically, memories relating to him. All it took was a little extra focus and concentration on his part and any trace of Blaine would be wiped clean from their memories.

So instead of using his talents just to make some easy pocket money or get laid, Blaine started to up the stakes. He got free meals and drinks at expensive restaurants. He stole from tourists and mugged people after they withdrew money from ATMs. He walked away with wallets and purses and credit card PINs without a single visit from a police officer.

People have a tendency to not press charges or identify you to the authorities when they not only can't remember what you look like but don't even remember meeting you.

This proved especially helpful when he started stealing prescription drugs at open houses, raiding medicine cabinets in the Upper West and East Sides for antianxiety drugs and insomnia medications, most of which list memory loss as a possible side effect. Blaine didn't know if his power would go away if he stopped volunteering and he didn't want to risk finding out, so he made sure to keep a steady supply of drugs on hand, just in case.

Once you have the power, the last thing you want to do is give it up.

But as Blaine soon discovered, the more drugs he took that

could cause memory loss, the stronger his power continued to grow. Not only could he remove memories of himself from others, he could make them forget just about anything, even their own identities. Blaine found this both ironic and amusing, considering that he'd started volunteering for clinical trials because he'd had his own identity stolen.

It didn't take long before the local papers started calling him Mr. Blank.

He likes the name. It has a sense of formality to it, a certain je ne sais quoi that commands authority and respect. As it should. He wouldn't be caught dead with a ridiculous name like Captain Vomit or the Rash.

While he enjoys stealing people's identities for kicks, Blaine has taken to chatting up well-to-do women at bars and going back to their luxury hotel rooms or uptown apartments. There he indulges in their physical charms before he wipes their memories clean and leaves with whatever money and jewelry and personal possessions he can take. And getting the combinations to their safes is as easy as getting them to spread their legs.

He knows eventually he'll get bored with this and want something more, something bigger and better. Even now, at this moment, he can feel his power increasing, expanding, pushing past the boundaries of what he thought was possible. In the meantime, he figures he'll continue to take advantage while the taking is good.

Bella appears at the back of the bar and makes her way toward him, her eyes catching his and a playful smile tickling the corners of her mouth.

Yeah, Blaine thinks. *This is going to be fun.*

"I was thinking," Bella says, brushing against Blaine as she sits down next to him. "Why don't we take this conversation some-place else?"

"What did you have in mind?" Blaine asks.

"Well, I have a room in the towers," she says, then sucks some of her mojito through her straw. "But that's just one idea."

Blaine gives her a smile and picks up his drink. "I think that's the best idea I've heard all day."

The clock on the ICU waiting room wall says it's 12:37 a.m., which means we've been at the New York Presbyterian Hospital for nearly three hours, but it feels more like three days. No one else is in the waiting room at this hour. On the flat-screen television mounted above us, CNN plays a relentless tune of death and disease and tragedy. Not exactly uplifting ambiance.

Maybe Sophie was right. Maybe the news needs to be less sensational and more inspirational. And right now, we could use some good news. But apparently CNN isn't in the feel-good business.

"Do you think Blaine caused Charlie's s-s-seizure?" Isaac asks.

According to the doctor, Charlie suffered what appears to be a grand mal seizure that put him into a coma. Isaac showed up at Randy's just before the ambulance and we all came down here together.

"I don't know," I say, as the death toll rises in some natural disaster somewhere. "I think it looked more like Charlie did it to himself."

"Kind of like how you thought Blaine was Illusion Man?" Frank says.

At least no one's assigning any blame.

"We all thought Blaine was Illusion Man," Randy says.

"I didn't," Isaac says.

Frank chugs down a Diet Coke and belches. "That's because you don't understand the concept of punctuality."

Frank found the vending machines not long after we got here and is eating his way from Almond Joy to Zebra Cakes.

"What does it matter who Blaine is?" Vic says, which is appropriate, considering he actually doesn't know who Blaine is. "Charlie's in a coma."

And that shuts everyone up.

The five of us sit in silence, watching the clock and trying to ignore CNN while listening to Frank eat a bag of Fritos.

"Do you ever stop eating?" Vic asks.

"I always eat when I'm stressed," Frank says before he shoves a handful of peanut M&M's into his mouth.

"You must be stressed a lot," Randy says.

Ten minutes later, the doctor finally comes into the waiting room and we all stand up.

"How is he?" Vic asks.

"Mr. Dinkins appears to have suffered from what is known as an ischemic stroke," the doctor says, whose name tag identifies him as Dr. Carey.

"A stroke?" Frank says. "But he's not even twenty-five."

"It is unusual for someone of his age," Dr. Carey says. "But it can happen, especially if he smokes or drinks regularly or uses recreational drugs such as cocaine or amphetamines."

"Charlie's not a smoker or much of a drinker," I say. "And as far as I know, he's never used any recreational drugs."

"Does anyone know if Mr. Dinkins is diabetic or taking any prescription medications?" the doctor asks.

None of us mention that Charlie takes prescription medications for a living. We probably should, but we don't.

A number of prescription medications can increase the risk of stroke. Beta-blockers and anticoagulants and contraceptives. Medications for ADHD and arthritis and Alzheimer's disease. Drugs approved by the FDA and then withdrawn after the manufacturer admitted to withholding information about the drug's risk.

"No," Vic says. "He's not diabetic."

"Is he regularly taking any over-the-counter medications for pain?" the doctor asks.

In addition to certain prescription medications, regular use of nonsteroidal anti-inflammatory drugs can increase the risk of stroke.

"Not that we know of," Vic says.

"Well, that rules out the more common risks for stroke," the doctor says. "It's possible he could have high cholesterol or some arterial abnormalities, perhaps an undiagnosed heart condition that could have contributed to the stroke."

"Could his seizure have caused the stroke?" Frank asks.

"Usually it's the other way around," the doctor says. "And true to form, Mr. Dinkins has experienced several light to moderate seizures since he was brought in."

"Shit." Randy sits down with his head in his hands and stares at the floor.

"While seizures can lead to unconsciousness, it's rare that we see a single seizure precipitate a coma," the doctor says. "However, continuous seizures can prevent the brain from recovering from one seizure to the next, which can lead to prolonged unconsciousness and, in some cases, coma."

No one says anything.

"Does Mr. Dinkins have a history of seizures?" the doctor asks, almost as if he knows we're hiding something.

We all avoid looking at one another as we try to come up with an answer that doesn't reveal Charlie's identity as a superhero and, consequently, our own.

"What would some of the symptoms be?" Frank asks.

"Fluttering eyelids, lip smacking, and hand fumbling are typical indications of a petit mal seizure," the doctor says. "In partial or focal seizures, staring episodes or lack of awareness are common, as are blackout spells that can last anywhere from ten or fifteen seconds to up to several minutes."

I remember how Charlie spaced out while staring at the window just before Blaine showed up. And again, during lunch at Curry in a Hurry. I wonder if those were the only times Charlie had an episode or just the ones I happened to notice.

"I saw something," I say. Then I tell the doctor about Charlie's episodes.

"Those certainly sound like they could have been seizures," the doctor says. "Until we have the chance to speak with Mr. Dinkins, we won't know for sure."

"So you think he'll wake up?" Vic asks.

"In spite of the damage from the stroke, his brain activity is positive," Dr. Carey says. "So we're optimistic he'll regain consciousness. It's just a matter of when."

Everyone takes a collective sigh of relief.

"So he's going to be okay?" Randy asks.

"At this point, it's too early to tell," the doctor says. "The CT scan shows that Mr. Dinkins suffered significant trauma to the motor cortex on the left side of his brain."

"What does that m-mean?" Isaac asks.

"It means that once he recovers from his coma, Mr. Dinkins is likely going to experience some loss of the use of his right arm and leg, as well as some paralysis of the right side of his face," the doctor says. "How much use he regains will depend on the severity of the stroke."

So much for the sense of relief.

"How much is all of this going to cost?" Frank asks, always the pragmatic one. "Charlie doesn't have any health insurance and he doesn't have any family."

"I'm not able to answer that for you," the doctor says. "But I can assure you that we'll do everything we can for Mr. Dinkins and won't discharge him until he's stabilized."

Dr. Carey asks several more questions, then indicates that we're free to visit Charlie but asks that we limit visitors to two at a time. Vic and Frank go first, leaving Randy, Isaac, and me in the waiting room.

The three of us sit in silence, alternately staring at the walls or watching CNN, which is now reporting on a massacre in some African country. This is followed by another story about a car bombing in Pakistan. Then a report on a sniper shooting at cars on the Los Angeles freeways.

Murder. Madness. Mayhem.

Wash. Rinse. Repeat.

It's enough to turn an eternal optimist's outlook from sunny blue to perpetual gray.

Isaac stands up. "I'm gonna get a C-C-Coke. Anyone w-want anything?"

Randy and I both shake our heads and Isaac goes to visit the vending machines, leaving me watching CNN while Randy continues to stare at the floor between his feet.

"This is all my fault," he says.

"No, it's not," I say. "If anything, it's my fault. I should have figured out something was wrong the first time I saw Charlie space out."

Randy shakes his head. "I called him out on being a superhero when he said he didn't want to meet Mr. Blank or Illusion Man, so he tried to show that he had what it takes."

"You don't know that," I say.

"Yes, I do," he says.

I try to come up with something to make Randy feel better, but I'm running low on anti-guilt remedy, having used up most of it on myself.

"I should have done something," Randy says. "We *all* should have done something."

"We couldn't," I say. "Blaine stole our memories. We didn't have any way to fight him."

"Sure we did," Randy says. "There were four of us and one of him. We could have taken him. Instead we just stood there and let that asshole get away."

"Vic doesn't even remember who Blaine is now," I say, trying to justify our inaction. Or maybe just mine. "And you've read the news reports. Some of these people who've run into Blaine have suffered permanent memory loss."

"So?"

"So even had we all rushed him, chances are at least one of us would have ended up losing our memories."

"That's the price of being a superhero," Randy says. "You have to be willing to make some sacrifices. Otherwise, you're just a guy wearing colored spandex and a satin cape."

And here I was thinking we were making sacrifices by not going out for a round of post-superhero beers.

On CNN, a young woman is talking about how her brother was killed by two men who beat him to death while a group of bystanders watched without doing anything to help. Then Isaac comes back into the waiting room with a Coke and some more vending machine bounty.

"Hey," he says. "Anyone want some S-S-Skittles?"

chapter 27

You're *who?*"

Sophie sits next to me on the couch, staring at me, her head cocked at a slight angle and her eyebrows pinched in concentration as if she's trying to understand me.

"I'm Dr. Lullaby," I say.

After what happened with Charlie, I decided it was time I told Sophie about my dual identity. There's nothing like having one of your superhero pals end up in a coma to make you come down with a severe case of honesty.

"Dr. Lullaby?"

"You know," I say. "The superhero."

Sophie shakes her head back and forth a couple of times, and it occurs to me that since she doesn't watch or read the news, she probably has no idea what I'm talking about, so I show her a recent copy of the *New York Post* with an article about our latest exploits.

Sophie looks up from the article. "Is this some kind of a joke?"

"No," I say. "No joke."

She gives me another puzzled look, then goes back to reading.

When she's done, she looks up again with something closer to concern. "You make people fall asleep?"

I nod and give a little smile, hoping she'll get the vibe that this is a good thing rather than something to be concerned about, but Sophie continues to wear her serious face.

"How is that possible? That you can make someone fall asleep?" She looks back at the paper, a single finger tracing along the text of the article. "Or vomit or gain weight or go into convulsions?"

"Well, I can't do *all* those things," I say. "That's Vic and Frank and Charlie, also known as Captain Vomit, Big Fatty, and Convulsion Boy. And Randy is the Rash because he makes people break out in rashes. And Isaac gives people erections, so we call him Professor Priapism."

"You didn't answer my question," Sophie says, apparently unimpressed by our pseudonyms. "How is it possible that you're all able to do these things?"

"Well," I say, trying to come up with some way to sugarcoat my answer, but at this point it's just a bitter pill. "We decided that it's probably a result of all the pharmaceutical drugs we've taken over the past five years. And possibly because of this one specific clinical trial we all volunteered for a few months ago."

Sophie stares at me through a long and uncomfortable silence that makes me wish I'd kept my mouth shut. I'd rather she get angry or yell at me. At least then I'd know what she was thinking. This inscrutable silence is worse. I just hope she doesn't ask me how long this has been going on.

"So . . . how long has this been going on?" she asks.

I don't have to be a mind reader to know that Sophie isn't going to be happy if I tell her the truth. But if I'm coming clean, I might as well bring out the soap and water.

"A few weeks," I say, using more water than soap.

"Really?" There's a sense of hurt and disappointment in her voice and on her face, which makes it that much more difficult to keep going.

"Give or take," I say.

"Give or take how much?"

I shrug and decide that my fingernails look fascinating at the moment. "Give or take a couple of months."

Sophie opens her mouth, then closes it and looks down at the newspaper. I'm guessing she's not doing it to get any more information. It's just someplace to look other than at me.

"Why didn't you tell me about any of this before?" she asks, her voice calm, almost comforting, like we're discussing a traumatic experience. Or erectile dysfunction.

"I didn't know how to tell you," I say. "And the longer I waited, the harder it got to say anything."

In my head, that sounded like a reasonable excuse. But hearing the words come out of my mouth, they just sound trite and pathetic and empty.

Something a coward would say, not a superhero.

"Lloyd . . . you should have told me," she says.

Sophie never calls me Lloyd, which isn't a good sign. It's more like CLOSED FOR REPAIRS. Or GOING OUT OF BUSINESS.

"I know," I say. "I'm sorry. I was afraid you wouldn't understand and would want me to go see a doctor."

"You're right. I don't understand. And you should go see a doctor." She stands up and grabs a bag of pixie dust off the side table. "Having the ability to make other people fall asleep isn't normal. And it's not natural."

"Not everything has to be natural," I say. "Look at Spider-Man. Or Captain America. Or any of a bunch of other superheroes . . . What are you doing?"

Sophie is sprinkling pixie dust over the plants. "This helps me to relax. And superheroes aren't real, Lloyd. They're make-believe. Comic book characters. You're not a comic book character."

"I know I'm not a comic book character," I say, then decide to appeal to her charitable and practical sides. "But I'm helping people, doing something that matters. Being more ambitious. I thought that's what you wanted."

"I wanted you to find something that you cared about," she says. "I didn't expect you to get dressed up in boots and a cape and go out to fight crime."

"We don't wear costumes," I say. "And I do care about this. As a matter of fact, it's the first time I've ever cared about anything in my life."

As soon as the words leave my mouth I want them back—like when you press SEND on an e-mail to your company mailing list and realize you've included a link to porn spam a second after you click the mouse.

"What I mean is . . . something other than you," I say. "Like a job or a hobby. Like the way you feel about working at Westerly or helping people to eat healthy or volunteering at the SPCA. That's how I feel about this."

She doesn't say anything but just continues to sprinkle her pixie dust over her plants.

"Don't you like the idea of having a boyfriend who's a super-hero?" I say.

"I don't want a superhero," she says. "I just want Lloyd."

"I *am* Lloyd," I say. "A new and improved Lloyd. You even said you noticed something different about me and that you liked it. You only wished you understood where it came from. Well, now you know where it came from. It's because I'm happy with who I am. For the first time in my life. And isn't that what you said? That was all you wanted for me? To be happy?"

Sophie's quiet for several moments, looking at one of the plants, a Chinese evergreen that isn't quite living up to its name.

"I do want you to be happy, Lollipop," she says. The fact that we're back to Lollipop is a good sign. "But I'm worried about this ability you've developed. Whatever is causing this to happen, you need to get it fixed."

"I don't know if I *can* get it fixed. For all I know, it might be permanent."

"You don't know that," she says. "Maybe if you tell someone about what's happened to you, they can figure out how to make it better."

"Maybe," I say. "Or I might end up in some kind of research facility where they would do tests on me and you'd never see me again."

Yet another example of something that sounded more reasonable in my head than coming out of my mouth.

"Besides, even if I wanted to get it fixed," I say, "even if someone could reverse this or make it stop . . . I can't do it now."

"Why not?" Sophie sprinkles pixie dust on a spider plant that looks closer to an actual web.

"Because we have to do something about Blaine."

"Blaine? What did he do?"

"He's Mr. Blank," I say. "A supervillain. He came over to Randy's and stole Vic's memories and may have put Charlie in a coma. By the way, I think all the pixie dust you're using is what's killing the plants."

Sophie turns to face me. "Charlie's in a coma? Why didn't you say something earlier?"

"Because I didn't want to upset you."

"Really?" She now most definitely looks upset. I think I prefer the calm and enigmatic Sophie. "Is that why you just told me you think I'm killing the plants?"

"It was more of an observation," I say. "But while we're on the subject, I think the pixie dust is also what's causing Vegan's upper-respiratory infections."

Maybe not the best time to bring this up, but eventually I was going to have to say something. And since I'm baring the truth, I figure I might as well let it all hang out.

"I also may have inadvertently used my superpower on Vegan and made him fall asleep," I say. "Which is probably why he's been so weird lately."

Sophie just stares at me, not saying anything. Then her face scrunches up and her brow furrows before she takes the rest of her pixie dust and thows it in my face, blinding me with sparkling metallic glitter. I can feel it stuck in my eyelashes as well as on my lips and up my nose, making it difficult for me to breathe.

No wonder Vegan gets URIs and all of the plants die. This stuff is like cosmic mucus.

By the time I'm able to get most of the pixie dust out of my eyes and nose, Sophie has retreated to the bedroom and locked the door.

"Sophie?" I say, knocking on the door.

No response. Just Simon and Garfunkel and the sound of silence.

I'm beginning to sound like Randy.

"Sophie . . . ?"

"I think you should go," she says through the door. Not with anger or resentment or muffled by tears, just a simple statement of fact.

"Okay," I say, thinking she just needs some time alone. "When should I come back?"

"No. I mean I think you should *go*. As in, *go* go."

I look around as if expecting to find an interpreter who can explain what she just said.

"You mean permanently?" I say. "As in never coming back?"

There's a long, drawn out silence before she answers: "Maybe."

While I didn't expect that Sophie would be happy when I told her the truth about everything, it never occurred to me that she might kick me out.

A moment later the bedroom door opens and Sophie walks out carrying her backpack, dressed in her Westerly shirt.

"Can we talk about this?" I ask.

"We already talked," she says, walking away from me and into the kitchen.

I follow along behind her, making sure to give her some

angry-girlfriend space as she prepares Vegan's dinner and puts fresh water in his bowl.

"Is this because of what I did to Vegan?" I ask. "Or because of what I said about your pixie dust?"

She pushes past me out of the kitchen without making eye contact and starts putting on her coat and scarf.

"Sophie?"

"It's because of everything," she says, her back to me, her voice low and subdued. "But mostly it's because you didn't respect our relationship enough to share what was happening with you. You didn't respect what we have enough to be *honest* with me."

As she puts on her coat and slips her arms through her backpack, I try to think of something to say to fix this, but I realize at this point I've said enough. Probably too much. While Neil Young might not be around to lament about needles, the damage is done.

Fucking Randy.

Sophie turns around and looks at me and I realize she's been crying.

"Can you stay with one of your friends for a while?" she asks.

"Yeah. I guess so."

She nods once and purses her lips. "When I come home from work, I think it would be a good idea if you weren't here."

I consider arguing that this is my apartment, too. That I've lived here for five years and I shouldn't have to leave, but that would just make things worse. So I nod and say, "Okay."

Sophie looks at me a moment longer, then turns and grabs her umbrella and walks out the front door.

chapter 28

S he kicked you out?" Frank says, then bites into his third piece
of pepperoni pizza. Or maybe it's his fourth. I've lost count.
We ordered two large pies from Domino's and had them deliv-
ered to the hospital. From the looks of it, Frank intends to eat at
least one of the pies by himself.

In the aftermath of Charlie's seizure and stroke, Frank has
ballooned to over 250 pounds.

I can't say I expected to be spending Thanksgiving in the
hospital cafeteria eating Domino's with Frank, Randy, Isaac, and
Vic, but it's nice to do something to support Charlie, even if he
doesn't know we're here.

"I'm staying at Charlie's until Sophie and I can work things
out," I say, taking a bite of pizza and wishing it was Sophie's
gluten-free vegan cornbread and wondering who she's spending
Thanksgiving with.

"Why'd she k-kick you out?" Isaac asks.

"She was upset that I waited three months to tell her about
everything," I say. "And that I wasn't honest with her from the
beginning."

I leave out how I told Sophie she was responsible for Vegan's health problems and that she was killing the houseplants with her pixie dust. And that I used my superpower on her cat.

There are some things your friends don't really need to know.

"So what are we going to do about Blaine?" Randy says. He's been mostly silent and serious and hasn't made any obscure references to classic rock bands or his sexual exploits.

"Who?" Vic asks.

Isaac snickers. "Every t-time you say that you s-sound like an owl."

"And every time you open your mouth, you sound like a jackass," Vic says.

At least we're all supportive of one another in this time of crisis.

The good news is that Blaine apparently didn't have enough time to permanently erase our memories about how to access our superpowers. The bad news, other than Charlie suffering a seizure and a stroke and being in a coma, is that Vic's memory of Blaine is still MIA.

"I have an idea about Blaine," I say.

"Let's hear it," Randy says.

It's an idea that's been brewing in my head for the last few days, something that started percolating when Vic and I took care of a couple of would-be muggers in Tompkins Square.

"Blaine and I used to play chess a couple of times a month," I say. The five of us are sitting far enough away from everyone else in the cafeteria so no one can hear our conversation. Still, I lean forward and speak in a conspiratorial voice. "We'd play at Tompkins Square, Bryant Park, all over the city. Sometimes we'd play for drinks or doughnuts."

"Dunkin' Donuts?" Frank asks, licking his fingers.

"Doughnut Plant," I say. "Jesus, who cares? It doesn't matter what kind of doughnuts. What matters is that most of the time, I'd win. Until he developed his superpower."

"What was his superpower again?" Vic asks.

"Memory loss," I say. "Anyway, I was thinking I could convince Blaine to meet me somewhere by suggesting we play for something a little more substantial than drinks or doughnuts."

"Like w-w-what?" Isaac asks.

"I don't know yet," I say. "But once I convince him to meet me, preferably somewhere with lots of people, then the four of you sneak up and surround him so he doesn't see you coming. Then we all hit him with our superpowers at the same time."

"I'm in," Randy says.

"Just like that?" Frank says. "You don't even know if it will work."

"It's like believing in a higher power," Randy says. "I just have faith."

"This coming from a guy who once had sex in a confessional booth with a virgin," Vic says.

"That he remembers," Randy says.

"So what do you want to discuss?" I ask Frank, who digs into the second pizza.

"For starters," Frank says, his mouth full of pepperoni and melted cheese, "we don't even know if Blaine will agree to meet you."

"I think I can convince him," I say.

"What m-makes you so s-sure?" Isaac asks.

"Blaine is power hungry and greedy," I say. "All I have to do is come up with something he wants. And considering that he wants everything, that shouldn't be too difficult."

"All right," Frank says. "Presuming you can get him to come out and play, what makes you think he'll be willing to meet in a public place instead of somewhere private?"

"Blaine knows that the five of us don't want our identities revealed, so meeting in a public place with lots of people around indicates we're not likely to try anything," I say. "Plus Blaine believes he's so much more powerful than us that I doubt he'd even consider we were plotting something against him. And even if he did, he wouldn't think he would lose."

"Typical supervillain hubris," Randy says.

"So we use his arrogance to our advantage," Frank says.

"Exactly," I say.

"If this Blaine can steal our thoughts," Vic says, "won't he know what we're planning?"

"Not if we pick the right pitch," I say.

"What does that m-mean?" Isaac asks.

"The pitch is where buskers and panhandlers set up shop to attract an audience," I say.

"Yeah, but we're not jugglers or musicians looking to fleece people out of their hard-earned money," Vic says. "And if we're off, we're not going to just drop a bowling pin or miss a note."

"The performance isn't always what matters," I say. "You can use the same sign or perform the same show in different locations with completely different results. But if you pick the right pitch, that can make all the difference between success and failure."

"So where are you thinking?" Randy asks.

"Union Square," I say. "There will be so many people around that Blaine won't be able to read everyone's minds all at the same time. There will be too much external noise for him to be able to focus on us."

"But you'll be sitting right across from him," Frank says. "Won't he be able to steal your thoughts?"

I hold up a single index finger, then reach into my backpack and remove five pairs of mirrored sunglasses and pass them out to everyone. "Blaine stared at Vic when he stole his memory and he looked all of us in the eye when he showed up at Randy's, which is when I think he temporarily blocked our ability to access our superpowers. I'm also pretty sure it's how he beat me at chess and won at poker."

"That fucker," Randy says. "I knew he had to be cheating."

"You think Blaine needs to make eye contact to use his superpower?" Frank says.

I nod and pick up the sunglasses. "I think if we all wear a pair of these, we should be okay."

"You think," Frank says. "But you don't know for sure."

Randy picks up his pair of sunglasses and puts them on. "How do I look?"

"Like a cop," Vic says.

Frank stares at his reflection in the mirrored lenses. "If we all gang up on Blaine out in front of a bunch of people, won't that essentially out all of us?"

"Maybe," I say.

"Don't we want to avoid that?" Vic says.

"Yes," I say. "But someone once said that in order to be a superhero, you have to be willing to make sacrifices and be willing to lose something you care about. Otherwise, you're just a guy in colored spandex and a satin cape."

I look at Randy, who gives me a nod.

As far as I'm concerned, I've already made my sacrifice. I've already lost something I care about. I just hope I can figure out a way to get her back.

"W-what if one of us ends up l-like Charlie?" Isaac asks.

"Good point," Frank says. "Maybe this is taking a physical toll on all of us and we don't even know it."

"I feel fine," Randy says. "And it seems like Charlie was having seizures for a while before he had his stroke."

"I agree with Randy," I say. "What happened to Charlie was probably going to happen with or without Blaine."

"But what if you're w-w-wrong?"

Everyone sits and mulls Isaac's question in silence, the only sound among us that of Frank's constant chewing.

"I'm still in," Randy says.

"Anyone else?" I say.

Frank finishes off another slice and sighs. I'm not sure if it's because he's thinking about his decision or just trying to make room for more pizza.

"I have my doubts," Frank says. "But I'll do it for Charlie."

Isaac tosses his sunglasses into the middle of the table.

"C-count me out," he says.

"What?" Randy says. "Why?"

"Muggers and s-stalkers is one thing," Isaac says. "That was f-fun. But this thing with B-B-Blaine . . . this is more than I signed up f-for."

"Come on," Randy says. "We need you. You're one of us."

"N-n-no, I'm not," Isaac says. "You g-guys have the ability to actually incapacitate s-s-someone. I just g-g-give guys erections. That d-doesn't exactly strike f-fear into anyone's heart."

"Unless you're homophobic," Vic says.

"I'm s-sorry. But I don't w-want to end up l-like Charlie." Isaac says. "I guess I'm just a guy in s-s-spandex and a c-cape."

Isaac stands up without looking at us, then turns around, his head down as he walks out of the cafeteria, leaving the four of us sitting at the table.

"Well, that sucks," Randy says.

"Vic?" I say. "What about you? Are you in or out?"

"I guess I'm in, too," Vic says, taking off his glasses and putting on a pair of the mirrored shades. "I don't want the three of you to have all the fun. Besides, what's the worst that could happen?"

chapter 29

W hat are you doing here?" Sophie asks in a low voice.

I'm standing just outside the employee break room at Westerly at the end of Sophie's shift while she gets ready to go home.

"I've been trying to get hold of you but you haven't returned any of my calls," I say.

"That's because we're on a break and I need some space," she says, putting on her parka. "And talking to you kind of defeats that purpose."

It hasn't even been two weeks since she asked me to move out and it already seems like two years.

"I thought the break was just temporary," I say.

"It is," she says. "But I still need some time to figure things out."

"Okay." I stand there looking at her, not knowing what to do or say next. "So what did you do for Thanksgiving?"

"I spent it with some friends," she says, brushing past me out of the employee break room.

"Who?" I ask, following her through the aisles, past the hormone- and antibiotic-free meat and poultry; past the organic produce; past the nutritional supplements; past the all-natural, environmentally friendly and cruelty-free body care products; past the self-service nut grinders and the bulk containers; past the checkout counter and out of the store.

"It doesn't matter *who*," she says once we're standing on the sidewalk, the foot traffic on Eighth Avenue light in the early hours of the first day of December. "All that matters is that we didn't spend it together and I don't really want to talk anymore about it."

"Okay," I say.

She looks at me a few moments, then lets out a sigh. "Good night, Lloyd," she says, then walks away from me across Eighth Avenue.

"Wait!" I say and catch up to her on the other side. "There's something I wanted to tell you."

"I'm tired, Lloyd," she says as she keeps walking along Fifty-Fourth Street. "And I don't really want to hear it right now."

"I know," I say. "And I'm sorry. But I wanted you to know that we're going after Blaine. Me, Frank, Randy, and Vic."

She doesn't say anything at first but just keeps walking until we reach Seventh Avenue, where she stops at the corner in front of the Famous Oyster Bar.

"Why are you telling me this?" she asks.

"I wanted you to know," I say. "Just in case."

"Just in case what?"

"In case anything happens to me," I say. "In case I don't remember you the next time I see you."

When Vic made his comment about the worst that could happen, I know he was just being Vic, using sarcasm to lighten the mood. But more than anything, the thought of forgetting Sophie and all of my memories of her is the worst thing I can imagine.

"Why are you doing this, Lloyd?" she asks.

I look around Seventh Avenue and notice several homeless people among the late-night deli patrons who are coming and going from Benash and Stage and Carnegie Deli.

I look back at Sophie and shrug. "Because I have to."

She lets out another sigh and nods, then steps forward and gives me a hug, holding on to me for several moments before letting go.

"Be careful, Lloyd," she says, then turns and walks away from me across Fifty-Fourth Street.

I watch her go until she's out of sight before I head in the opposite direction to catch the subway.

chapter 30

When I get to Union Square just past noon on a relatively warm day in early December, the Hare Krishnas are camped out across from the subway entrance, burning incense and playing an incessant melody on drums and bongos and finger cymbals to accompany their Maha Mantra.

"Hare Krishna, Krishna Krishna!"

On the opposite side of the subway entrance, several dozen young men and women sit on the steps beneath the statue of George Washington on a horse—eating Subway sandwiches, reading books, or plugged into their cell phones or iPods. Near the statue, a bearded man in baggy pants and a sweater plays the "Skye Boat Song" on the bagpipes, the low, droning sound and the high-pitched melody mixing with the Hare Krishnas' chanting and drums to create an oddly harmonious tune.

At the foot of the steps below the statue at street level, a dozen chessboards are set up on small folding tables and plastic dairy crates, with players sitting on either side on folding chairs or portable stools. Everyone's playing speed chess. This isn't a competition. It's just something people do here. Like eating lunch or playing bagpipes or chanting a mantra to a Hindu deity.

I walk past the chessboards, all of them occupied by men caught up in the intricacy and strategy of a fourteen-hundred-year-old Persian board game, until I come to a chessboard with one empty seat facing Fourteenth Street. Without waiting for an invitation, I sit down behind the white pieces and look across the chessboard at Blaine from behind my mirrored sunglasses.

Maybe it's just his helmet of hair, but I swear his head looks bigger.

"Hey Lloyd," he says from behind his own sunglasses, which are, appropriately, black. "I see you came prepared."

I shrug. "I thought it might be a good idea if I accessorized."

While I wasn't positive about Blaine needing to make eye contact to steal my memory, I'm feeling pretty good about my plan. Still, I avoid thinking about anything but the game, just in case.

"Should we play one for fun first?" Blaine asks.

"Why not?" I say, then move the pawn in front of my queen out two spaces. "So I hear you've been busy."

Since I last saw Blaine, there have been increasing reports of people getting robbed and burglarized or losing their valuables without any memory of what happened. In addition, numerous people have experienced a complete loss of their own identity and preexisting memories. Retrograde amnesia, they call it.

"You know what they say about idle hands," Blaine says and brings out one of his knights.

I move my bishop to threaten his knight and Blaine counters with one of his pawns.

"So what should we talk about?" Blaine says. "Holiday plans? The Jets' chances of making the playoffs? World domination?"

"Let's just stick to chess," I say, taking his knight and making sure I keep my focus on the match.

"Fair enough," he says. "By the way, I dig the salt-and-pepper look you've got going on. Very distinguished."

Why does everyone keep saying that?

We continue playing, both of us setting up our pieces, preparing for the attack. It almost feels like old times. Except that Blaine's a supervillain and I'm here to depose him.

I initiate a series of attacks, which Blaine counters, and when the exchange is over, he's taken one knight, a bishop, a rook, and a pawn, while I've taken one of his pawns along with both of his knights and bishops.

"You're more aggressive than usual today," he says. "What's gotten into you, Lloyd? Or should I say, Dr. Lullaby?"

I look around to see if anyone heard him, but no one is paying attention.

"Worried about someone finding out who you are?" Blaine takes another of my pawns. "Don't believe your press. No one cares about you or your little band of super zeroes."

"I think you underestimate the power of our positive message," I say.

"It's an ADHD world, Lloyd," he says. "And you're nothing more than the latest distraction. Tomorrow everyone will have moved on to the next most interesting thing and you'll be yesterday's news."

"What about you?" I say, taking one of his rooks with my remaining knight. "Won't the public get tired of you?"

"That's what I'm counting on," Blaine says, taking my knight. "Unlike you and your band of super losers, I don't want people to know I exist. I want them to think they're safe and that I was just something the tabloids used in order to sell some papers. You know that quote about how the greatest trick the devil ever pulled was convincing the world he doesn't exist?"

"Yeah. Kevin Spacey says that in *The Usual Suspects*."

Blaine shakes his head like a disappointed sensei. "The French poet Charles Baudelaire said it in a story he wrote back in 1864 about meeting the devil. Or he said something nearly similar, but the wording is inconsequential. The point is, no one's going to think I exist, because they won't remember me. I'll be a forgotten memory, a figment of a dream that exists just beyond their grasp. After that, I'll be able to do everything I've always wanted without having to worry about anyone catching me. Or even knowing I did it."

"Sounds like you've got it all figured out."

"Everyone needs a hobby," he says. "Mine just happens to be taking over the world."

We keep playing, making moves and taking pieces. Whenever I feel my mind beginning to drift from the game, I think about baseball.

"Baudelaire also said that the unique and supreme delight lies in the certainty of doing evil, and that men and women know from birth that all pleasure lies in evil," Blaine says. "That's a philosophy I've learned to embrace, Lloyd. You'll learn to embrace it, too."

"Don't get ahead of yourself," I say. "We still have another match to play."

When I called Blaine to convince him to meet me for a game of chess, I told him that if he won, I would join him in his pursuit of world domination. He said he didn't work well with others, so I suggested I could be his personal minion, instead.

"Every supervillain needs a loyal minion," I told him. "Bob the Goon. Mini-Me. Darth Vader."

"I don't think Vader is the best example of a loyal minion," Blaine said. "He ends up throwing Palpatine into the Death Star's reactor shaft."

"I promise not to throw you into a reactor shaft," I said. "Or any other shaft."

We also agreed that if I won, Blaine would be my Boy Wonder.

"Just so long as I don't have to wear a leotard and tights," he said.

I think we both knew Blaine didn't expect to lose. But then, supervillains never do.

"I'm not the bad guy," Blaine says, taking one of my rooks. "I'm just the one who's smart enough and has the vision to see which side is most likely to win."

"I think I'll stick with trying to help all of the people you seem intent on taking advantage of," I say before I take his queen.

"Don't paint yourself as some heroic white knight in shining armor," Blaine says, returning the favor. "Darkness exists in all men. It's their default setting, even if they don't know it or won't admit it."

"That's very nihilistic."

"There are no heroes, Lloyd," he says. "Only villains and liars. And if you ask me, the liars are worse. At least the villains are willing to own up to who they are."

At this point we're down to a skeleton crew of pieces, but soon the remaining pawns are gone and all that's left are both kings, my bishop, and his rook.

"Looks like a draw," Blaine says. "Shall we do this for real?"

"Ready when you are."

As we reset the chessboard, I allow myself a quick glance around Union Square. The lunchtime crowd has thickened, the tourists and the locals out to soak up every moment of sunshine and warmth the day has to offer. A lot of people are wearing sunglasses. I don't see any that are mirrored, but I know they're out there.

"How about we make things interesting," Blaine says. "Take off our sunglasses. Play it straight up."

"You afraid you can't beat me without being able to get inside my head?"

He stares at me and smiles. Or at least I think he's staring at me. I can't see his eyes behind his black lenses. But then, he can't see mine, either.

"Have it your way," he says. "But how about we up the ante?"

"Name your price."

He cocks his head and appears to think it over a moment, though I get the feeling it's just for show.

"In addition to having you as my minion," he says, "I get to erase your girlfriend's memory of you and make her my personal sex slave."

I know he's just trying to bait me, but I remind myself that it doesn't matter what we wager. This game won't reach its conclusion. And even if it does, I don't plan on living up to my end of the bargain.

"All right," I say. "And if I win, you give yourself up. Turn yourself in to the police."

"That seems like an awful lot for me to risk over a game of chess," he says. "But sure. Why not?"

It's his arrogance I'm counting on to make this work, and Blaine doesn't disappoint. Now all I have to do is keep his focus on the game so he won't sense what's coming.

"And just to make sure we cover all the bases," he says, "what if it's a draw?"

"Then things stay as they are and we see who ends up being the last man standing."

"A gentleman's agreement." Blaine sticks out his right hand. "Or should I say, a guinea pig's agreement."

When we shake, I have a moment to wonder if Blaine has somehow manipulated me into grasping his hand because he's developed the ability to read minds through touch. Then the moment passes. Still, I can't help wiping my hand on my pants before I move the pawn in front of my king out two spaces.

"You're so predictable." Blaine moves the pawn in front of his king out a single square. "It's like you learned how to play chess from a YouTube video for beginners."

"Maybe I'm just baiting you," I say. "Making you think I'm predictable when I have some new moves you haven't seen."

I bring my queen-side knight out to protect my pawn.

"I doubt that." Blaine counters by bringing his queen out beside his pawn. "The only new moves you're likely to have are the ones you're going to want to take back."

I can't threaten his queen, so I move my bishop two squares forward next to my knight. I glance at my watch.

"Someplace you have to be?" Blaine asks as he brings out his bishop.

"No," I say, moving my knight to threaten his bishop. "This is exactly where I need to be."

"Then why don't you stop worrying about the time and start thinking about the expression on Sophie's face when I'm fucking her like a monkey?"

"Aren't you getting a little ahead of yourself?" I say, trying to keep my focus on the game.

He moves his queen forward and takes the pawn in front of my bishop. For a moment I don't understand what he's doing, why he's sacrificing his queen, until I realize his queen is protected by his bishop. There's nowhere for my king to go.

"That's checkmate," Blaine says. "You really are easy to read, Lloyd."

I stare at the board, trying to see my way out of this, but there's no denying that Blaine just managed to beat me in four moves.

"You didn't really think mirrored sunglasses would keep me out of your head, did you?" he says.

I look up at Blaine and realize I just might have underestimated him.

"I told you before that you had no idea who you were dealing with," he says. "I've taken so many drugs for insomnia and anxiety that my powers have grown exponentially. Nothing can stop me. Not even you and your band of mystery misfits. Now if you'll excuse me, I have some business to attend to."

Blaine stands up and turns to his right, his finger pointed at Vic, who stands near the corner of Fourteenth Street. I'm expecting Blaine to start vomiting or at least dry heaving but he just stands there with his index finger leveled at Vic, whose face turns from surprised to blank to slack in a matter of seconds.

Everything's happening too fast and I don't have time to give the signal to Frank and Randy, so I access my trigger, my lips turning numb and a yawn working its way into my jaw. In my peripheral vision, Frank moves toward us from the direction of the Hare Krishnas, lumbering against his own inevitable gravity. The next moment, Blaine swings around toward me and shouts in a voice that sounds like thunder.

"We have an agreement!"

I'm about to unleash Dr. Lullaby when Randy grabs Blaine from behind in a full nelson and twists him away from me toward Fourteenth Street. I redirect my superpower to avoid hitting Randy and a woman walking past on her cell phone drops to the ground in an unconscious heap. An instant later, a guy playing chess at the table next to us lets out a shout of surprise as he inflates like a balloon.

Then Blaine starts screaming.

INTERLUDE #5

All's Rash That Ends Rash

Randy stands on the sidewalk in front of Whole Foods across from Union Square, smoking a cigarette and watching Lloyd and Blaine, waiting for the signal. He checks his watch. Five more minutes. If Lloyd doesn't give the signal by then, they're supposed to abort. Walk away. Regroup and try this another time. But Randy has already decided he's not going anywhere.

Today is the day and it will never come around again.

For most of his life, Randy has been a happy-go-lucky kind of guy, living in the moment and not worrying about tomorrow. He just took what life gave him and made the most of it, choosing to act on impulse rather than thinking about any potential consequences. This philosophy led to more than a few uncomfortable situations, most of them involving women who had thought they were going to have a relationship with Randy that would last more than a single night.

Randy has never considered himself a player, more like an

opportunist. And when it comes to women, there are plenty of opportunities to be had if you know what to look for. And Randy always seemed to have a knack for looking.

But over the past couple of months, Randy has had a chance to reflect on the path he's chosen and the decisions he's made, which has caused him to come to the conclusion that he's more or less wasted the past ten years of his life. He's willing to give himself a break about the one year of high school included in that period because as far as Randy is concerned, high school is a waste of everyone's time. Even if you were a jock or a rah-rah or one of the popular kids, going to high school is like eating a bag of popcorn.

It has no nutritional value.

But the nine years he's spent as a legal adult could best be summed up as self-indulgent and aimless. At least until recently.

He looks across the street from behind his mirrored sunglasses as people walk past and glance his way, and he thinks about how the past few months have given his life a sense of purpose beyond getting laid. He just hopes he can find a way to make up for lost time.

Randy takes another drag on his cigarette, wondering what compelled him to pick up this habit again after nearly a decade. The strange thing is, while smoking has helped to calm his nerves and keep his mind focused, it has also seemed to have an effect on his superpower. Each time he inhales, he can almost feel something igniting inside of him.

He takes a final drag and exhales, watching the smoke disappear like a phantom in the winter air, then he drops the cigarette to the sidewalk and crushes it beneath the toe of his Doc Martens. Vic would probably give him shit for using the sidewalk as a cigarette-butt depository, but Randy isn't concerned about his douche-bag status at the moment. His attention is on Lloyd and Blaine as he channels his superpower, turning up the flame on the heat that is burning inside of him.

He can feel his ability simmering just below the surface, building up energy, waiting to boil over. He takes several deep breaths, using the meditation techniques Vic taught him to help keep his superpower under control. But this feels different than the other times he's summoned the Rash. That was just training camp and preseason. Today there's more at stake. Today they're playing for real. Today is when everything matters.

Randy stares across the street, watching Lloyd and Blaine, trying not to think about what he's going to do or how he's going to do it, but trusting that he'll know what to do at the time it needs doing. Then the M14A bus pulls up at the stop in front of Whole Foods, temporarily blocking Randy's view of Union Square.

He glances at his watch. Two minutes until Lloyd is supposed to give the sign. The bus should continue on its route before then, but Randy senses that if he doesn't act now it's going to be too late. And if there's one thing Randy has learned over the years, it's to trust his instincts.

Randy leaves the shadows and runs around the back of the bus, checking to make sure he's not going to get flattened by traffic before he runs across Fourteenth Street. Even before he reaches the sidewalk, he knows something has gone wrong.

Blaine is standing up and pointing at Vic, who is frozen in place, like he and Blaine are playing a game of Red Light, Green

Light. When Blaine spins away, Vic looks around, his eyes blinking like he just woke up. Then Blaine shouts something at Lloyd about an agreement, his voice filled with rage, while Frank struggles to move his overburdened frame through the lunchtime crowd.

Randy doesn't think about what he's doing—he just sprints toward Blaine and grabs him from behind, slipping his arms under Blaine's armpits and clamping his hands behind his neck, then spinning him away from Lloyd in a single move. It's something he learned in wrestling during his phys ed classes and put to good use during his nights as a bouncer, though he never thought he'd use it in a situation like this. Turns out high school wasn't a complete waste after all.

Blaine struggles against him, twisting and squirming, elbows pistoning into Randy's ribs, hitting their target, but Randy is bigger and stronger and he doesn't let go. He can't let go. If he does, he knows Blaine will win.

Nearby a woman on a cell phone stops talking and collapses to the ground, her head hitting the concrete with a hollow *thunk*, while a guy playing chess cries out and turns into a sumo wrestler. In the background, the Hare Krishnas chant and play their drums and cymbals while accompanied by the mournful wail of bagpipes.

Deep inside of him, Randy's superpower continues to heat up, hotter than it's ever been—like a geothermal geyser. Or a volcano about to erupt.

This time when he releases his superpower, Randy is pretty sure it's going to cause more than just a rash. And it's not going to be temporary.

Blaine continues to yell and thrash against him. For an instant Randy thinks about all of the things he's done wrong in his life, the mistakes he's made and the regrets he's had and the women to whom he wishes he could apologize. But mostly he thinks about Charlie and how he wishes he could take back his criticism of his friend's resolve.

Then it's all wiped away in a searing flash as he unleashes his superpower.

It starts out as a rash, red and angry, but quickly turns to boils that erupt and explode on Blaine, causing him to scream out and thrash harder. Except it's not only Blaine who's affected. Randy can feel his own skin burning, the flesh starting to bubble, and it's all he can do to hold on.

Blaine's shrieks of pain and anger fill Randy's ears, mixing in with his own screams, but Randy doesn't let go. His hands dig into the back of Blaine's neck, his fingers fusing with Blaine's flesh, the two of them melting together. Randy has a moment to wonder how long this is going to last and if his soul will be linked with Blaine's in the afterlife.

Then he and Blaine both burst into flame.

From the front page of the *New York Post*:

UP IN SMOKE!
SUPER HOLIDAY SPECTACLE AT UNION SQUARE

The lunchtime crowd at Union Square bore witness to a spectacular and deadly exhibition yesterday as New York's newest superheroes descended upon Manhattan's iconic intersection to do battle. Two innocent bystanders caught up in the preholiday showdown experienced the telltale side effects induced by Dr. Lullaby and Big Fatty, while two others burned to death in what several witnesses described as spontaneous combustion.

Ben Vincelette, a Boston native spending the holiday in Manhattan, was playing chess next to one of the men.

"This guy stands up and yells something at his playing partner, then this other guy runs up and grabs the first guy from behind," Vincelette said. "Next thing I know, the guy I'm playing chess against blows up like a puffer fish and the two guys wrestling each other go up in flames. Strangest damn thing I've ever seen."

Although neither of the two men who died in the unexplained fire has officially been identified, the popular consensus among those interviewed is that the Rash was one of them.

Greg Magill, a retired firefighter from Queens, was an eyewitness.

"I saw the two guys wrestling from the start," Magill said. "The one holding the other from behind in a full nelson started glowing, and the guy he was holding broke out in hives, as if he was suffering the mother of all allergic reactions. A few seconds later, they both turned as red as lobsters and started peeling and blistering. I never seen anything like it. But that was the Rash. I know it was, God rest his soul."

John McCormack, an off-duty police officer from the Bronx who arrived at Union Square moments before the two men burst

into flames, believes the other man involved in the human con-
flagration was none other than the infamous Mr. Blank.

"I talked to at least a dozen people who were frontline witnesses," Officer McCormack said. "Half of them couldn't remember what happened. Others couldn't even remember what
they were doing there. Now I don't know for sure what happened, but having that many people unable to remember anything . . . Let's just say it's out of the ordinary."

While there are those who remain skeptical of the motives
of New York's newest superheroes and believe this latest episode indicates that Dr. Lullaby, Captain Vomit, and their crime-
fighting cohorts have gone rogue, Patricia Goggin echoes the
opinion of many of Manhattan's homeless and less privileged.

"I don't believe they were there to cause any trouble. I believe they were there to stop Mr. Blank," Goggin said. "They're
good boys. All they want to do is help people. I believe in them.
A lot of people do. They're real-life heroes. And it breaks my
heart to think that one of them may have died."

Whether the Rash, Dr. Lullaby, and the rest of New York
City's other vigilante crime fighters were at Union Square yesterday to wage battle against Mr. Blank is yet to be determined.
But what appears obvious is that something supernatural took
place.

The NYPD, however, has its own interpretation.

"This is just another example of what happens when ordinary citizens take matters into their own hands," Captain James
Goudrealt of the Thirteenth Precinct said. "Innocent people get
hurt."

The man who suffered from rapid and excessive weight gain
courtesy of Big Fatty was taken away in an ambulance, while the
woman allegedly assaulted by Dr. Lullaby regained consciousness at the scene and was evaluated by medical personnel for
concussion-related symptoms.

chapter 31

It's a week before Christmas and I'm standing on the sidewalk in front of Citibank in the fading twilight with several dozen men and women in holiday winter garb, while across the street several hundred people have gathered at Union Square in front of the George Washington statue. Some hold hands or candles in reverent silence while others play guitars or drums and sing ballads and hymns, paying respect in their own way, as tourists and news crews and amateur videographers document the event. The Hare Krishnas are out in full force, chanting their Maha Mantra, adding their own unique flavor to the evening.

A middle-aged woman in a black overcoat and matching beret stops and stands next to me to watch the tribute. "What's everyone doing over there?"

"It's a memorial," I say.

"Who for?" she asks.

I almost say Randy's name, then I catch myself. "A local hero."

The woman continues to look toward Union Square. "It looks like he had a lot of friends."

When I heard someone was organizing a memorial for the

Rash, I didn't know what to expect. I figured a few dozen people would turn out to pay their respects—maybe a hundred or so, tops. But I never imagined anything like this. It's humbling. And inspiring.

While I always felt like the six of us were trying to make a difference and doing something worthwhile, I had no idea what it meant to the people we were helping. Until now, I had no idea how much what we were doing mattered.

I wish Randy were here to see this. Of course, if Randy were here, none of this would be happening, which only emphasizes the fact that I feel responsible for his death.

Guilt is a merciless instrument of self-torture.

As the daylight continues to fade, more candles appear among the gatherers. Those without candles raise lighters in the air. Here and there homemade signs appear above the crowd, thanking the Rash in one way or another. Most of the people who've come to honor the memory of Randy just stand and look around, not exactly sure what to do. I'm guessing this is their first superhero memorial. I know it's mine.

A few of the signs in the crowd decry Mr. Blank and thank Randy for getting rid of him. While I know better than anyone what Blaine was capable of doing, and I realize that his death probably saved countless others from his diabolical plans, the signs strike a chord on the strings of my conscience. I know I'm not to blame for what happened to Blaine or what he'd become, but I still wish there had been something I could have done to change how things turned out.

For all of his annoying know-it-all facts and his desire for world domination, Blaine was still my friend. Or at least he used to be once upon a time.

A dozen feet away from me, a guy starts playing "Christmastime Is Here" on his guitar, adding some holiday spirit to the somber mood. Several people walk past and throw singles into his guitar case, which after less than two hours appears to have at least forty bucks in it.

I should really learn how to play a musical instrument.

After watching the faithful memorialize Randy for a few more minutes, I decide to beat the crowds and head back to Charlie's apartment.

A month after his stroke, Charlie is still in a coma. Apparently he's experiencing continuous seizures, something called status epilepticus—which sounds like something out of a Road Runner cartoon. In any case, the seizures are preventing Charlie's brain from recovering, leading to his prolonged unconsciousness.

This doesn't help to improve my spirits, holiday or otherwise.

The fact that Charlie doesn't have health insurance and won't be able to pay his bills isn't precipitating his hasty exit from the hospital. Even in an age when health care seems to be more about profit margins than about compassion, the hospital won't discharge Charlie or move him to another facility until his health is stabilized. Then they'll hit him up with a seven-figure invoice for services rendered.

On my way to Charlie's apartment, I pay a visit to Frank.

"Lloyd," he says, greeting me at the door and waving me in with one hand while holding a slice of pepperoni-and-sausage in the other. "Pizza?"

"No thanks," I say. "I don't have much of an appetite."

"We seem to be on opposite ends of that spectrum." Frank closes the door, then waddles over to his couch and sits down with a grunt and a creak and a cloud of dust in front of his coffee table, where an open cardboard Domino's box holds the remaining slices of what used to be an extra-large pie.

Frank looks like he could play right tackle for the Jets. If he's not pushing three hundred pounds, then I'm a Patriots fan.

I sit down in the mafia chair at the end of the coffee table, my back to the wall, and watch Frank finish off the slice he was holding.

"So how was the memorial?" he asks.

"Overwhelming," I say, and tell him how many people showed up. "You should have been there."

"I'm not a big fan of crowds," he says. "Especially since I tend to stand out in one."

Frank hasn't left his apartment since the events at Union Square. I don't think it's because he's afraid he'll be recognized, but more because, like me, he's suffering from a severe case of the guilts.

While I know rationally that Charlie and Randy made their own choices, I hold on to my personal responsibility for them like a security blanket. In a strange way, it's the only thing that gives me comfort.

Frank and I chitchat for a few minutes, talking about nothing of substance while Frank powers down another slice, both of us ignoring the elephant in the room. And that's not a fat joke.

"So I was thinking . . ." I say.

"That's never a good thing," Frank says. "What about?"

"I was thinking we should keep going."

"Going where?" he says. "I didn't realize we were in motion."

The image of hundreds of people in Union Square holding candles and lighters plays back in my head.

"I think we should keep going with what we started," I say.

Frank stares at me, his chin covered with grease. "You can't be serious?"

"I think it's what Randy and Charlie would have wanted."

"I don't give a rat's ass what Randy and Charlie would have wanted." He grabs another slice. "I've had enough."

Obviously he's not talking about pizza.

"But think about all that we've done," I say. "Think about all of the good we could do. Think about Randy and Charlie and Vic."

"I do think about them," Frank says. "That's all I do. Every day. Every hour. And do you know how I feel?"

I shake my head but I'm pretty sure I know the answer.

"I feel responsible," he says, his mouth full of meat and cheese and dough. "I should have talked all of you out of this superhero insanity in the first place. I should have been the voice of reason. Instead I enabled the fantasy. I participated in it. And now because of that Randy's dead, Charlie's in a coma, and Vic is missing."

After Randy and Blaine went up in flames, Frank and I searched everywhere for Vic. Neither one of us saw him leave, and in the chaos of the moment we couldn't find him. So we did the only thing we could do—we got the hell out of there.

We've called Vic's home phone multiple times but he hasn't answered. Since he doesn't have an answering machine or voice mail, we can't leave him any messages. And neither of us knows where he lives.

I can still see the blank, slack expression on Vic's face after Blaine leveled his finger at him, and I wonder how much damage might have been done to his memory.

"What about all of those people who are at Union Square right now?" I say.

"What about them?"

"They believe in Randy and what he stood for. They believe in all of us."

Frank takes another bite of pizza. "What's your point?"

"My point is that Randy's death shouldn't be the end of it," I say. "We should honor the sacrifice he made, both him and Charlie, and take vengeance on all of the would-be muggers and rapists."

"Honor isn't something I'm interested in pursuing," Frank says, letting out a belch. "And vengeance isn't good for the soul, Lloyd. It just eats it up."

Frank finishes off another slice while I sit there contemplating his words and what it must be like to be his lower intestine.

"What about all of the people who still need our help?" I say. "Don't you want to make a difference?"

"I've helped enough people," Frank picks up the last slice of pizza. "I'm done being a superhero, Lloyd. Big Fatty is hanging up his cape."

chapter 32

The New Year comes and the New Year goes and Frank is still retired, Sophie still isn't talking to me, and Charlie is still in a coma. While the doctors don't know how much longer he'll stay that way, the occurrence of seizures is decreasing and they're monitoring him with the hope that he'll eventually regain consciousness.

I wish I could get excited about their prognosis, but at the moment I'm not exactly glowing with optimism.

There's still no word from Vic. I've placed multiple calls to police stations, telling them Vic might be suffering from amnesia, but no one has been able to help me. So for the past month I've been checking the homeless shelters, starting with those closest to Union Square and working my way south, but so far no one has seen anyone who matches Vic's description. I'd post flyers except I don't have any photos of Vic and I'm not much of a sketch artist. I'm more Paleolithic cave painter than Renaissance artist.

It's not easy trying to find an amnesiac superhero in New York City.

When I'm not looking for Vic or volunteering for clinical

trials and panhandling to pay Charlie's rent, I keep working on Frank to get him to change his mind about hanging up his cape, but he isn't interested in changing anything, including his T-shirt and sweatpants. So I go out on my own to fight crime a few nights a week, but it's not the same without the others. When it comes to being a superhero, I work better in a team setting.

It would be easier if I had someone to talk to. Someone who knows me and cares about me and who could offer me emotional support and physical comfort, but Sophie hasn't returned my calls let alone offered me a hug.

Eventually I start scouring the tabloids and local news websites, looking for any odd or unusual stories about people experiencing vertigo or insomnia or uncontrollable flatulence. I wander through Tompkins Square and Washington Square and other parks after nightfall, looking for kindred crime-fighting souls. I go back to Curry in a Hurry hoping to run into the guy who said he was Karma. But the only superhero to be found is the one staring back at me in the mirror. And he could use a vacation.

I look exhausted. Emotionally and spiritually. And a good ten years older than my age. More if I catch my reflection in the wrong lighting. The fact that my hair has nearly turned completely gray doesn't help.

I think part of my haggard appearance has to do with the guilt and depression that are hanging around like sycophantic sidekicks. But I'm beginning to think that the cumulative experience of being a guinea-pig superhero is a significant contributing factor. Whatever it is that allows me to project sleep onto others seems to have taken a physical toll, which means I should probably stop.

The problem is, being a superhero is the only thing that makes me feel better about myself. If I stop, I'm afraid I'll end up like Frank. Not morbidly obese, but depressed and lonely and feeding my guilt with something that isn't good for me.

It doesn't take me long before I realize that's exactly what I'm doing.

So January comes and January goes and I hang up my cape and go back to living the same life I did before I became a super-hero: just guinea-pigging and panhandling, living on the fringes of society in order to survive. Only this time I'm doing it without Sophie, which makes my existence that much less glamorous.

Winter is always bad for panhandling. While you can usually count on some benevolent souls taking pity on you, most of the time people are just too damn cold to care. And two of the clinical trials I've signed up for are lockdowns, one of which requires me to wear a catheter, but this is what I know how to do. It's where I'm comfortable. And human beings are nothing if not creatures of comfort.

Every now and then I find myself haunting Seward Park, eating a doughnut from the Doughnut Plant and looking across the street, waiting to catch a glimpse of Sophie coming home or leaving for work. I've seen her a couple of times, but I'm afraid to let her see me, so I make sure to keep my distance, sometimes not catching more than a glimpse of her figure bundled up in her coat and scarf and knit beanie.

Sometimes I ride the Staten Island Ferry back and forth, listening to the symphony of foreign languages and thinking about violins and clarinets and saxophones, remembering the joy on

Sophie's face as she listened to the orchestra of voices and hearing her buoyant laughter as we would run to try to catch the return ferry.

It seems lately that everywhere I look all I see and hear are the memories and ghosts of Sophie. And none of them is anything but a weak, unsatisfying substitute for the real thing.

Sometimes I walk along the Mall from the Bethesda Terrace to the Olmsted Flower Bed, hoping to find Sophie in her seafoam-green sleeveless dress with matching green wings and yellow chiffon skirt, holding a single rose in one hand, standing perfectly still like the day I met her. But the only statues I ever find are those of Christopher Columbus and William Shakespeare, neither of whom is either alive or my type.

Sometimes I approach Sophie's pitch from the Wollman Rink or from Fifth Avenue, thinking that maybe by mixing things up she'll be there and I'll be able to re-create the magic of that moment when we first met. It's silly, I know, but you tend to do such things when you're lonely and depressed and desperate.

I know I could just wait for Sophie outside her apartment or show up at Westerly when she gets off work, but I don't have the courage. I'd rather find her as a living statue. That way I could do all of the talking and say everything I need to say and she couldn't walk away or ignore me or tell me how much I disappointed her. She wouldn't have any choice but to stand there and listen and not say a word.

I never claimed to be adept at relationships.

In early February, the canopy of elms lining the Mall is gone, the limbs a tangle of skeletal arms that reach toward one another beneath the dismal gray sky. The wind blows in off the Hudson, scattering a few dead leaves across the ground and hibernating lawns. Other than a few hardy green shrubs, the Olmsted Flower Bed is devoid of any color.

While the weather has been unseasonably warm and pleasant, today seems to be a more fitting reflection of my current state of existence.

I've brought a flower, a single red rose, as a peace offering. I probably should have brought a lily, since that's Sophie's favorite, but it was sort of a last-minute purchase, an impulse buy, and the only flowers the guy on the street corner was selling were roses. But as has been the case every other time I've come here, my gesture is made to a nonexistent audience and an empty theater.

I think about the day I met Sophie, how she stood there wearing her faint smile like she had a secret. Like she knew something I didn't. I remember how I walked up to her and told her I believed she'd appeared to me for some divine reason and that I could use a little pixie dust to change my luck.

As I stare at the Olmsted Flower Bed, it occurs to me with no small amount of chagrin that I'm back right where I started more than five years ago, trying to figure out what I'm supposed to do and how I'm supposed to do it. Except this time there's no fairy to sprinkle pixie dust over me.

I never believed in the power of Sophie's magic, that she or anyone could change someone else's life simply by sprinkling metallic glitter over them. But standing here in my own personal time warp with the benefit of hindsight to slap me in the face, I'm hit with an epiphany that makes me realize how wrong I've been.

When Sophie sprinkled her pixie dust over me and offered me a place to live, she changed my life. Everything good that has happened to me over the past five years came from that one single moment. If it hadn't been for Sophie, I don't know what I would have done or where I would have ended up or who I would have become.

Without any sense of hyperbole, Sophie saved me. She's my own personal superhero. The Fairy. Defender of lost causes and champion of cats. Able to tolerate slacker boyfriends for longer than expected.

If only I'd been smart enough to figure this out before I decided to screw it all up.

||| chapter 33 |||

While I've never been to Paris, I'm guessing it's the only city in the world that's a more romantic place to spend Valentine's Day than Manhattan. In addition to all of the restaurants, nightclubs, and museums that offer the opportunity to ignite or rekindle your love, you can canoodle at the top of the Empire State Building, hold hands while ice skating at Rockefeller Center, go window-shopping at Tiffany's, take a ride on the Staten Island Ferry, and, of course, go for a stroll through Central Park.

If you have someone to romance, that is. If you didn't screw up your relationship and aren't single and pathetic and lonely.

It's been more than two months since I've seen Sophie, and my hopes that we can reconcile dim with each passing day. Still, that doesn't keep me from imagining various scenarios where I sweep her off her feet with roses or poetry or a steady job with benefits.

For the past five years I've spent Valentine's Day with Sophie. But this year, rather than canoodling, skating, or strolling, I'm panhandling at the Bethesda Terrace in Central Park, sitting near the arcade with a sign that says:

ALL YOU NEED IS LOVE . . . AND CHOCOLATE

I know I'm recycling one of my other panhandling signs and substituting *chocolate* for *Ben & Jerry's*, but my creativity has waned of late. Besides, what better way is there to celebrate Valentine's Day than with love and chocolate?

So far my take for the day is pretty good. The near-record winter temperatures help, but it's a lot easier to make money when your targets are men and women drunk with love, who tend to lose their inhibitions when it comes to emptying their pockets. Especially if they're trying to impress their dates.

Twenty feet away from me, Marcus the Magnificent, the reigning magician of Central Park, performs tricks for the sweethearts and passersby, many of whom have stopped to enjoy his show. He's already done his coin and card tricks. Now he's doing his Professor's Nightmare rope trick, soon to be followed by his Rainbow Handkerchief trick, and he'll eventually work his way up to his grand finale, where he makes everyone's money disappear. As usual, he has his spectators enthralled and manages to elicit laughter and the occasional *ooh* and *aah*.

Marcus can sometimes be a bit of an asshat, but when it comes to putting on a good show, he knows how to bring it.

On the opposite side of the Terrace, a bearded homeless man in dirty khakis, a sweatshirt, a yellow rain slicker, and a wool ski cap sits on a bench watching the magic show and eating a hot dog. I suppose he could be an eccentric millionaire who doesn't give a shit about fashion, but from the looks of it I'm guessing he's homeless. Could be he's been at it a while or maybe this is his new reality, but becoming homeless isn't something that just happens to strangers and people who are screwups or mentally ill. It can happen to anyone. And it happens more often than you'd think.

You need a lot of money to survive in this world, at least in the United States, and most definitely in New York City, where the rent alone on a one-bedroom apartment could feed an entire village in Ethiopia for a week. But no matter whether you're living in a city or on a tree-lined suburban street or on a quiet piece of property out in the sticks, no one is immune to life-altering financial hardship.

All it takes is an accident or an illness, getting divorced or downsized, losing all of your life savings due to bad advice or a bad investment and the next thing you know, you can't pay your bills. Your insurance costs pile up. You get behind on your mortgage or you can't cover your rent. Before you know it, you've lost everything and instead of trying to figure out which bills to pay, you're trying to figure out where you're going to live.

I watch the homeless guy with bad fashion sense and wonder what his story is, how long he's been on the street, and if there's some way I can help him—not by inviting him to sleep on the couch at Charlie's but maybe by sharing my Valentine's Day bounty with him or teaching him some basic panhandling skills.

For the past couple of weeks I've been living by the mantra WWSD: *What would Sophie do?* It helps me feel like I'm still doing something useful without accessing my superpower, which I've managed to keep subdued for the past several weeks using a combination of meditation and self-control, and by avoiding clinical trials that involve medications for sleep disorders. It's the new me. I don't know if it's much of an improvement, but it feels like I'm pointed in the right direction.

Just think of me as a new superhero. Captain Panhandler, defender of the homeless and champion of slackers. Able to make awesome cardboard signs with a single Sharpie.

In a way I'm channeling my own version of Sophie, only without the yellow chiffon skirt and fairy wings.

I'm about to get up and go spread my proverbial pixie dust when a sexy redhead approaches me, dressed in the color of Valentine's Day and temporarily distracting me from my noble purpose. She's wearing a form-hugging red silk sweater, a short red skirt, red tights, and red midcalf boots. She stops a few feet away and looks down at me over the top of her red sunglasses.

"I like your sign," she says.

"Thanks." It's all I can think of to say. One word, six letters, one syllable. It's as if her breasts have short-circuited my brain.

I once heard that a man's level of intelligence drops significantly when he's talking to an attractive woman. If that's the case, then I just went back to remedial school.

"How's business?" she asks.

"Not bad," I say, attempting to raise my IQ. "Love is a pretty easy sell, especially on Valentine's Day."

I gesture toward the couples sharing personal space with one another, walking past and sitting by the fountain, getting all googly-eyed and schmoopie-pied.

"I prefer chocolate myself," she says.

"So I take it no moon has hit your eye like a big pizza pie."

"Not yet," she says, then she opens her red handbag and tosses a twenty-dollar bill into my hat. "But you know what they say: In true love, destiny awaits."

I just stare at her, unable to even offer up a thank you for the Andrew Jackson.

"Happy Valentine's Day," she says, then walks over and sits down next to the homeless guy with the hot dog and starts talking to him.

I pull out my wallet and remove the fortune I received at the Buddhist temple. I already know what the fortune says, but I still have to check it, just to be sure. Then I glance over at the redhead as she sits with the homeless man, who spreads his arms in a grand gesture like he's making a point about something. A moment later he starts laughing like the redhead said something hilarious. The redhead never once glances over at me or gives any indication that she's aware of the connection between her words and the fortune I keep in my wallet.

In true love, destiny awaits.

I read the fortune once more before returning it to my wallet. While I still have my doubts about the whole destiny thing, considering how well it's worked out so far, I can't help but think that someone or something is trying to make sure I get the message that I'm supposed to be with Sophie. It's not like I need a whole lot of convincing, but at this point, it's not up to me. It's up to Sophie. And I don't think she's getting the same cosmic memo.

I continue panhandling, scoring some pocket change and singles, with the odd fiver thrown in, when the redhead walks away from the homeless guy and saunters past me.

"Thanks for the donation," I say.

She gives me a smile and a wink before she disappears into the shadows of the Bethesda Arcade.

When I look back, the homeless guy has abandoned his bench and is walking across the terrace in the direction of Strawberry Fields. Before he can get away, I grab my hat and my earnings and run after him.

"Hey!" I call out. "Hold up!"

He turns around and watches me approach with a look that's a mixture of apprehension and curiosity.

"I wanted to give you this," I say, and hand him the twenty bucks Red Hot gave me.

"Why?" he says.

I shrug. "I just thought you looked like you could use the help."

For a second, I think I'm mistaken. He's just some slob who needs a shave and a bath. Then his face brightens a little, a wry smile touching his lips as he takes the money. "Thanks."

This is followed by that awkward silence that always occurs whenever you give a twenty to a stranger in Central Park.

"Hey," I say. "Do you know how to pick a pitch?"

A week and a half later, on my way to check a few homeless shelters for Vic before heading to Central Park to take advantage of the continuing warm spell, I run into Sophie.

This isn't one of those figurative moments when we cross paths or metaphorically bump into one another at a local cafe or on some street corner. I actually run into Sophie coming out of Charlie's apartment and knock her on her ass.

At first I don't realize it's her. I just think I've knocked over some woman in a sweatshirt and shorts who was unfortunate enough to get in my way. But when I reach down to apologize and help her up off the sidewalk, she looks up at me and our eyes meet. That's when I realize all of the daydreaming I've done over the past several months about what I would say to Sophie when I saw her again hasn't prepared me for this moment at all.

"Hi," I say, helping her up.

The excitement and awkwardness of being around her again make it hard enough for me to get out a simple greeting, so I hope the fact that I don't say her name isn't weird. I say it about five seconds later just in case, which probably makes me sound like I have brain damage.

"Sophie."

She brushes herself off, then gives me a look as if she doesn't recognize me. Her reaction probably has something to do with the fact that my hair has gone completely gray and I haven't shaved in a couple of weeks.

I half expect her to ask me who I am. Instead she says, "Hi, Lloyd."

In all my imagined permutations of this moment, I always pictured myself saying something suave or romantic like *You look beautiful* or *You have no idea how much I've missed you* or *But soft, what light through yonder window breaks?* What comes out instead is:

"How are you?" I say.

So much for suave and romantic.

"Good. Things have been good," she says. "How are you?"

Telling her that I'm lost and struggling to keep myself together on a daily basis sounds too desperate, so I go with the gold standard response.

"Good," I say.

I can tell by her expression that she doesn't believe me. Probably because I look like I should be taking Centrum Silver.

"How are the boys?" she asks.

This doesn't seem like the appropriate time to discuss details of my friends burning to death or disappearing with retrograde amnesia, so I tell her they're fine.

"Are you still at Charlie's?" she asks, motioning to his apartment building.

I nod. "The landlord thinks I'm Charlie's stepbrother, so he's only charging me an extra two hundred a month to stay there until Charlie gets out of the hospital."

She doesn't ask me how I'm earning the money to pay for Charlie's rent, and I don't tell her. We both know how that discussion would play out.

"How's Charlie doing?" she asks.

"He's still in a coma."

She nods and bites her lower lip and says. "I'm sorry."

Fortunately the Emergency Medical Treatment and Active Labor Act provides for Charlie to continue to receive treatment—at least until he regains consciousness and is able to take care of himself or has someone who can take care of him.

Sophie and I stand and stare at each other, neither of us speaking or probably knowing where to go from here, people and traffic moving past, the two of us sharing the same three feet of space but standing on opposite sides of a relationship chasm.

I'm trying to come up with the perfect thing to say, something sweet and poignant that will lift me up and carry me across the divide to Sophie, like a hot-air balloon built for two.

"I should be going," she says.

And my hot-air balloon deflates and plummets into the abyss.

"Sure," I say, with a forced smile. "It was good to see you."

"You too," she says, and walks away.

I watch her go, thinking I should call out to her, ask her if she'd like to get together sometime for a cup of organic tea or fair-trade coffee. My treat. Instead I watch her go, unable to find the courage, and I realize it's probably for the best. She deserves someone better than me. Someone who can treat her with honesty and respect and who has the ability to earn a living without taking experimental drugs or wearing a rectal probe.

So much for my destiny.

After running into Sophie I'm feeling maudlin, so I decide to feed that feeling and head down Canal Street to Sara D. Roosevelt Park, past the bench where Randy, Charlie, Vic, Isaac, and I first gathered to test out our superpowers. I stop and look around, remembering how Vic made the douche-bag smoker with the cell phone throw up; then I cut over to Bowery and stand in front of the Royal Jewelry Center and reminisce about our first unofficial foray as superheroes.

I remember the smell of vomit like it was yesterday.

Because I'm feeling awash in nostalgia and sentimentality, I follow Bowery to Fourth Avenue until I reach Union Square, where I stop at a flower stand and buy a red carnation and pay my respects to Randy before heading up Broadway to Madison Square Park. With the early-afternoon sun shining and the mercury threatening to top out in the mid-sixties, the lines at Shake Shack are longer than normal for the last week of February, but I'm not interested in ordering a ShackBurger or any cheese fries.

This is the last place I remember feeling good about my life. I had a girlfriend and a purpose and a group of friends who were at the top of their superhero game. Destiny had come calling and I'd embraced it and made it my own. But when your girlfriend breaks up with you and kicks you out and your friends end up dead, comatose, or missing, or become depressive, obese, pizza-eating hermits, the idea of destiny doesn't seem like much of a comfort anymore.

I leave Madison Square Park and walk along Fifth Avenue past the Empire State Building, stopping at a nearby Starbucks to order a double latte. While I'm waiting for my drink, I look around and notice a couple of people reading the *New York Post*. On the cover is the headline:

SUPER POOPER . . .

HEROES ABANDON MANHATTAN

For the most part I've managed to stay away from reading the papers or watching the news. I don't want or need the media's shame heaped on to my preexisting guilt. But every now and then I see a headline or hear a story that makes me feel like I've abandoned the people I'd once wanted to help.

In addition to the headlines and stories about us, I'm aware that while there haven't been any more reports of Mr. Blank's memory shenanigans, Illusion Man continues to terrorize New York City, branching out into Queens and the Bronx and Brooklyn, leaving no borough safe from his hallucinogenic reach.

The thirty-something guy holding up a copy of the *New York Post* catches me staring at him.

"Sorry," I say. "I was just reading your paper."

He checks the front page as if he can't remember what the headline said, then opens the paper back up. "Politicians. Professional athletes. Superheroes. They're all disappointing," he says. "I guess you can't count on anybody these days, right?"

Once my latte is ready, I head back outside and continue up Fifth Avenue, planning to cut through Bryant Park to reminisce about some of the good times we had fighting crime there, when

I notice emergency vehicles on the street in front of the New York Public Library. An ambulance and a fire engine and a single NYPD cruiser are on the scene as traffic backs up from what looks like an accident involving a couple of taxis.

A crowd has gathered on the sidewalk, so I stop and ask a few people on the outskirts what happened.

"Some homeless guy ran out into the middle of the street and got nailed by a cab," a guy says. "Caused this whole fuckin' mess."

I'm not in the mood to rubberneck, so I leave the gawkers and the chaos of the accident behind and continue on my way, when I see Isaac sitting at the top of the library steps, holding a Starbucks container and watching everyone with that odd little smirk of his.

I stop and stare at him, not sure what I should do. It's been three months since I last saw Isaac and I don't know how to feel about seeing him now. On the one hand, he's a friendly face and someone I've known for nearly five years of my life. Maybe not as well as Charlie or Randy or Frank, but still a friend. On the other hand . . .

Isaac sees me and holds up a single hand in a stillborn wave and says, "Hey Lloyd," as if there's nothing wrong. As if he didn't abandon us on Thanksgiving in the hospital where Charlie was in a coma and never called to see what happened to everyone.

On the other hand . . . I obviously still have some unresolved issues about Isaac.

I can't decide if I should ignore him and keep walking or return his greeting. Eventually I do neither and sit down on the steps next to him a few feet away—the two of us drinking our coffee, not saying anything, the promising blue sky above us a contrast to the aftermath of the accident on Fifth Avenue.

"You've gone gray," Isaac says, breaking the silence.

I shrug and hope he doesn't say anything about how it makes me look distinguished.

"Charlie's still in a coma," I say. "In case you were wondering."

Isaac just nods and drinks his coffee, the silence settling over us once more as the lifeless body is loaded into the ambulance.

"And Randy and Blaine are dead," I say.

"I heard," he says, like we're at a cocktail party or a backyard barbecue, drinking beers and making idle talk. No *What happened?* or *Are Frank and Vic okay?* or *Sorry I wasn't there.*

I want to lay into Isaac, but I just don't have the energy. Instead I take a deep breath, let it out, and go with a more lighthearted approach.

"Give anyone a boner lately?" I say.

He shakes his head slowly back and forth.

"Decided to hang up your superhero cape?" I say.

Isaac gives a wry little smile. "I was never a superhero."

"Sure you were," I say. "You were Professor Priapism. Giver of erections. More powerful than an aphrodisiac. Able to—"

"I never gave anyone a boner."

"What?" I say. "You didn't?"

"No," he says, like it's the most ridiculous thing in the world.

"Then why did you say you could?"

"I wanted you guys to think I was like you."

There's something different about Isaac, something I can't quite put my finger on, but at the moment I'm more focused on his admission that he didn't have any supernatural abilities.

"So all those times you went out with us, you were just *pretending* to be a superhero?" I ask.

"Not pretending," he says. "*Performing*."

It must be an actor thing.

"Is that why you didn't want to come with us when we went after Blaine?" I say. "Because you didn't have a superpower?"

"No, it just seemed like a really bad idea," he says. "Plus it wouldn't have been in character."

"What does that mean?" I ask, ignoring for the moment that he called my plan a bad idea. Even if it's true.

"Think about it."

It strikes me again that there's something different about Isaac. It's not just his confident demeanor, but there's something else. Something right in front of me that I should be able to see but that I just can't figure out.

"Come on, Lloyd," he says. "Cat got your tongue?"

Then it hits me.

"Hey," I say. "What happened to your stutter?"

Isaac cocks his head as if thinking about his answer, but before he can respond, a hot-dog vendor on the corner across Fifth Avenue starts shouting at everyone to get away, threatening them with his wiener tongs. A moment later he discards his tongs and starts shoving wieners and buns into his mouth as fast as he can like he's trying to unseat Joey Chestnut as the Nathan's Hot Dog Eating Champion.

"Jesus." I stand up and scan the crowds on Fifth Avenue, not sure who I'm looking for, but hoping I'll know when I find him.

"What's the matter?" Isaac asks, still sitting on the steps.

"I think Illusion Man is here."

It's been nearly a month since I've attempted to access my trigger, so I'm a bit out of practice. While in a way it's like riding a bike, it's also a bit like kick-starting a stubborn motorcycle.

"Illusion Man?" Isaac says.

A police cruiser sits parked diagonally on Fifth Avenue, with one of NYPD's finest standing near the cruiser and the other directing traffic. The one standing by the cruiser starts walking toward the hot-dog stand, pulls out his gun and shoots the hot-dog vendor, then puts the gun in his mouth and pulls the trigger.

People start screaming and running off in multiple directions as a red VW Jetta runs through the intersection and hits a cab before it veers across Fifth Avenue, drives up onto the sidewalk, and crashes into the front window of Capelli.

I give my trigger one final kick, imagining dentists and drills, and my lips start to tingle and my eyes grow heavy as a pressure builds in the back of my throat. I look around, trying to locate Illusion Man, figuring he has to be somewhere nearby, when I notice Isaac just sitting on the steps and drinking his coffee while the chaos unfolds, wearing a smile as if he's watching his favorite movie.

Then the proverbial penny drops and I realize Isaac wasn't as bad an actor as I thought.

My lips go numb and my throat tightens. Before I can open my mouth to release my yawn, Isaac looks at me and cocks his head and everything goes "Lucy in the Sky with Diamonds."

INTERLUDE #6

Welcome to the Grand Illusion

Isaac sits on the steps in front of the New York Public Library, drinking a grande black Pike Place Roast in the afternoon sun and watching the tourists and locals walk past, imagining that they're actors in a play or a movie and he's sitting in the audience, enjoying the show. He does this a lot. Just sits and imagines and pretends. It's what he likes to do more than anything.

Isaac watched a lot of television when he was a kid, pretending the lives of the characters on sitcoms and dramas were his, imagining that he had the perfect life with the perfect family and that his parents hadn't divorced when he was eight years old and his mother didn't leave him home alone on a regular basis while she slept her way through a series of drunken one-night stands.

As he grew older, Isaac's attention shifted from television to the big screen and he spent as much time as possible in movie theaters, watching adventures and romantic comedies and fairy tales where everyone lived happily ever after. Eventually he decided that if he wanted his life to have a fairy-tale ending, he was going to have to become an actor.

So he joined the drama club in middle school, where he played minor roles and bit parts before graduating to high school theater and landing the lead or supporting role in half a dozen plays, including *The Laramie Project* and *Rosencrantz and Guildenstern Are Dead*. People told him he was good, that he had talent, and he believed them. He had It, with a capital *I*. His destiny was written on the wall in twenty-four-karat gold, and the road ahead was paved with diamonds.

After high school he moved to New York to become a star on Broadway, only to burn out and develop a stutter and discover that life isn't like a movie. Life doesn't wrap up with the hero or the main protagonist overcoming obstacles in order to succeed. Life is about loss and disappointment and all of the things that can go wrong.

To paraphrase Jim Morrison, life is about heartache and the loss of God.

In real life, there is no happily ever after.

At least, that's what Isaac used to think.

For most of his adult life he'd been a serial failure, killing one opportunity after another, working temporary night jobs and volunteering for clinical trials so he could afford to pay the rent on his crappy studio apartment in Alphabet City while he auditioned for plays so far off Broadway that they might as well have been in New Jersey. Not that it would have mattered. His stutter always betrayed him and the role eventually went to someone else.

Then, six months ago, everything changed.

The first thing he noticed was that he stopped dreaming, which was weird because Isaac always dreamed, ever since he could remember. Sometimes the dreams were so vivid he would wake up thinking that his nocturnal visions had followed him into the real world. Occasionally, in the brief twilight between being asleep and awake, Isaac would have trouble differentiating between what was reality and what was fantasy.

As night after night passed without a single snippet of a dream, he began to wonder if their disappearance was a reflection of his waking life, a metaphor for how his real-world dreams of being an actor had never materialized. But Isaac soon discovered that their absence was due to something more monumental and life-changing than he could have ever imagined.

He had developed the supernatural ability to make other people hallucinate.

Isaac had once seen a cicada molt and emerge from its nymph exoskeleton as a fully formed adult with wings. That's how he felt when he discovered his new talent—as if he had finally cast off the detritus of his previous existence and was ready to fly.

At some point Isaac's stutter vanished. He's not sure exactly when it happened but one day it just wasn't there. *Poof*, like magic. But like a good magician, Isaac didn't reveal his secrets and kept up the pretense of his stutter so that no one would suspect anything had changed.

When he found out that Vic and Lloyd and the other guinea pigs had all experienced their own metamorphoses, Isaac initially felt a sense of disappointment that he wasn't a unique butterfly.

But he soon learned that their new abilities, while amusing and effective, didn't come close to his ability to manipulate the fabric of reality.

So he decided to play along with them and use his acting skills to make the others believe he could give people erections. None of them would ever know the truth, because no one would ever want to check. And they believed him. He fooled them all. It was the performance of his life. He should have won a Tony. Or an Oscar.

Maybe once he's grown tired of Manhattan, he'll head out to California and see if they appreciate his talents any more in Hollywood than they did on Broadway.

Isaac takes another sip of coffee and continues to watch the giant movie screen on Fifth Avenue, hundreds of men and women playing out their roles in a never-ending script. But this particular scene is beginning to grow a bit boring, so Isaac decides to liven things up.

At the bottom of the library steps, a homeless man dressed in a red coat, dirty tan pants, and a pair of white tennis shoes roots through a garbage can like a raccoon. Next to him is a shopping cart filled with an assortment of clothing and artifacts that probably constitute the homeless man's life savings. It's obviously been a while since he's been the leading man, so Isaac decides to make him a star.

The world around Isaac dims and goes out of focus for a moment, the sounds of the city a murmur of background noise and conversation. Then Isaac cocks his head and the murmur turns into a hum. Tires on asphalt. A high-powered fan. The incessant drone of ten thousand bees.

The homeless man whips his head around, startled and confused, then looks up into the sky and his eyes go wide.

"Go away!" he shouts and starts waving his arms around his head.

A moment later, he screams in pain and starts running back and forth on the sidewalk in front of the library, continuing to wave his hands in the air as if batting at some unseen attacker. Then he lets out another scream of pain and terror before he runs away up the sidewalk and dashes out into Fifth Avenue, where he gets hit by a taxi speeding to make it through the stoplight.

The man flies across the hood of the taxi and slams headfirst into the windshield, then launches over the roof as the cab driver slams on the brakes. Rubber screams on asphalt, the body somersaults through the air, someone shouts out in horror and surprise just before another taxi slams into the rear of the first, glass exploding and metal crunching, the sound jarring and insistent and final. The homeless man continues to tumble through the air, once then twice, before he finally falls to the asphalt in a sprawl of broken bones and flesh and blood in the middle of Fifth Avenue.

The crowds converge on the accident, men and women reacting with shock and grief and horror, a wide range of human emotions playing out on the screen in front of him.

Much better, Isaac thinks, then he takes a sip of his coffee and settles in to enjoy the show.

I've never dropped acid or eaten psilocybin mushrooms. I've never even smoked pot. And after five years of testing pharmaceutical drugs, you'd think I would have had at least one hallucinatory episode to add to my life experience, but until now I've managed to avoid seeing any Plasticine porters with looking-glass ties. Hell, I don't even know what Plasticine is.

So while there aren't any newspaper taxis waiting to take me away, my reality has definitely taken a turn for the psychedelic and surreal.

Faces and people melt and blur together. Buildings laugh and street signs wave. A giant balloon floats by that looks like Frank. For all I know it *is* Frank. I haven't seen him in over a month, so maybe he's turned into a blimp. In my present reality, anything is possible.

The rational part of my mind knows none of this is real, but that doesn't make it any easier to cross the street when the asphalt is bubbling like hot lava while Viking ships populated by all of the characters Eddie Murphy has ever portrayed float past and fire cantaloupes at me out of licorice cannons.

This is not how I thought my day would turn out.

Clouds become disembodied faces. Streetlamps turn into the stilt-like legs of giant aliens. Everything melts or expands or otherwise breaks the rules of physics. It's as if I'm living inside a Salvador Dalí painting.

I look around and try to figure out where I am, but there aren't any recognizable landmarks to help guide me. The last thing I remember I was standing next to Isaac on the steps of the New York Public Library. I don't recall walking away, so for all I know I'm still standing there and this is all in my mind. Except I feel my arms and legs in motion and the ground moving past beneath my feet, which means I must be mobile. But in my current state of mind, I can't be sure of anything.

At some point I realize the sun is gone and I'm wandering in the dark through a haunted forest, with barren, skeletal limbs reaching out and voices whispering in the darkness, so apparently I've transitioned from Dalí paintings to Disney cartoons.

For some reason, my hallucinations are predominated by pop culture references.

Sophie appears, laughing and running, hiding behind tree after tree, but as soon as I catch her she turns to vapor and vanishes like a breath in the winter air. Someone taps me on the shoulder and I turn around to find Randy floating six feet off the ground wearing a Led Zeppelin T-shirt, his flesh melting, so naturally I scream and run away. Charlie and Vic and Frank and Blaine show up here and there, more demons and ghosts to haunt the landscape of my newly warped reality.

Even the monochromatic redhead who gave me twenty bucks

makes an appearance, standing in the path ahead of me wearing a red lace teddy and beckoning me toward her with an alluring wave of an index finger. Then her index finger morphs into a serpent and I turn and run in the other direction.

Like I said, I'm pretty sure none of this is real, but I'm not taking any chances.

I reach a clearing in the forest and look up and see the moon glowing like a giant eyeball in the black sky. I'm waiting for it to turn into a face and wink at me, or start bouncing across the sky like a cartoon sing-along ball.

Look out! Look out! Pink elephants on parade!

Instead, the moon starts to look less like a lifeless satellite reflecting the sun and more like the opening at the end of a circular tunnel. The longer I stare at it, the bigger the moon grows, until I feel myself hurtling through the tunnel and into a universe of white, blinding light.

Then something pops and everything goes black.

chapter 36

I wake up shivering on the ground, curled up in the fetal position, wearing rumpled khakis and a pullover hoodie, covered in dirt and leaves. I get to my feet and brush myself off and look around, trying to figure out where I am. There's not much light but it's enough for me to decide that I'm in the Ramble in Central Park. Or at least I think I am. At the moment I'm still not sure of anything. Scratch that. I'm sure of one thing: I'm staying as far the fuck away from Isaac as possible.

How he managed to fool all of us for so long is beside the point and not something I'm going to beat myself up about, because I already have enough guilt on my plate to feed an entire congregation of Catholics. But it's obvious that when it comes to superpowers, I still have my training wheels, while Isaac is in the pole position at the Indianapolis 500.

I start walking, rubbing my hands together and trying to warm myself up, waiting for the trees to uproot and follow me or for Randy to come jogging past wearing a *Dark Side of the Moon* T-shirt and spitting balls of fire. Instead I see a man in a jacket walking a black standard poodle. At first I think my hallucinatory experience from yesterday has run its course and that my reality has returned to normal, but then the man waves back at me with three hands and his poodle starts barking in German.

Hallo, Ich sah nur ein Vogel. Ein Vogel! Ich bin so aufgeregt! Vogel!

Eventually I make my way out of the Ramble, past the Shakespeare Garden, and end up by the Delacorte Theater, where Romeo and Juliet embrace in an eternal prelude to a kiss. While the statue captures an innocent moment of the star-crossed lovers frozen in time, I notice that one of Romeo's hands has shifted to Juliet's ass while his other hand cups her breast. He squeezes Juliet's breast as she lets out a moan of pleasure. Then I blink and the statue returns to normal.

The last remnants of night are holding on in the shadows as the first hint of blue sky appears above Queens. I'm hoping the daylight will bring some relief from my hallucinations, though I wouldn't be surprised if the sun rose wearing Ray-Bans and singing "I Heard It Through the Grapevine."

I walk past the Great Lawn on my way toward Fifth Avenue, blowing into my hands and rubbing my arms, trying to ignore the miniature Loch Ness Monster that keeps surfacing in the Turtle Pond. A couple approaches, a young man and woman walking hand in hand, either getting an early start to their day or putting the finishing touches on a late night. When they kiss, their faces melt together and drip onto the sidewalk like hot wax.

Apparently Isaac's superpowers are longer lasting than Extra gum.

I walk through the Greywacke Arch and sit down on a bench out behind the Met. Other than joggers running past on their way to a healthy lifestyle, and a homeless person digging through a garbage can, there's no one else around. So I sit there in the early-morning cold, trying to warm myself up and pull myself together, wondering what I'm going to do if my new state of mind turns out to be permanent.

A few minutes after I sit down, a man in a long black coat and freshly pressed slacks sits down on a bench across from me. He's holding a bouquet of daisies in one hand and looking around expectantly, an expression of anticipation on his face, as if he's waiting for someone. He looks familiar, though I don't know from where or when. If you live in Manhattan long enough you're bound to run into someone you recognize. In my current state of mind I wonder if he's real or a figment of my imagination; an odd coincidence or my subconscious coming out to play on the jungle gym of my hallucinating mind. There's a good chance it could be either.

There's also a good chance his bouquet of daisies will jump out of his hand and start dancing to the *Saturday Night Fever* soundtrack. So I put my head in my hands and stare at the ground, then take several deep breaths and hope no one comes up to talk to me. Right now, I just want to be left alone.

I don't know how long I stay like this. It seems like a few days but I'm guessing it's more like a few minutes, since the sun continues to inch its way above the Upper East Side. Plus, when I look up, the guy with the daisies is still sitting across from me, and I doubt he'd still be there after three days.

A woman comes jogging along the pedestrian path toward us and the man stands up, a nervous smile playing at his lips. From the expression on his face, it's obvious he came here to surprise her. And it occurs to me that this is one of the scenarios

I fantasized about when I imagined running into Sophie, only she wouldn't be jogging. And I would have brought lilies. But otherwise it's pretty close. So I watch out of curiosity to see what happens, hoping my hallucination has a happy ending.

"Hi Sara," the man says, raising his right hand in greeting, his left hand wrapped around the bouquet of daisies, which he holds out to her like a peace offering.

Sara doesn't look thrilled to see him, which isn't a good sign, for me or for him. Instead, she keeps running as she reaches into her waist belt and pulls something out with her right hand. For a moment it's concealed by her fingers; then I see that she's holding a small pink canister. As she runs past him, she raises her right hand and sprays the man in the face.

The man drops the daisies and starts screaming and clawing at his eyes, stumbling and nearly running into a garbage can before he staggers away through the Greywacke Arch toward the Turtle Pond as the woman continues her morning jog and disappears from view.

So much for happy endings.

I look back at the daisies scattered on the ground, the sun still waiting to peek over the high-rent homes and offices lining Fifth Avenue, and I can't help but think that my hallucination does not bode well for a reconciliation with Sophie.

"That looked like it hurt," a woman says as she walks past me.

Her red mane of hair cascades over her red turtleneck and her red leather jacket, which match her red leather pants. A red scarf and a red cable-knit beanie finish off the ensemble. She walks over and stands with her hands on her hips, looking toward the Greywacke Arch. "Did that look like it hurt?"

I stare at her, standing there like a giant red exclamation point, and like with everything else that's happened to me since I woke up this morning, I wonder whether or not she's real. Considering that the rest of my subconscious is making an appearance this morning, I'm guessing not.

After a moment, I realize my hallucination is waiting for an answer.

"I'm sure he's fine," I say. "He doesn't really exist anyway."

"Oh, I don't know about that," she says, then walks over and sits down on the bench next to me. Her lips are so red it's like they're made of candy apples.

"You're not real, are you?" I ask. "You're just my imagination fucking with me."

She shrugs. "I guess that's all up to interpretation."

I'm still pretty sure she's a hallucination, but I figure if I have to hallucinate, at least I picked an attractive figment of my imagination.

We sit in silence a few moments as she taps her foot to some silent beat and the sun finally peeks up over Fifth Avenue, the rays shooting out of the clouds like an homage to God. Then my hallucination stands up and walks over to the bouquet of scattered daisies, picks them up, and comes back and sits down next to me.

"I don't know why he brought her daisies." She gives them a light sniff and makes a face as if she just smelled someone's dirty feet. "He should have brought roses."

"I don't think roses would have made a difference," I say, thinking about the confrontation that was an imaginary representation of my inadequacies as a boyfriend.

"Probably not." She tosses the daisies aside with an unceremonious flick of her wrist. "He should have brought her lilies, instead."

And now I know the redhead is just a product of my own subconscious. Otherwise, how would she know Sophie's favorite flower?

"But enough about his mistakes," she says. "What we need to focus on is you."

"Why?" I ask, though I realize she's really just me talking to myself.

"Because you've lost your way and I want to help you get back on the path you were meant to take," she says. "Back to the person you were born to be."

It's as if I've hallucinated up my own imaginary therapist.

"I didn't realize there were multiple versions of me," I say, playing the role of the patient.

"More like versions that are better and worse," she says. "And I want to help you reach your full potential."

"Sounds good," I say. "But I have to warn you, reaching my potential has always been an issue with me."

"We'll work on it," she says and stands up. "But first we need to get you to the hospital."

I stand up and walk along beside my hallucination.

"So are you my subconscious?" I ask. "A manifestation of my guilt? Or are you just a chemical reaction in my brain brought on by Isaac's superpowers?"

"Why don't you think of me as your fairy godmother?"

"You mean like in *Cinderella*?" I ask.

"More like in *Sleeping Beauty*."

This is one of our poker-night discussions all over again.

"I hope that doesn't mean I'm going to get raped by a king," I say, and wonder what this conversation looks like from the outside.

"I'm not going to put you to sleep for a hundred years," she says. "I'm here to help you get back on your path."

"In case you haven't noticed, staying on my path has never exactly been my strong suit."

"That's because you lack discipline," she says.

"Tell me something I don't know."

We walk out of Central Park and onto Fifth Avenue, where a couple of police cars come racing down the street, sirens wailing.

"The trick to staying on your path is believing in it," my fairy godmother says. "It's one thing to seek out your path but it's another thing to make it your own."

The neurons in my brain fire, bringing up the memory from Curry in a Hurry and the guy who claimed he was Karma.

Man creates his own destiny. The path you seek is your own.

"We're talking about my destiny?" I say.

"Sure," she says. "Why not?"

I stand in front of the Met watching the traffic drive past on Fifth Avenue and think about my destiny. I think about Sophie and the wrinkled fortune in my wallet. I think about Dr. Lullaby and all the people he helped. I think about the love I had and the friends I've lost and the confrontation with Isaac that brought me to this moment.

Man creates his own destiny. The path you seek is your own.

"Okay," I say to the hallucinatory manifestation of my subconscious. "So what's my destiny?"

Two and a Half Months Later

'm sitting on a table in an examination room—not in a doctor's office on the Upper West Side with framed diplomas and family photographs and a window overlooking Riverside Park, but in a health clinic in Long Island City with framed cartoons and posters of reproductive organs and no windows.

"How are you feeling today?" the phlebotomist asks as she draws a sample of my blood into an evacuated tube.

The phlebotomist is female. Mid-thirties. Dark brown hair. She's wearing just enough makeup to highlight her features. Her breath smells like onions.

"I'm fine," I say.

"Any problems sleeping?" she asks.

"Every now and then."

"How often?"

"Couple times a week."

"How's your appetite?"

"Good," I say.

She looks down at her list of questions.

"Any nausea?" she asks.

No.

"Seizures?"

No.

"Rashes?"

No.

"Any cognitive issues?" she asks. "Problems with memory?"

I shake my head.

"Have you been hallucinating?"

"No," I tell her. "No hallucinations."

That's not exactly the truth. I'm pretty sure I saw a squirrel follow me onto the subway a few days ago but other than that, my last hallucination was nearly a month ago.

Once she finishes drawing my blood, the phlebotomist hands me a sterile plastic specimen container.

"Remember to put your name and date on it," she says. "And try to catch the urine midstream."

I just nod and walk into the bathroom.

After I leave my urine sample, I head to the waiting room and check out with the receptionist, who gives me a smile along with several prescription drug vouchers.

The receptionist is female. Early twenties. Bleached-blond hair. She's wearing too much eye shadow. Her breath smells like Red Bull.

"Thank you, Mr. Prescott," she says. "We'll see you in two weeks."

∘   ∘   ∘

For the past two and a half months I've been going to the health clinic in Long Island City for bimonthly appointments. The blood and urine tests are to check for any signs of bipolar disorder and to test my liver and kidney functions to make sure there's nothing going on physiologically that may have contributed to my hallucinations.

While I know Isaac's superpower is responsible, the medical community is a little more pragmatic in their diagnosis. But at least Sophie's been supportive about everything.

"How was your appointment?" Sophie asks and gives me a kiss before she takes off her work apron.

We're in the employee break room at Westerly, where Sophie just ended an afternoon shift on her day off covering for a sick coworker. Normally she still works nights, which means we get to spend most days together from morning breath to late-night snack.

"It was good," I say. "Everything looks normal."

"Yay!" She gives me a big hug. "How much longer do they think you'll have to keep taking your medications?"

"Another month or so. They want to continue to monitor my blood and urine, just in case."

Megan pops into the break room to grab her jacket.

"Hey Lloyd," she says. "How's the drug biz?"

"You say that like he's a cocaine dealer," Sophie says.

"If he was, he'd be making more than all of us combined," Megan says. "You're not holding out on us, are you, Lloyd?"

"Sorry," I say. "I'm just as financially challenged as you."

"Too bad. Catch you lovebirds later," Megan says, then exits, stage left.

"So what's going on in the world of Westerly?" I ask Sophie.

"We got in a big shipment of fresh organic spinach and asparagus," she says, putting her apron into her backpack. "Oh, and rhubarb. I'm thinking of making a pie."

"Sounds yummy."

I'm not a big fan of rhubarb pie, but considering it's the closest to a doughnut I'm probably going to get, I'll take it.

"I'm meeting Leslie for dinner in Koreatown and then we're thinking of catching a movie," Sophie says. "Do you want me to bring you something to eat?"

"I'll grab something on my way home."

"Okay." She gives me another kiss. "I love you, Lollipop."

"I love you, too," I say, then watch her go.

Once she's gone, I put on my own apron and walk out into the store, past the hormone- and antibiotic-free meat and poultry; past the organic produce; past the nutritional supplements; past the all-natural, environmentally friendly and cruelty-free body-care products; past the self-service nut grinders and the bulk containers, until I reach the front of the store, where Tony, the Monday-night shift manager, is waiting

"Evenin' Lloyd," he says. "Ready for another awesome night?"

"Absolutely," I say, then take my place behind the counter.

For the past month I've been a full-time cashier at Westerly, working nights and weekends six days a week. Sophie got me the interview with her boss and vouched for me. Another two months and I'm past my probationary period and eligible for benefits, including health insurance. That's a big deal, considering that I've been depending on my prescription-drug vouchers.

The afternoon after I was admitted into Mount Sinai Hospital to get treated for my hallucinations, Sophie showed up. She was still my emergency contact, so she came as soon as she could and stayed with me most of the night while I shared my hospital bed with the Seven Dwarfs and watched purple monkeys swing from the ceiling.

At least they didn't fling any poo at me.

The next day Sophie helped to sign me up at the Long Island City health clinic for their treatment program. While she wasn't happy with the idea of me putting more drugs into my system, I didn't have any other options to combat the aftereffects of Isaac's superpowers. Since I needed to stay with someone who could keep an eye on me, Sophie let me stay at her place and sleep on her couch.

After a week of treatment with antipsychotics, my hallucinations started to tail off. After another week of heart-to-heart talks and a lot of apologizing and truth telling, Sophie invited me back into her bed. Vegan wasn't thrilled with my return at first, but after I started sneaking him bacon from Flowers Cafe, he warmed up to me.

So for the second time, Sophie came to my rescue and saved me from an existence that would have been far less enjoyable without her in it. I understand how fortunate I am to have her back in my life, and this time I'm determined to not screw it up.

"Welcome to Westerly," I say with a smile to a fiftyish woman with gray hair who steps up and places a bottle of probiotics and spirulina powder on the counter. "Did you find everything you were looking for?"

Except for the occasional odd squirrel following me onto the subway or phantom crows diving at me from trees and rooftops, my reality has more or less returned to normal. That's due in large part to Zeprocol, the antipsychotic medication I've been taking.

While it's good to be able to have a conversation with Sophie and not think she's a talking water buffalo or to walk down the street without encountering a herd of Eddie Murphys, controlling the hallucinations that Isaac inflicted on me doesn't come without a price. Like any antipsychotic drug, Zeprocol has a litany of side effects, including restlessness, fatigue, dizziness, irritability, constipation, increased appetite, weight gain, runny nose, trouble swallowing, apathy or lack of emotion, impaired judgment or motor skills, seizures, diabetes, and liquid discharge from your nipples.

Fortunately the only side effects I've experienced so far have been restlessness, some fatigue and irritability, and an increased appetite, which has led to the expected weight gain. Sophie says it's not a big deal, that there's more of me to love, but I don't like having a muffin top.

I've also experienced some mild depression, which isn't all that surprising when you think about it, so I've been prescribed Norvox, which can cause constipation, heartburn, diarrhea, sleeplessness, and an inability to get an erection.

I'm thinking I need to switch to another antidepressant.

But all in all, things are good. True, I never grew up thinking I would be a cashier in an organic health food store, and it's not the Yankees or *Playboy* or *National Geographic*, but it beats sitting in a cubicle all day. Plus I get to work with my girlfriend *and* fulfill my destiny. How many people get to say that?

"Welcome to Westerly," I say to a twenty-something guy with dreadlocks who is supporting his low-carb, gluten-free lifestyle. "Did you find everything you were looking for?"

||| chapter 38 |||

After work, I take the Q train down to Union Square to pay my respects to Randy. It's not something I even think about anymore, just something I do. Every day, one way or another, I find myself at the George Washington statue. Sometimes it's just a quick visit. Sometimes I park myself at the foot of the statue with a latte for a half hour or so and tell Randy what's going on with me. Sometimes I watch the people playing chess and I consider sitting down to play against one of them, but I never do.

Eventually I say good night to Randy and walk along Fourteenth Street to First Avenue, where I stand at the corner in front of Papaya Dog, trying to convince myself this is a bad idea and that I should double back and walk down Second Avenue, instead. Or walk down one more block and go home through Alphabet City. But I was never good at listening to my common sense.

As I walk down First Avenue, I catch a glimpse of my reflection in the window at Subway and stop to take a look. Even though my hair has begun to reclaim some of its natural color and the wrinkles and bags around my eyes have cleared up, sometimes I still catch myself looking in the mirror and wondering who the stranger is wearing my skin and my face. At moments like this, when I see my faint image looking back at me, I feel like I'm just a ghost of the person I used to be.

Or maybe that's just the Zeprocol, which in addition to drooling, slurred speech, trembling, clumsiness, unsteadiness, and difficulty with swallowing and breathing, can cause blurred or impaired vision along with a mask-like face.

I stare at my unfamiliar reflection a few moments longer, then continue along First Avenue.

Another side effect of most antipsychotics is insomnia, which is a bigger problem for me than it is for your average person, since insomnia causes my inner Dr. Lullaby to want to come out and play. And that's something Sophie and I have agreed isn't a good idea.

So in order to combat my insomnia, I'm taking Somnata, which comes with its own host of side effects. These include dizziness, nausea, cotton mouth, loss of appetite, headaches, problems with memory or concentration, mild skin rash, agitation, aggression, thoughts of hurting yourself, anxiety, and depression.

At least I'm already taking Norvox.

One of the other side effects of Somnata is the possibility of hallucinations, which makes me wonder if pharmaceutical companies make sure their drugs have side effects that require the cross-pollination of their other drugs. Fortunately the only side effects I've experienced on any regular basis have been indigestion and some occasional nausea.

And I can't help but think about Vic.

I continue along First Avenue for another few blocks until I come to Stromboli Pizza and look through the window. Past midnight on a Monday, most of the customers are ordering slices rather than entire pies, and there's a line of about six ahead of me. While I'm hungry and looking forward to sneaking in a couple of slices of pepperoni pizza without Sophie knowing, that's not the main reason I came here.

I know it probably won't make a difference and that I'm just going to leave here feeling worse than I did before, but after staring through the window another moment, I walk through the door and get in line.

Vic stands behind the counter, taking someone's order; then he rings them up and gives them their change before helping the next customer, then the next and the next. While I know not to get my hopes up, by the time I get to the front of the line my heart is pounding.

"Hey," Vic says. "How's it going?"

"Good," I say. "How about you?"

"Couldn't be better," he says, flashing a smile that looks genuine rather than forced, like he's happy to be working here. For all I know, he is.

I still don't know what happened to Vic after his encounter with Blaine. I don't know if he ended up on the streets or in a shelter or got married. But no matter how many times I've come in here, he hasn't told me where he's been or what happened. Not because he doesn't want to, but because he doesn't know who I am.

I ran into Vic about a month ago on my way home from work.

When I saw him, I was so happy I started crying and asking him where he'd been all this time, but he just stared at me and shook his head and told me he didn't know what I was talking about before he asked if I wanted to order some pizza. It didn't take me long to realize that Vic doesn't remember anything about me or his life as a guinea pig or what we went through together. None of it.

Whatever Blaine did to him, it seems to be permanent.

Even so, I stare at Vic another moment, looking for some glimpse of recognition in his eyes, some hint that buried deep in the recesses of his psyche he knows who I am. But like every other time I've come in here for the past month, there's nothing more than common courtesy lurking behind his expression. To Vic, I'm just a guy who comes into Stromboli's a few times a week to order some pizza, and the extent of our conversation revolves not around our shared history but what's on the menu.

"So what'll it be tonight?" he asks.

I know what I want but I look at the menu anyway, stalling for time like I always do, hoping that something somewhere in Vic's memory clicks into place.

"Two slices of pepperoni pizza and a root beer," I say. "And while you're at it, how about throwing in a couple of douche bags."

Vic gives me a sideways look. "I don't follow."

For just a second I convince myself that I catch a flash of recognition in his eyes. A spark plug trying to fire up his memory. Then it's gone. Or maybe it only existed in my imagination.

"Nothing," I say. "Just making a joke."

"Got it," he says. "Two slices of pepperoni and a root beer, coming up."

He rings up my order and I pay him like we're just a couple of ordinary guys living ordinary lives who never did anything out of the ordinary together. Once my order is ready, I take it to a table and sit down, eating my pepperoni pizza and drinking my root beer in silence without enjoying a single bite or sip. When I'm done, I stand up and walk outside, pausing at the door to raise a hand in the air to Vic on my way out, but he's preoccupied with another customer and doesn't see me or return the gesture. So I head home hoping that maybe next time he'll remember me.

chapter 39

H ey CB," I say. "What's shakin'?"

Charlie smiles and his left eye fills with tears when I walk into the room. Unlike Vic, Charlie still remembers me, and I can see the combination of familiarity and pain in his expression. But whereas Vic and I are at least able to hold a meaningless conversation, Charlie still isn't able to form an intelligible sentence.

"Ay Llld. S gd tcu," he says.

Listening to Charlie talk is like hearing a teenager's text message spoken phonetically.

"It's good to see you, too," I say.

After Charlie came out of his coma, it was obvious the stroke he'd suffered had caused some significant permanent damage, so he was transferred to a long-term care facility in Queens, where he's been a resident for the past couple of months. I don't know who's footing the bill or how much it's costing, since Charlie doesn't have any health insurance or the ability to pay for any of this, but I'm guessing it's not going to be cheap.

I sit down in the chair next to his bed and Charlie reaches out with his left hand, his right hand motionless and curled up next to him on top of the covers, his fingers halfway curled into a claw, a patch covering his right eye so he looks like a pirate in a nursing home. When I take his good hand he smiles at me, or at least he tries to. The right side of his face still droops, as if someone turned up the gravity on one side of his body.

"How are you feeling?" I ask.

Charlie's mouth twitches and his left eye blinks, like he's trying to answer in facial Morse code. He mumbles something that I can't make out, which only seems to make his mouth and eye work harder. Finally I hand him the pen and pad of paper on the bedside table and he scrawls out something with his left hand.

When he's done I look down at what he's written. Charlie is right-handed, so his penmanship looks like that of a six-year-old with cerebral palsy, but I can still make out his answer to my question.

I hate being like this.

Charlie never was one to hide his feelings. And I'm so struck by his honesty that I don't know how to respond, so I just give his hand a little squeeze and tell him that I'm sorry.

We sit in silence for a few minutes before Charlie lets go of my hand and wipes away the tears that have coursed down his cheek. Then he takes a deep breath and seems to get himself under control.

"Hss ic?" he says.

I've only seen Charlie a handful of times since he regained consciousness, and I feel guilty about not coming to see him more often. Part of my absence stems from my own work schedule and the fact that it's tough for me to get out to Queens, since the long-term care facility is all the way over in Whitestone. Plus most of the spare time I do have I try to spend with Sophie. But each time I've come to visit him, Charlie has asked me the same question.

How's Vic?

"He's good," I say. "He seems happy."

I've told Charlie about Vic, about how Blaine blew away his memory and how Vic now works at Stromboli Pizza and doesn't remember anything. I haven't told Charlie that I've seen Vic several times a week for the past month in the hopes of triggering his memory. Instead, I just keep my answers simple because it's easier that way.

Charlie nods and gives a half smile, which is a trick no one should ever have to learn how to do.

"I iss I ood c m," he says.

Seeing the pain on Charlie's face and knowing how much he hates being like this makes it that much harder to be here. Plus there's the awkwardness of not knowing what to say that makes visiting him an exercise in learning how to manage my own guilt, which makes me wonder if maybe Blaine didn't do Vic a favor by erasing his memory.

"Nn hss ank?"

"Frank's good," I say.

Frank's been at a weight-loss boot camp in Long Island for the past six weeks after ballooning up to over three hundred pounds. Apparently he had some rainy-day money stashed away that he decided to use to get his weight under control after he hit bottom and couldn't manage to get through his bathroom door.

"I'm going to see him next week," I say.

Charlie nods again and I can see his lips twitching and his left eye filling up with tears again, so he grabs the pen and writes another note.

Tell him I said hey.

I sit with Charlie for a while and try to think of things to talk about, telling him about Sophie and my job at Westerly and how I've started volunteering one day a week with Sophie at the SPCA, which, in addition to the bacon, seems to have improved my relationship with Vegan. I try not to make it sound like things are all that great, but I know that no matter how much I downplay my life, it's an all-expenses-paid trip to Tahiti compared to Charlie's.

After I've run out of things to say, Charlie and I sit there in silence for several minutes, staring at each other and pretending to smile. Charlie's lips twitch again like he wants to say something, then he picks up the pen again and starts writing. When he's done, I see a new question that he hasn't asked on my previous visits, but one that was inevitable.

What about Isaac?

"He's still out there," I say.

For a week or so after my encounter with Isaac there were a few reports in Brooklyn and Staten Island about people suffering from hallucinations or exhibiting delusional behavior, but other than that the news around New York City has been hallucination-free. However, over the past couple of months, there have been reports about people having hallucinations in Philadelphia, Baltimore, and Pittsburgh, with a slew of them cropping up a few days ago in Columbus, Ohio.

From what I can tell, Isaac appears to be working his way west.

chapter 40

Would you like some more asparagus?" Sophie asks.

"No thanks," I say, then take another bite of my Tofurky kielbasa.

While Sophie's not a big fan of fake meat, she's okay with me eating veggie sausages and hot dogs and sandwich meats, so long as I don't eat Boca Burgers, which contain *hydrolyzed wheat protein, disodium guanylate, disodium inosinate, methylcellulose,* and a bunch of other ingredients I can't pronounce. Not to mention that they're owned by Philip Morris. But she's okay with me eating Tofurky, since it contains organic, non-GMO ingredients and hexane-free soy. And Sunshine Burgers, which contain only ground raw sunflower seeds, brown rice, carrots, herbs, and sea salt.

Still, every now and then, I need a slice of pepperoni pizza or a couple of pieces of bacon.

I glance down at Vegan, who looks up at me and licks his chops as if he can read my mind. For all I know, he can.

We finish our meal and do the dishes together, enjoying each other's company as much as possible. Instead of letting Sophie cook, I do it with her. Rather, I help where I can. Sophie's the one with the culinary skills. But I'm present instead of watching TV or reading the paper or surfing the Internet. And likewise after meals, she helps me clean up. It's like we're a team instead of two people with separate responsibilities. Maybe that was part of the problem before. I didn't work hard enough to be part of a team.

At least not with Sophie.

After we finish cleaning up, Sophie waters her plants. She no longer sprinkles her pixie dust on them or throughout the apartment, which has made for healthier plants and a healthier Vegan. So at least my eruption of honesty wasn't a complete disaster.

Afterward, we sit down on the couch to watch *Annie Hall*.

While Sophie and I get to spend a lot of our days together, we don't get very many leisurely nights to ourselves, since both of us work six nights a week, so date nights are few and far between. The occasional night we do get together, we usually stay at home to watch a movie. At some point, foreplay and sex enter into the evening, but I'm not always able to hold up my end of the bargain, causing me to experience some mild anxiety, which is also a side effect of Somnata. So I've been prescribed Pacifix.

The side effects of Pacifix are similar to those of some of the other drugs I'm taking, including the inability to get an erection and loss of interest in sex. So taking Pacifix to help relieve my sexual performance anxiety makes about as much sense as drinking a beer to cure alcoholism.

At this point, I'm on so many medications that I might as well be popping Viagra or Cialis or some other drug for erectile dysfunction. Sophie suggests we consider trying a more natural sexual enhancement remedy or aphrodisiac, like ginseng or ginkgo biloba or horny goat weed. But the last thing I want to attract is a horny goat. Besides, I'm already a walking pharmacy. What's one more prescription?

Vegan jumps up onto the coffee table and stares at me. He's been doing this regularly over the past couple of weeks, staring at me for a minute or two and then walking away. While I am the giver of bacon, he's still wary of me when I'm not at the table or in the kitchen. But tonight, rather than turning around and showing me the ass end of his feline disposition, he jumps onto my thighs, where he sits and stares at me for another thirty seconds or so before migrating to Sophie's lap.

It's just a drive-by lapping, but at least it's progress.

Sophie laughs with delight at *Annie Hall*, even though she's seen the film a hundred times, and then we retire to the bedroom, where Sophie attempts to coax me into an aroused state without much success. We still manage to get in some kissing and touching and I do what I can to please Sophie, but while my heart's in it, the pertinent part of my anatomy is a disinterested bystander.

When we're done, Sophie curls up next to me and wraps one of her legs over mine and tells me she loves me into my shoulder.

"I love you, too," I say, then turn and kiss her on the forehead.

She lets out a contented sigh and snuggles in closer, like she's trying to find a way to burrow into my genetic structure. After less than five minutes, her breaths start to slow and deepen and I know she's fallen asleep.

I stare at the ceiling, thoughts chasing each other around inside my head, and I realize I forgot to take my Somnata. I don't want to get up and disturb Sophie, so I close my eyes and take deep breaths, then slowly let them out, focusing on the field of black on the inside of my eyelids. I don't bother counting sheep or backward from one thousand. Instead, I imagine the word *sleep* when I inhale, drawing the word into me like it has magical power—which, it turns out, isn't too far from the truth.

Every time I inhale and imagine the word *sleep*, my lips start to tingle. I don't even have to think about going to the dentist; my trigger is right there, waiting to be called up, and I can feel my superpower vibrating like a steady hum of electricity. Only it feels different than before. Stronger. More powerful. As if it's been working out at the gym. Or taking steroids.

This isn't something that's been going on for the past few days or building up over a couple of weeks. This is, to channel my inner Randy, total INXS. A new sensation.

I don't understand how this happened and spend the better part of five minutes trying to figure it out, until I remember how Blaine claimed to have taken a bunch of prescription drugs to increase the strength of his superpower, and I wonder if that's what's happening to me. I wonder if by taking all of these medications I've awoken Dr. Lullaby rather than tucking him into bed and singing him to sleep.

I'm still wondering this when the sun comes up the next morning.

chapter 41

Lloyd," Frank says, embracing me in a bear hug. "It's been too long."

Once he releases me, I step back and check him out. "You look great."

In the six weeks he's been at the live-in boot camp, Frank has dropped more than a hundred pounds from his high of 310. While he's still a little chunkier than the Frank I've known for most of the past five years, he's slimmed down to the point where I can almost imagine he was never a superhero named Big Fatty.

"Come on," he says, opening the front door. "Let's get some fresh air. I was just about to take a walk."

We head outside into the late spring, the calendar about to turn from May to June, and it's not lost on me that nearly a year has passed since all of the events that transpired were set in motion. It seems more like ten years. I don't know if Frank feels the same way, but I'm pretty sure he's aware of the upcoming anniversary, since most of the weight he gained after Randy's death was the result of guilt therapy.

When it comes to Charlie, Randy, and Vic, I know Frank feels more responsible than I do about what happened to them. For all I know he even feels guilty about Blaine and Isaac, though he hasn't said as much. As far as I'm concerned, he's still the patriarch of our little guinea pig clan, even if there are only five of us left and one of us is partially paralyzed, another has amnesia, and a third is a supervillain.

Hey, every family has its issues.

"I still have another twenty pounds to lose," Frank says as we walk along the grounds, which are located in Ronkonkoma, halfway to Montauk. "But even with the extra weight, I notice how much better I feel without the toxins of all those experimental drugs coursing through my system. It's as if I've been cleansed. No. *Purified*. I tell you, Lloyd, I feel better than I have in years."

I smile and nod and give him a congratulatory pat on the back, but I can't relate. If anything, I feel just the opposite. I'm a walking pharmaceutical lab.

Frank continues to talk about how far he's come and when he expects to get out of here and how excited and nervous he is to get back to living a normal life again.

"But enough about me," Frank says. "How's Lloyd these days?"

"I'm good," I say, and elaborate with anecdotes about Sophie and my job and my volunteer work at the SPCA. I leave out the part about how I'm taking so many drugs that my side effects have side effects—including a really big one.

When I'm finished with my rose-colored Lloyd update, we walk for a few minutes along the sidewalk that winds through the grounds surrounding the boot camp, chatting about nothing of consequence. Finally I decide to bring up the topic that's been on my mind.

"Are you still able to access your trigger?" I ask.

Frank shakes his head. "Not in a while."

"How long is a while?"

"I don't know. A couple of months? Why?"

"I'm just curious if your superpowers went away once you stopped participating in clinical trials," I say.

"Yes," he says. "They went away. They're gone."

"So you can't access them?"

Frank stops and turns to look at me, a crack appearing in his façade of good humor. "You can't be serious?"

I shrug. "Can you?"

"No."

"You're sure?"

"Yes," he says, as several more cracks appear. "I've put all that behind me. Big Fatty is history."

He starts walking again, probably to get away from me. But I didn't come here to let him get away.

"So if you thought about Famous Ray's or Dunkin' Donuts, you wouldn't get all gassy and floaty?"

Frank turns around, the façade crumbling, his old anger flaring up. "What the hell are you trying to do here, Lloyd?"

"I'm not trying to do anything," I say. "I'd just like to know if you can still access your trigger."

"Do you have any idea what you're asking me to do?" He walks up to me, a single angry finger pointed at my chest. "Do you know how hard I've worked to feel good about myself? How hard

I've worked to get my life back? I don't need you coming here and making me feel guilty about the choices I've made."

"I'm not trying to make you feel guilty about anything," I say. "I just wanted to find out if Big Fatty is still lurking around inside of you or if he's gone for good."

"He's gone for good."

"You're sure?"

He stares at me, his face flushed and his nostrils flaring; then he closes his eyes and takes a couple of deep breaths. When he opens his eyes, he gives me a smile that looks more forced than genuine.

"It was good to see you, Lloyd," he says and gives me a cool pat on the shoulder. "Take care of yourself."

Frank walks past me and makes his way back to the boot camp dormitory. Before he can get out of earshot, I call out to him.

"By the way, Charlie says hi."

He stops but doesn't turn around this time, just stands there for a few beats as if contemplating the repercussions of beating the shit out of me. Then he starts walking again and doesn't look back.

A few days later, I'm in Washington Square Park, sitting in the shade on the west side of the fountain as the sun drops toward the Hudson. It's a beautiful spring afternoon in Manhattan, with everything green and the flowers in bloom and the promise of a sweltering summer just around the corner.

You haven't experienced New York until you've smelled the garbage in August.

My sign today reads:

IF YOU WERE IN MY SHOES, I'D BE BAREFOOT

In the two hours I've been here I've only earned fifteen dollars and change. A far cry from what I used to take in and not enough to pay Time Warner or T-Mobile. It would buy half a dozen black-and-white cookies from Greenberg's, but I don't panhandle for personal profit anymore. Instead, I use the money I make to help out the homeless and the hungry I see on the streets of Manhattan.

Usually I buy them lunch or dinner, sometimes a pair of shoes or some clean underwear. Unfortunately I haven't had as many bullish days as I used to, mostly because I haven't been able to use my WILL TAKE VERBAL ABUSE FOR MONEY sign since I started taking my brew of prescription medications. Having someone insult and verbally abuse you while you're experiencing the side effects of a strong antipsychotic isn't the best way to avoid jail time for assault and battery.

I've already started to discontinue some of my medications, though it's a gradual process that might take up to a month. Once I've been weaned off of my meds, I'm hoping my mood swings will balance out and allow me to get back to living a normal life. Except at this point, I'm kind of wondering just how "normal" that's going to be.

Although Frank told me he couldn't access his superpower, I'm not sure I believe him. Even though he's no longer volunteering for clinical trials and has all of those drugs out of his system, I believe Big Fatty is still lurking beneath the surface of his newly trim figure. I don't know what it would take to bring him out, but he's there. I'm sure of it. Almost as sure as I am that my own superpower is being nourished by the drugs that are coursing through my system. The only question is how strong it will be once I've been weaned off my concoction of prescriptions.

After another hour of earning less than minimum wage, I gather up my money, put on my hat, toss my sign into the nearest garbage can, and pick up my prescription vouchers at Duane Reade. With a little over an hour to kill before meeting Sophie, I take a walk through SoHo and Little Italy and Chinatown as the sun heads for New Jersey and the nine-to-six crowd transitions from work to play.

I wander along the streets, past stores and restaurants and subway stations, past men and women and teenagers, laughing and shouting and minding their own business. Some of them happy, some of them sad, some of them destitute—either because of their own failed choices or bad luck or because life dealt them a shitty hand.

A homeless man talks to himself on the corner by Famous Ben's Pizza.

A woman moves her belongings down Wooster Street one bag at a time.

A drunkard lies passed out on the sidewalk near Tribeca Park.

Any one of them could have been me, given the right set of circumstances. Or the wrong ones. Had Sophie not rescued me three months ago or five years before that, I might have ended up as one of New York's anonymous homeless, lost and forsaken, stranded on the streets with no one to care about me.

I walk past a homeless woman sitting out in front of the Burger King on Canal Street, no sign asking for help, just a pleading look on her face. No one who walks past offers her anything, and most just ignore her, so I stop and ask her if she'd like something to eat.

"Bless you," she says with a smile, her voice soft and sweet, as if I'm offering to solve all of her problems.

I order a TenderGrill Chicken Sandwich meal, with fries and a vanilla shake, along with a large Coke for me, paying for it with my panhandling earnings. Sophie would probably encourage me to find something vegetarian for the woman, or at least something healthier, preferably gluten-free, but I'm focusing on carbohydrates and protein and sustenance rather than lifestyle choices.

When I walk outside and hand the bag of food and the milkshake to the homeless woman, she thanks me and reaches into the bag, her hand coming back out holding two French fries, which she eats as though they were a rare confection. I stand there a moment and watch her, then reach into my pocket and give her the rest of the money I earned in Washington Square Park.

She takes the money and gives me another smile. "You're my hero," she says, then takes a bite of her sandwich.

That's the first time anyone's said that about me in months.

I walk away wishing there was more I could do to help her, wanting to make sure she's taken care of and protected but knowing I can't do everything for everyone. In this case, at this moment, I did what I could. And maybe that's all I need to do in order to make a difference: show some warmth and compassion to the people who need it the most. I don't need to have a supernatural superpower to be a superhero. I just need to care.

Inevitably I find myself visiting several locations where Frank, Vic, Charlie, Randy, and I performed our own inimitable brand of community service that involved more than being fast-food heroes. I meander through Foley Square and Columbus Park, stopping for a moment to reminisce, remembering every moment, right down to each nap, rash, and seizure.

I'm getting sentimental again.

I make my way through Chinatown and stop out in front of Bayard Street Obstetrics & Gynecology across from Charlie's old place, thinking about friendships and superheroes and destinies.

I wonder if Charlie's destiny was to end up paralyzed by a stroke or if Vic's destiny was to lose his memory or if Randy's destiny was to die while battling a supervillain. Considering all the good the three of them accomplished, it doesn't seem fair that they drew the short straws when it came to fame and fortune. But like Randy said, maybe in order to be a superhero you have to be willing to make some sacrifices. Otherwise you're just a guy in colored spandex and a satin cape.

Sophie texts me to find out what time I'll be home. Tonight is date night and Sophie's making spicy peanut butter tempeh and brown rice. I text back that I'll be home in ten minutes and then head up Elizabeth Street, wondering if there's someplace I could grab a steak along the way.

At the corner of Elizabeth and Hester, I stop outside of the Ho Won Bake Shoppe and consider going inside to grab a couple of pineapple buns for dessert. Sophie won't be happy about it, but I'm craving a pastry and their pineapple buns are the epitome of my confectionery desire.

While I'm contemplating the fallout of bringing them home, I notice a couple of young trolls standing across the street and whistling at girls as they walk past, calling out to them, making suggestive comments. With daylight lingering and witnesses around, they're inclined to stick to verbal harassment. But when the moon comes out and shadows rule the streets, they might decide to escalate from verbal to something else. I don't know this for sure. It's just a look they have.

Someone needs to teach them some manners.

As if some cosmic force is tapping me on the shoulder to re- mind me of my path, Sophie texts again and asks me to pick up some toilet paper on the way home. This is followed immediately by another text that simply says, *I love you, Lollipop.*

I smile and think how lucky I am to have Sophie and how much she means to me. More times than I can remember, I've wondered what I would do without her. She's the best thing that has ever happened to me.

The two creeps harass another woman and leer at her as she walks past, causing her to quicken her pace. They watch her go, then look back at one another and exchange a nod and a smile before they slink off after the woman in the growing shadows. I watch them go and think about Charlie and Randy and Vic. I think about everything they sacrificed in order to try to make the world a better place. I think about what they would do if they were here instead of me.

I'm waiting for another cosmic tap on the shoulder but when it doesn't come, I take out my wallet and remove the fortune from the Buddhist temple and unfold it, reading the words that I know so well.

In true love, destiny awaits.

Sometimes I do this to remind myself of my destiny and how much I love Sophie. Other times, I take out the tattered fortune and read it and wonder if destiny is something you pick out of a basket for a dollar and read every now and then to help you to stay on your path. The more I think about it, the more I believe that destiny isn't a combination of five words written on a piece of paper. It's something you feel. Something you own. Something you create for yourself.

Man creates his own destiny. The path you seek is your own.

I take one more look at the fortune in my hand, the paper wrinkled and frayed at the edges, the words solid and black and poignant. My own personal destiny. After a few more seconds, I close my hand around the fortune and wad it up into a little ball and throw it in the garbage can before I follow the two assholes down the street.

In order to be a superhero, sometimes you have to be willing to make personal sacrifices and lose something you care about. Otherwise you're just a guy in colored spandex and a satin cape. And I don't look good in spandex.

chapter 43

They call me Dr. Lullaby.

Author's Note

Back in October 2003, around the same time I was discovering the ideas that would eventually evolve into my first two novels, I saw an advertisement on television for a new drug that promised to help cure abdominal cramping, with one of the side effects of the drug being that it might *cause* abdominal cramping.

Intrigued by the comical irony, I wrote the gist of the commercial down in my journal and filed it away, but I didn't come back to it until 2009 after reading about people who made their living on the fringes of society by testing drugs in clinical trials. That's when the idea for a superhero story about professional guinea pigs was born, although it would have a long gestation period while I wrote my third and fourth novels.

While *Less Than Hero* is filled with social commentary on the proliferation of pharmaceutical drug use in the United States, it's also a story about figuring out what it is you're supposed to do with your life. That's a common theme in my novels. Finding your role. Your purpose. Your reason for your existence. It's not something I set out to do when I sit down to write. It just sort of happens.

There's also a running commentary on fate and destiny in this novel, which was also the major theme of my second novel, *Fated*. Because both novels are set in Manhattan, I thought it would be fun to have the stories and universes overlap in a few places. For those of you who've read *Fated*, hopefully you enjoyed (or will enjoy) encountering some of the familiar characters and scenes that I incorporated here. For those of you who haven't read *Fated*, it's not required reading.

Now, on to the acknowledgments.

I'd like to thank the following people who helped to make this book possible:

Michelle Brower, my agent, for her continued guidance, and the team at Folio Literary Management for all of their support.

Ed Schlesinger, my editor, for his invaluable feedback, and the gang at Gallery Books for all of their hard work.

Clifford Brooks, Ian Dudley, Heather Liston, Lise Quintana, and Keith White for their ruthless and honest criticism.

I'd also like to thank my parents, my family, and my friends, who have all been instrumental and supportive in my writing over the years. While there are too many to name, hopefully you all know who you are.

Finally I'd like to give a big shout-out to my readers and fans. Thanks for the love. You are awesome.